GIDDYAP TIN LIZZIE

THE LONG ROAD BACK TO THE PLOW

Book I of The O'Shaughnessy Chronicles

by HAROLD WILLIAM THORPE

D1490824

LITTLE CREEK PRESS®
AND BOOK DESIGN

Mineral Point, Wisconsin USA

Little Creek Press and Book Design
A Division of Kristin Mitchell Design, Inc
Mineral Point, Wisconsin
www.littlecreekpress.com

Second Printing August 2018

For more information or to order books:
Harold William Thorpe: e: haroldthorpe@hotmail.com
or online at www.haroldwilliamthorpe.com

Printed in the United States of America

Library of Congress Control Number: 2012944434

ISBN-10: 098492454X
ISBN-13: 978-0-9849245-4-7

This book is dedicated to my mother, Laura Annette Fitzsimons,
who in her memoir, From High on the Bluff, provided a wellspring
of people, places, and events that flowed into
The O'Shaughnessy Chronicles.

INTRODUCTION

I call the O'Shaughnessy stories Family Fiction. Will, Mary, the other Mary, Michael, Sharon, Ruby, Catherine, and Gusta are fictionalized versions of Laura Annette Fitzsimons' closest family members, but the experiences, interactions, and persuasions are the way I imagined them happening. All other family members in *Giddyap Tin Lizzie* are fictitious characters and any resemblance to the living or dead is purely coincidental. All non-family members are fictitious, too. Although the names are different, people who have read Laura's memoir, *From High on the Bluff,* will recognize the villages of Ashley Springs, Hinton, Willow, and Logan Junction. And anyone who has read Laura's book will relive in comprehensive detail the many events she described in that memoir.

LOOKING AHEAD

Now that you've read *Giddyap Tin Lizzie*, look to the next book in the O'Shaughnessy Chronicles, *BitterSweet Harvest*, which will appear soon. Follow Will and his family's fortunes as they struggle through the depression and World War II years on their Wisconsin River valley farm. A Texas cousin arrives to turn the family's harmony on its head, Jesse reappears, while Will organizes his farm neighbors into a co-op that helps them struggle through these difficult years. But it's not easy. Will's fortunes zigzag and, through it all, he remembers Grandpa Duffy's admonition, "You're not hard enough to make a living at farming." Is Grandpa right?

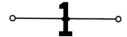

1

outhwest Wisconsin, Summer, 1913.

Sooks said hogs would eat a downed man, but Will O'Shaughnessy had never seen it. Not before now.

He ran to the barn for a pitchfork to beat them off, and after he dragged his grandpa's body from the pen, he couldn't bear to look any more.

After Will's grandmother, Doris Duffy, had died in an accident, the O'Shaughnessy boys took turns helping their grandpa keep the dairy farm going. Every week, one of the three came to their grandpa's. This was Will's week.

After Doris's death, Will's grandfather, Walter, had hired Sadie, a neighbor woman, to cook for him. As soon as Sadie rang the dinner bell, Will came straight from the barn to wash up. When the old man didn't appear, Sadie said, "I got it all ready to dish up, Will. Better go see what he's up to."

Will searched all around inside the milking parlor, hallooed down the pasture, and poked his head in the door of the shadowy machine shop. Finally he thought of the hog pen, and when he saw his grandpa there, motionless and face down in the mire, his knees buckled and he grabbed a fencepost so he wouldn't collapse.

They'd gone for the soft places—the face, the throat, even ripped through the old man's shirt and pants to his belly. Will ran back to the barn to find the canvas his grandpa kept in the feed room. Hurrying, he tossed it over the old man's body, and then he covered the ground to the house in great strides to get to the telephone.

But at the back door he pulled up short to steady himself against the wall. What was the use of calling anyone? Grandpa was gone. He'd known it the moment he saw him.

"That you, Will?" Sadie peered out the door, a pan of biscuits in one hand. "Didn't you find him?"

"I found him." Will gasped from his efforts. He shook his head and stared at his boots. "He won't be needing his dinner after all."

Walter's mutilated body lay three feet above his head, but the cows still had to be milked. Will heard thunder in the distance. He looked up and shuddered.

He had wanted to bring Walter into the back parlor, but Sadie planted her ample frame in the doorway and said, "Not in here, not like that. Take him to the barn. I'll go get Frank and your dad."

So Will dragged Walter's body toward the barn, but he twisted to look away from the grisly remains. When Walter's coverall strap hooked a nail on the loft door, Will quickly turned away, threw a tarp over the old man, and then slammed the doors and ran to the milk barn below.

Will hurriedly stripped the last drops of milk from a stubborn teat. Lightning flashed through the isinglass window of the milk barn door. He knew he should shed tears, but Walter wasn't a man you cried over. Hadn't his grandpa told him, "You don't let nothin' stand in way of the milk'n'." Walter had then spat a wad of Red Man to where he pointed his gnarled finger. "If I fall dead in that gutter, you finish the cows before you pick me up."

The farm would be his now. But was he ready? He had planned to be a farmer all his life, had excelled in high school agriculture classes and attended university courses, but he didn't even know how much income Walter made from ten cows.

"Move over, Bess." Will pushed his shoulder into this half-ton milk factory and slipped the one-legged stool under him while he reached down for her soft, supple teats. Bess, a heifer, lost her first calf when she freshened last month. The syncopated rhythm of milk splashing the bottom of the tin pail calmed Will. Lightening flashed through the window, once, twice, a third time, and thunder shook the barn on its foundation. Will looked up toward Walter above and hoped the roof didn't leak down on him. He jumped off his stool and stepped across the gutter but knew it wasn't necessary. This was Walter's barn, not his dad's. Rain pounded down around him, but no water seeped through the door.

Will knew that Walter had thought he could outdo him at milking, but Walter hadn't milked so fast near the end. Why, he used to tease the milk from three cows and strip them dry before Walter finished two. Will supposed it was the arthritis that had slowed the old man down.

Will dumped Bess's milk into the eight-gallon can and moved across the aisle to Mazy. He was surprised the old man hadn't butchered her long ago. She hardly earned her keep these days. Will shifted his weight to lean under Mazy and strip the last milk from her with a flurry of tugs on her teats. The pail was only a quarter full, less than half what the others gave.

Of course, he didn't have the farm yet, but his father said he'd get it. Farms always went to the oldest male heir, and Grandpa had no sons of his own. His youngest brother, Jesse, was convinced of that. He'd pestered Will for a share ever since agriculture classes—wanted to farm the back forty until he had earned his own grubstake. And Will agreed to half shares, but he didn't give it much thought. Walter was healthy as the barnyard bull, and with Jesse's fondness for the bottle, he probably wouldn't get very far with his crops anyhow.

Bess let out a mournful bellow. Her first cry pierced the wind and driving rain. The second one came soon after, and then a series of quick, desperate calls stabbed through the night air.

Will hoped they could get through this without trouble. He knew that Jesse had been drinking again. His dad was flushed from drink as well, but liquor didn't change Thomas's disposition.

Family, friends, and neighbors filed past the closed coffin. The men looked grim. Women cried. All paused a moment; some bowed, some kneeled, and some crossed themselves. They then offered condolences to Walter Duffy's only child, Will's mother, Gertrude, and Walter's three grandsons, Will, Frank, and Jesse. Will, the family's scholar, was twenty-four, a year older than Frank and two years older than Jesse. Frank looked and acted so like his grandfather that, despite the age difference, people sometimes called him Walter. And Walter only grudgingly acknowledged his ne'er-do-well grandson, Jesse. The three boys, with fresh cut hair, slouched and buried their hands deep into the pockets of rarely worn suits.

Jesse edged over to Will who stood alone and, in a slurred voice that shattered the silence of the large room, said, "Who'd have thought this many'd mourn the old fool?"

"At least wait till the funeral's over to berate him," Will said. "He may have been hard, but he didn't deserve this."

Will thought about how the family would change with him and Jesse gone. Could Thomas get by? He'd had his down times, too. Of course, losing Jesse wouldn't be noticed. Lucky for his dad, Frank would still be there, and Frank was always sober.

"Look at Frank," Jesse said, and he nodded toward their brother, who stood by the coffin as he received condolences. "Crying like a baby. His kowtowing won't get much now."

Father Murphy strolled to his pulpit and looked down on the gathering. "Please bow your heads. Dear Lord, we gather to remember Walter Duffy, not to mourn his untimely death, but to consider his life. Walter was an industrious man, an honest man, a man you could rely on," the priest said.

Yes, but a hard man, narrow minded and unyielding.

Father Murphy raised his voice. "He gave his tithe and helped his brethren when there was need."

That he did—but always by his terms.

"And we know how difficult it was for him after he lost his beloved Doris."

The priest's words droned on, and Will lost touch with the present—the minister, the mourners, the casket. Will remembered that time. It had been the worst day of his life, the day grandma died.

After five years, the specter of his grandma under the overturned buggy still haunted his dreams.

The morning had started bad. A cow had calved during the night, but Walter hadn't finished the calf pen he was building.

"But, Walter," Doris said, "we never miss Mass."

"Well, I'll be miss'n today. If I don't get that little one outa the rain and mud, she'll not be see'n the sunset. That's money lying out there on the cold ground."

"She made it through the night. The Good Lord'll see her through His Mass."

"If the Good Lord chose the Sabbath to put her in my hands, He probably expects me to tend her on the Sabbath." Walter grabbed his slicker off the entryway peg and stepped out into the rain. "Come on, Will. Help me finish that pen."

Will was carrying a keg of nails toward the barn when he heard shouts coming from the lane and saw Jesse limping toward him—trousers torn, leg bloodied, and mud-caked from top to bottom.

"Get Grandpa! Grandma's under the buggy!"

Jesse collapsed before he took another step, but Will ignored him, dropped the keg, and raced toward the barn to get Walter.

They ran a half mile down the road, and when they rounded the curve next to the alder trees, Will saw Doris ahead, under the buggy, face down in water that collected in the ruts. Will hadn't run so fast since his school sprint medleys, but he couldn't keep up with Walter. "I'll lift the buggy, Will. Pull her out."

When he pulled Doris from the mud, Will saw the deep gash on her bloody temple.

Walter dropped the frame and bent over his wife. "Doris, are you okay?" He lifted Doris upright.

But when his grandma's head fell limp, Will knew that she'd never be okay again.

For a moment, Walter held her head erect while he rung water from his dirty shirt and washed the filth from her face, his tears mixing with the stream that ran down her forehead.

"Run to the phone, Will. Get Dr. Ruggles out here." He cradled Doris in his arms as if he were about to carry her across the threshold on their wedding night, and he stumbled through the mud toward home.

Will never learned whether it was the blow or the water that killed her, but he remembered the moment Dr. Ruggles pronounced her dead. In two steps Walter raced through the door and surged down the hall to the bedroom where Jesse whimpered in his misery, clutching his untreated leg. Walter snatched him off the bed as if he were a half-full flour sack and slammed him into the bedroom wall.

"You drunken sot." He bent down until their brows almost touched. "You killed my Doris. I told you not to race down those rutted roads, and now you've gone and killed her. I hope you rot in hell."

Will knew that Doris would still be alive if Walter had gone to Mass. And he knew that Walter thought it was the Devil's work, and the Devil lay at his feet.

"Turn to page 423 in the hymnal and follow Annabelle Murrish as she sings Walter's favorite song, 'The Old Rugged Cross'."

Will knew the song by heart and he sang a few words into the refrain—"So I'll cherish … " the word turned Will's thoughts to Mary Tregonning. He could hardly get her off his mind lately. He blushed when, "Mary, will you marry me?" slipped through his lips, a ditty that he found himself repeating often.

But deep down, he worried that this lovely lady from Hinton, with her fine clothes and soft hands, wasn't meant to be a farmer's wife. She knew that he lived at home and worked for his dad, but that was different than being tied to his own farm. Would he have time to date her? Would she want to quit teaching to work by his side, work as hard as a mule while trying to get their future secured? That thought hadn't crossed his mind until now. But what could he do? He didn't know anything else, and, besides, he loved the farm.

Jesse rode to the burial with Will. "Now that you're about to get his farm, don't forget our agreement."

"You've reminded me often enough. Yes, you can farm the back forty until you get your grubstake."

"Grandpa wouldn't even do it on shares, and I offered him sixty percent."

"Grandpa did things his way. Did you ask Dad?"

"You know he's not got enough tillable land, and not paid for, either." Jesse slammed his fist into the wooden seat. I'll not get anything. You'll get it all."

"I've not got anything yet." Will snapped the reins. "Giddyap, Maud. It's not your age, Jess; it's the liquor. Grandpa would have forgiven you if you hadn't been drinking."

"To hell with him!" Jesse pounded the board again, took another swig from his flask, and tottered on his seat.

2

W ill, Jesse, and Frank paced the floor while Gertrude sat quietly, hands in her lap. The room—big enough for wall shelves, the lawyer's huge desk, a table, and a half dozen padded chairs— smelled like cigars, even with the windows open.

Will walked toward the window, glanced out, then continued to stride across the room. "He said he'd be here at ten o'clock. It's past ten-thirty."

Miss Hennessey, Attorney Brower's secretary, looked toward the window. "He's coming now," she said as she grabbed the coffee pot. "Will you have a cup, Mrs. O'Shaughnessy?"

Before Gertrude answered, Attorney Brower lumbered into the office, his face and armpits wet with sweat. Out of breath, he wheezed as he tore off his suit coat and threw it on a chair. Then he sorted through papers piled high on his desk. As he rummaged through the pile the overhead fan blew the documents into more disarray.

Brower nodded toward the boys. "We'll get right to it." He dug into the disheveled paper pile. "It should be here someplace." He rummaged through a stack of papers and ledgers. "Aw, here it is. I never lose 'em for long." The attorney pulled out of the pile a large envelope and tossed it onto his desk.

Brower settled into his cushioned, roll-back chair. He straightened his tie and cleared his throat. "As you know, I've handled Mr. Duffy's legal affairs since I first came to Ashley Springs. More than twenty years now, hard to believe." He rolled his chair tight to his desk—as tight as his ponderous belly allowed—and latched onto the envelope. "I tried to get him to make a will, but he avoided it until Doris's death. Lots of people do, you know. But five years ago, he caved in." Brower tapped the envelope against his desktop. "Maybe you knew the provisions—all pretty standard. Then last August he barged through those doors and demanded a change. I tried to get him to wait, to think about it, but he insisted. He seemed pretty worked up. Said if I wanted to keep his business that I'd do as he asked, and do it right now."

August, Will thought. The cow.

"So I did what he wanted. Said I shouldn't say anything until after his death. Of course, I wouldn't, even though it went against custom."

Brower lit a cigar, puffed three times, turned away, and blew smoke across the room. Then he lifted his letter opener, inserted it under the seal, and sliced the envelope open.

Will felt the blade's sting.

Brower slowly drew the paper out. He cleared his throat before he began to read. "Last will of Walter Duffy. I, Walter Duffy, a resident of Ashley Springs, Wisconsin, being of sound mind and memory and over the age of eighteen, and not being actuated by any duress, menace, fraud, or undue influence, do make, publish, and declare this to be my last will, hereby expressly revoking all wills and codicils previously made by me."

Jesse poked Will in the ribs and whispered, "Remember our agreement."

"Shush, it's not what you think," Will said.

Brower puffed on his cigar until the room filled with smoke. Will's eyes burned.

Then he read, "As for tangible personal property; my furniture, furnishings, household equipment, and personal effects, it should go to my only child, my daughter, Gertrude Duffy O'Shaughnessy."

Brower set the papers down and removed his glasses. "Miss Hennessy, where's that addendum that Walter brought in when I was on vacation?"

Miss Hennessy rushed to her desk and pulled out a crumpled envelope, tried to smooth it, then raced back to Brower. "You told me to hang on to it until you found the file with the will." She smoothed the envelope again, and handed it to Brower. "It looked like this when he brought it in."

"You witnessed his signature, didn't you, Miss Hennessey? It's dated?"

"Yes, just like you said it should be done. And I stamped it, too."

Brower opened the envelope and withdrew a sheet of perforated paper that had been ripped from a spiral notebook. "Let's see." He turned toward Gertrude who, hands in her lap, sat unruffled on her chair. "Your father wrote this in his own script."

Brower smiled as he turned the paper in his hand. "He had a bold hand. Easy to read." He cleared his throat. "My red settee goes to cousin Mabel. She always insisted on sitting there when she came to visit—which wasn't very often. The old ice box in the back room goes to Jake Witherspoon. I always said he should keep his food on ice, but he never wanted to spend the money. Told him he's going to poison himself one of these days if he's not more careful. And the kitchen chairs stored over the tool shed to Esther Spencer. Mother's costume jewelry to her sister Alice. Her dresses to Alice, too, unless Gertrude wants them, which I greatly doubt. My fishing gear to Thomas. Maybe more time fishing will keep him away from the tavern, but that's 'bout as likely as Gertrude wanting her mother's dresses."

Brower droned on.

"Now, let's get to the important parts," he said. He puffed and blew more smoke that now hung so heavy that it slipped off the ceiling and curled around the table and chairs. He glanced in Will's direction, sighed deeply, and shook his head.

Will knew that Jesse would be outraged. He should be, too, but he just couldn't get the hog pen from his mind. The smoke teased his nose and burned his eyes, floated around his head and taunted him. Will never understood why anyone smoked cigars. Cigars didn't please the senses like the pipe tobacco he enjoyed. He dabbed at the tears that filled his burning eyes.

Brower paused a long while, then continued reading. "I bequeath all my property—my farm land, its buildings, cattle, and equipment—to my grandson, Frank O'Shaughnessy."

Will heard his mother gasp.

Jesse grabbed the paper from Brower's hand. "He can't do this. Will's the oldest and it's rightfully his!"

"It's all legal, son. I tried to talk him out of it, but he insisted. It's signed and witnessed properly." He took the will from Jesse and pointed at the signatures.

Will felt drained.

"That's all?" Jesse shouted. "There's nothing for us?"

But Walter Duffy left nothing but hard feelings for Jesse and Will.

"There is a sealed letter," Brower said. He picked up an envelope and pushed it toward Will. "He said I should give it to you."

Brower puffed on his cigar as he handed the letter across the table.

Will tapped the envelope on the desk, tore off the end, pulled out the letter, and scanned the short message. He handed the paper to Brower. "Isn't there anything I can do?"

Brower read Grandpa's note, then handed it back. "I'm afraid not. He isn't required to do this much. He didn't have to give a reason."

Will stuffed the letter into his pocket. "Come on, Jess. Let's get out of here."

Gertrude started toward Will, but Frank grabbed her hand and tugged her out the door. Will walked silently from Brower's office. Jesse stayed behind, and Will heard Jesse's shouting as he unhooked Maud's reins from the hitching post. Jesse caught him before he turned his horse onto the road.

"What'll we do, Will? You shouldn't have let this happen. You gotta fight it. What'd he say in the letter?"

Will removed the crumpled envelope from his pocket and read. "By rights, this farm should go to you, Will, but I've decided to give it to your brother Frank. I'm sorry, but that's the way it's got to be. I spent too many years building it up to chance losing it out of family. You may be the smartest grandson I've got, and you work plenty hard, but farming's a business, son, make no mistake about that. You've got too many high-minded ideas. Too much schooling. And just when I needed you most, you went traipsing south to see that black fella teacher. All your book learning's not worth a hill of beans if you've not got the disposition for business. And I don't think you do. You're too sensitive, not hard enough to make a living at it."

Will stepped up to his seat. He reined Maud until Jesse settled next to him. "I knew the outcome as soon as Brower said Grandpa'd changed the will last August. That's when he wanted me to take the cow back from old Mr. Jacobson, but I wouldn't do it."

"Jacobson didn't make the payments," Jesse said.

"He couldn't make the payments. Why, the old man's almost blind."

"That's why Grandpa gave our farm away?" Jesse said. "Over a cow? He's a cantankerous old coot, but I don't believe it. Not over a cow. He probably knew our agreement."

"We had lots of disagreements."

"Frank's been angling all along. He took advantage."

"Maybe you're right."

"Well, what are you going to do about it?"

"Not much I can do."

"You'll let Frank get away with it?" Jesse grabbed Will's wrist with a grip that turned his hand white. "Well, I'm not so easy. I'll make Frank pay if it takes a lifetime. You can bet your sweet ass on that. And you're no better, you weak-kneed bastard."

Will threw the reins down and exploded off the seat. "I lost the most, you ingrate. I'd have helped you, and you blame me for this?"

He'd shook free of Jesse's grip, but when his brother grabbed him again, Will pushed back hard, so hard that Jesse flew off the seat and sprawled in the road's dust.

"A weak-kneed bastard, you say?"

But when Jesse didn't move, Will jumped to his side. "Are you okay?" He saw blood running down Jesse's chin as he lifted him and brushed dust off his suit. "I didn't mean to hurt you."

Jesse pulled away, staggered, fished a flask from his vest pocket, and, without a word, turned toward town.

The next day Will was in a desperate hurry to get started. Morning milking done, he led his horse, Fanny, from the barn. "We only have a half hour." Will hoped it would be no more than a half hour. "I've got to get to the field, old girl."

Two years old, Fanny was too young for field work, but Will had been preparing her by hitching her to the empty wagon and walking her around the barnyard. Fanny snorted, tossed her head, looked toward him, and whinnied. She'd be a fine horse, already good on the buggy. He wished the sun would show, but clouds hung heavy, and the nighttime mist seemed content to linger in the steaming grass.

"Fanny, if I can't get to the field soon, I'll never see Mary tonight." With Frank gone and Jesse out all night feeling sorry for himself, and the next day sleeping it off, Will and his father couldn't keep up with the field work. "Do you think Mary could take to this life?" Will asked Fanny.

Fanny stopped, looked back, and neighed.

"You understand, don't you, old girl?"

Will wasn't sure why he called her old girl, but supposed it was out of habit after driving Maud so many years.

He knew that the loss of Walter's farm left him no prospects, no significant source of income. He couldn't support a family on $15 a month. He had to increase that somehow. "Do you think Frank will hire me?"

Would Frank want him? Could he find the time to work two farms?

"What do you think, old girl?"

Fanny remained silent.

"You don't seem very enthusiastic about it, now do you?"

Hard to get enthused over Frank, Will knew. Suppose he shouldn't count on his brother. Maybe he could try beef. Raise a few steers for market. He had never done it before, but it couldn't be too hard. He could pay his dad a little for the feed and still make a profit. Maybe some chickens, too. But no pigs. He'd seen enough pigs for his lifetime.

Will took one more swing around the barnyard, unhitched Fanny, and stabled her. He found his father behind the barn greasing the hay loader. "Let's get a move on, Dad. I need an early milking tonight."

"Oh? Must be seeing that Tregonning girl again. Getting serious, is it?"

"Let's get going or we'll never finish."

"Hay's still damp."

Will looked at the sky. "We better git it in while we can."

"We can't put damp hay in the barn. Do you want to burn it down?"

"I want to finish before seven."

"Use your head, Will." He handed the grease gun to his son. "Here, grease the loader while I hitch Jake and Billy."

Will shot lubricant into every fitting that protruded from the labyrinth of metal parts. Will thought about how hard it was before the loader, the days when they pitched loose hay into the wagon. That was when Frank, Jesse, and his dad helped. And Walter Duffy, too. He had greased so often, he was sure he could lubricate the machinery while taking a nap. And he probably did that a time or two, but not today. Today he better not leave any dry serks, that's for sure. All he needed was a breakdown to completely screw up his plans.

His father returned with the horses and wagon. "Hook the loader to the wagon, Will. By the time we hit the field it should be dry enough."

Will didn't stop to discuss the matter but flew to the horses, backed the wagon to the loader and hooked it on. Thomas pulled a flask from his coverall pocket and took a long swig. That was no surprise to Will.

Thomas always lubricated his throat as thoroughly as he greased his machinery. It would be a long day.

Thomas drove Jake and Billy while Will pitched hay away from the loader that spewed the day's harvest into the wagon's hinder. While the horses followed the grass snake across the uneven field, Will lurched over the pitching deck until he gained his sea legs, stopped on each wave's peak and stepped through the trough. But the unending flow of hay from the machine's giant maw filled the deck with hills and valleys that thwarted his every move. He staggered a step or two, paused, then threw his forkful of timothy and broom into the low spots. Over and over he repeated this task until hay piled high above the wagon's rails, his legs were weary, and his drenched shirt gripped his back.

Then, when his father stopped the wagon to unhitch the loader and head for the barn, Will peeled off his shirt. He knew the hay stubble would sting like a thousand needles piercing his skin and bloody his arms, but he needed to escape from the wet heat caused by the sun and his sweat.

Will thought about Mary. The longer he was away from her, the more frenzied with desire he felt. After two weeks without a break, he'd see her tonight, and he planned to make an impression. Plenty other fellows had an eye for Mary, and they'd be there, too, but he'd prepared for a month and now he had an ace up his sleeve. Walter had taught him the violin and he'd practiced all week. And the band leader, Uncle Billy, said he could call a square. He knew Mary would be impressed. She loved music; why, she played a lively piano herself.

Thomas pulled his flask and tipped it longer than most men would, but when his father offered him a drink, Will shook his head. "Not today. I'll be seeing Mary tonight, and she's death on liquor."

"Oh?"

"She's Methodist."

"Might as well wed a temperance woman."

Will didn't say it, but he thought she was that, too. "Who said I was going to marry her?"

"It sounds serious to me."

"Now that I don't have claim to Grandpa's farm, I've been thinking." Will twisted his shirt, wringing out the wet, and wiped it across his brow. "Well, I've been thinking."

"Get on with it."

"Will you give me this farm? Not right now, you know. I mean. When you retire."

"You'll wait awhile for that. I still owe on it."

"I'd pay for it. Pay a fair price."

"And where'll you get that kind of money?"

That was a problem. How'd he ever save enough on his fifteen dollar salary?

"Son. It wasn't right what Walter did. He never told me. Didn't tell anyone. Wasn't right." Thomas lifted his bottle again. "When I retire, you can buy this farm. If you're able. Wish I could give it to you, but I'd not have enough to get Gertrude a house in town. But don't plan on it for a while."

The ride back to the barn was way too slow for Will's liking, but he knew they couldn't go fast down the slopes. An overturned wagon would cut a swath through the day's progress. It was almost noon, and they hadn't put a load in the barn yet. Six more loads and milking. How'd he ever be ready when George May stopped to pick him up at seven?

After driving the loaded wagon under the hay door near the top of the barn's gable, Thomas, now atop the load, thrust a huge fork into the pile; then he jumped up and down on the fork's crossbar to drive it deep into the loose hay. Will waited in the haymow for the first stack to arrive.

From back to front, a track traversed the barn below its highest peak, protruded through and past the hay door. After Thomas buried the steel tentacles into the hay, he shouted at Gertrude to drive Fanny ahead, to pull the rope that lifted a mountain of hay upward to where the large fork snapped into the track's carriage. Thomas pulled the carriage rope that slid the hay along the track until the mountain poised over Will, who then shouted at Thomas to pull the trip rope. He hoped he was agile enough to avoid the falling stack. While Will spread the hay through the mow, Gertrude backed Fanny to their starting point and Thomas pulled the hayfork back through the hay door and down to the wagon. Then the process was repeated until the hayfields were shaved clean and the last wagon emptied.

Jesse usually ran the horse on the rope, but he was nowhere to be found, so Thomas had recruited Gertrude. Gertrude could do most of the farm jobs if she had a mind to. But, today, she didn't.

"I don't know where that no good son of ours is these days. If he expects a bed and three squares, he should do his work."

Will knew that his mother was onto Jesse, even if she didn't admit it. How could she not be?

Gertrude pointed in Thomas's direction. "If you had any gumption, you'd have him out here on the horse. I've got house work to do. Don't got time for this. I should have known better, but I married a farmer anyhow."

Thomas slipped into the well house and Will saw him take a long swig from the bottle that he hid behind the door. Then he offered his wife a dipper of ice cold spring water. She turned her back and marched toward the house.

His mother intimidated him, just like her father had. But farm life was hard. Could Mary take it? She wasn't a farm girl, had never been a farm girl. He looked down at his calloused hands and sunburned skin. He'd have to find a way to keep her out of the barn and fields. Then he smiled to himself. Maybe they'd have a passel of sons.

Without Gertrude's help, Thomas had to jump off the wagon and lead the horse, and that brought them closer to milking but farther from an empty field. Bloodied and tired, Will knew they'd never finish in time. But after a half hour of drudgery, Will got his legs, the horses their second wind, and his father, having emptied his flask, sang something about happy days while hay poured into the wagon and out again at the barn. At this rate, maybe they could begin milking by five o'clock, and he could be ready by seven. Happy day, for sure.

While he rode the wagon back to the field, Will scanned the sky. The heat drove salty rivulets down his neck, arms, and back. And there was no breeze to whisk it away. Will blinked to clear his eyes, to refocus through the shimmering heat waves. He inhaled, gasped to fill his lungs with air. It felt as if the sun demanded all the earth's oxygen in exchange for its gift of daylight. It was the kind of day that spawned summer storms. That worried Will, but he soon forgot the weather as he piled hay high in the barn's loft. They had begun to strip the first windrow of the day's last load when Will heard a metallic rattle followed by a loud clang, then the chain fell loose and hay stopped piling into the wagon. He knew immediately that the worst thing possible had happened: The loader's drive chain broke. It was then he saw lightening in the far western sky.

"Unhook the loader!" his father shouted. "We'll have to pitch the rest into the wagon."

Load the hay by hand? Will knew who'd do the pitching. And it was a slow job, even when his brothers helped. He jumped from the empty wagon and pulled the pin from the loader.

"Let's get on with it," Thomas said. "There's a storm heading this way."

And Will knew they must get this hay off the field before the storm hit. Wet hay in the field rotted. Wet hay in the barn burned. Thomas edged forward along the windrow, stopping whenever Will couldn't keep up. And Will was bushed. But tired was an occupational hazard for those who started each day at sunrise and worked into the night. Will read that some people worked a ten hour day, but he'd not seen it.

Will heaved fork after forkful into the wagon while his father drove and pitched it around. With luck they could still load all the hay that Thomas had downed three days before. The storm moved closer. Will, engulfed in hay and dust, seldom noticed the lightening, but the thunder assaulted his fatigue, reminded him that his night with Mary was rapidly slipping away. Will damned the loader, damned the weather, damned his farmhand existence.

They returned to the barnyard in time to see George May's buggy disappear down the road, but not in time to avoid the rain. Their hay was soaked before they reached the buildings.

"Might as well dump it," Thomas said. "Can't put it in wet. Have to use it for bedding. Tomorrow, we'll scatter it and hope it doesn't mildew. Better get to milking."

"Damn the milking!" Will screamed into the night. "Damn the farm." He had to find a job, any job that paid a decent living. He wanted Mary.

Will woke early and finished milking, but when Thomas told him to clean the calf pens, Will snarled, "I stayed last night, but not today. I'm going to town."

Thomas took a swig from his flask and said, "Will, I need you here. Those pens are filthy from the scours that hit the calves this week."

"Sorry, Dad. Put that bottle down, buck up, and do it yourself."

"But, Will—"

Will pushed past Thomas and headed into the house to clean up. He found his best tan cotton trouser, pulled his buttoned-down plaid shirt—the one he'd gotten for Christmas but has never worn—from the closet, and polished his brown oxfords until his fingers hurt.

Mary wasn't his first sweetheart. The girls liked Will, but there was never time to get serious. Friends began to call him "Batch." But Mary was special. Many a fella chased after the young teacher from Hinton, so Will worried that his absence the night before might push him back in line. But today, he intended to reestablish his lead status. He worried most about Fred Schmidt. Fred was persistent, and he had money. He had a motor car, too. Will didn't think Mary was interested in him, but he knew that Fred wouldn't hesitate if he saw an opening, and money bought lots of things.

When Will led Fanny from her stall, he passed his dad. He looked so sad that Will wished he'd not been so harsh. "The gate between the barnyard and lane is sagging like an old cow's milk-heavy udder," Will said. "I'm going to buy some bolts so I can fix that old barnyard gate." Calling the trip business made him feel better about running off like this.

"I need those calf pens cleaned."

"Not today, Dad." Again, he was about to tell Thomas to do it himself, but his father looked so miserable—"Later, Dad. I'll do it after I get back from town."

Will jumped into the buggy and shouted toward Fanny, "Giddyap, old girl."

Where would Mary go? He thought about driving to her apartment at the west edge of Ashley Springs, but that was farther, and he knew she usually went shopping on Saturday morning. Most farmers took their families to town Saturday night, but she had told him, "I love those kiddies, but five days a week is enough."

Sometimes Mary rented a horse and buggy and drove eight miles down the dirt road to her mother's in Hinton. He hoped this wasn't one of those weekends. If she was in town today, he'd find her—even if he had to check every store in the village. Ashley Springs' main business district, High Street, ran uphill a half mile from Commerce Street at the lower end of town to the state road on the village's northwest perimeter.

Samuels' Department Store seemed as good a place as any to start his search. So he raced down High Street and entered the door underneath the cast-iron dog.

"Mr. Samuels, has the school teacher been in today?"

"Miss Tregonning? She's been looking at a dress. Thought she might be in, but haven't seen her. Not today."

"If she stops, tell her I'm going to the library."

Will dodged people as he dashed past sturdy rock buildings, some more than fifty years old, some with painted facades and signs that advertised their wares. Maybe she stopped at Sandby's grocery. Will pushed through the front door. He looked up and down the aisles, but the store was empty. "Mr. Sandby, I thought I might find Mary Tregonning in here."

"I haven't seen her, Will. My daughter heard her say she was going to Hinton this weekend. Mirabelle's in her third grade class, you know." Sandby pointed toward a display case behind him. "I got some new corncob pipes yesterday. The salesman said they smoke real good." He pulled one from the case and offered it to Will. "Interested?"

"Only if you have a Meerschaum. I always wanted a Meerschaum." Will looked back as he pulled open the door. "Gotta go."

"Maybe she went to Hinton last weekend," Sandby said. "Memory's not so good anymore."

Will wasn't sure where to try next, but he wasn't about to quit now. He waited for two buggies to pass, then crossed the cobblestone street and looked in Silvia Antoine's Beauty Salon, but it was empty.

He remembered that Mary said her pens were smearing ink, so he raced back up High Street to Andrews' Stationary Store. That was a long shot, but he knew that Mary sometimes bought her pen nibs there. But she wasn't there. He raced back down the street toward Warner's Book Store, waved through the open door at Bennie as he passed the bar, but didn't stop when Bennie hollered, "Come on in, Will. Have a cold one."

Will turned the corner on Iowa Street and walked three blocks to Josh Whittington's Music Emporium. Maybe she was in the market for some piano music. But she wasn't there either. He began to think that Sandby's memory wasn't so bad after all.

Out of breath and his shirt soaked, Will slowed as he returned to High Street. Darn. How could he be so unlucky? Could Fanny make it to Hinton and back? He had never taken her that far before, and it was hot today; probably too hot to risk it. But he felt desperate. He looked into Mason's Hardware. Might as well buy those bolts.

Will liked Bob Mason. He liked to shoot the breeze and talk village gossip with him. Everyone liked Bob. And if anyone knew who was out and about, it would be Bob Mason.

"Bob, I hear you're going to run for mayor."

"Mayor? Nah. Not interested."

"You have lots of customers out there."

"I couldn't beat Tommy, you know that."

"He doesn't need the job. Municipal judge work keeps him busy."

"I've got more than enough with the store and family."

Will supposed eight kids would keep a man home—that and the loveliest wife in town.

"I saw your lady heading down the street a while ago," Bob said.

"Mary?"

Will forgot the sagging gate as he rushed out the door and ran toward his favorite place in town, the library at the bottom of High Street, the last stop on his route down the hill. If Mary was there, he hoped she hadn't already left. He glanced through store windows as he ran toward the library, but didn't see Mary, and he didn't stop to ask.

Will took the library's steps two at a time to the little rock building's door, but he stopped and removed his cap before entering. The library smell was distinct and fresh, but old, too. He supposed it was because of all the history stored there. He looked around the large room but didn't see a familiar face.

Will loved this room. He would read the latest editions of *The Breeder's Gazette*, *Hoard's Dairyman* and *Farm Journal*, or catch up on world news. He would read the *Wisconsin State Journal*, and sometimes he'd pull *The Chicago Tribune*, or maybe the Sunday editions of The *New York Times* or The *Wall Street Journal*. So many choices that he couldn't possibly read them all, but mostly they wrote about the same stuff anyway.

He glanced up the nearest rows of neatly stacked books, but he saw no one. She must not have come here. He pulled the *Wisconsin State Journal* from the newspaper rack and saw that Europe was aflame with hostilities. It wouldn't take much to embroil the Old World in war.

Then, from the corner of his eye, he saw a floral covered dress emerge from the far stacks. He looked up, and when he saw it was Mary, he felt a little light headed. The newspaper slipped from his fingers. "Why, Mary, I heard you went to Hinton. I never expected to see you today."

"Oh." She cocked her head and smiled.

Will was certain that she saw through his little white lie. "I'm so embarrassed that I missed the dance last night. We had a breakdown in the field, and—"

"That Fred Schmidt, he pestered me all night long."

Jealousy overcame Will. "I suppose Fred—"

"Don't you worry about Fred. The other boys kept me so busy, I only gave him one dance."

Will tossed a shoulder and forced a smile. "You don't know what you missed, what I had planned for you."

"Oh, tell me, Will."

"You're so pretty in your new flowered dress."

Mary lifted the dress to show her ankles, and then tiptoed a circle.

Will's eyes followed her movement across the floor. "Mighty nice."

"Will! You didn't even look at the dress."

He felt himself blush. "I did. I liked that, too!"

"You should be ashamed." She wagged her finger. "I spent my hard-earned money and you didn't even look at it."

But Will knew that Mary was pleased. "Why, it's prettier than the dress in Samuel's front window. And he puts his finest out there."

"Will! It's the dress from Samuel's front window. I bought it an hour ago."

"How'd I not notice? It can't be the dress then. Must be the girl wearing it. But I don't miss everything, my dear. I've noticed that you're a beautiful lass whatever you're wearing."

"You're not Irish, are you, young man?"

"No indeed, ma'am." Will tossed a shoulder and flashed a sly grin. "We O'Shaughnessys are as German as Kaiser Bill."

"And I suppose you think the Tregonnings are English like that man Churchill."

"You aren't?" He stepped back in feigned shock.

Mary took a swipe at him. "You better be careful about calling me names." She tossed her head and laughed—a soft deep throated laugh that made Will feel weak with pleasure.

Will scooped the newspaper off the floor, hung it on the rack, and took Mary's hand. "Will you join me across the street at Shopley's? I'll buy you a root beer float."

"Make it a cherry phosphate and you've got a date. First, let me check out this book. I've wanted to read Fielding ever since school started, but I couldn't find the time. Too many papers, but I'm more organized now."

They paused to let a wagon pass; then they walked hand-in-hand across the street to the soda fountain and candy store. Shopley's had three light bulbs hanging over the counter and one above each aisle. And they left them lighted all day long. But Will mostly loved the smells that permeated the store—cinnamon, wintergreen, chocolate, peppermint—all blended into an amalgam that floated out the door and fanned in all directions. Shopley's didn't need a sign to tout their wares.

Will ordered one cherry phosphate and a root beer soda.

"Tell me, Will, what was the surprise?"

"I planned to play my fiddle, a tune just for you. I've been practicing 'Listen to the Mockingbird' every night for the last month." Will believed he could charm the birds right out of the meadow with his sweet music. "And Uncle Billy said I could call a square, too. All for the most beautiful, most elegant, and smartest lass in Iowa County."

Mary blushed. "And you say you're German. Sounds like Irish blarney to me."

"'Tis nothing but the unvarnished truth."

Mary slapped Will's hand ever so lightly, then rested her fingers on his for so long that he wanted to drop to his knees and proclaim his love, right there in Shopley's.

"Mary, I—" but only gravel came out. Excitement surged through his body, but he didn't dare express his feelings, not yet anyhow. He cleared the huskiness from his throat. "Did you like Uncle Billy's Hayseeds? About the best we've got 'round here, don't you think?"

"I do wish you'd been there. Can you really call squares?"

Will stood, pretended to raise a fiddle to his shoulder and take a bow in hand; then he bowed low to his sweetheart.

He bowed right. "Honor your partner." Bowed to his left. "Honor your corner."

Then he fiddled away while he called:

Allemande right and allemande left
All hands round.
Ladies in the swill barrel
Upside down.

"Will O'Shaughnessy, that's indecent!" She slapped at his arm and turned away, but coyly looked back. "You were really going to call that?"

But before he could answer, the attendant set the soda in front of Will and handed a cherry phosphate to Mary.

"I thought you favored ice cream sodas," Will said.

"Yes, but I like anything cherry." She averted her eyes. "I'm avoiding ice cream."

"Avoiding ice cream? A dairy farmer's wife can't avoid—" Will turned red.

Mary reached across the table and caressed his hand. "Is that a proposal?"

He clasped her soft hand between his two burly ones, regained his composure, and looked into Mary's blue eyes. He thought they were the most beautiful eyes he had ever seen, bluer than the cornflowers his mother grew alongside her house.

"I wish—but not yet, Mary. You deserve better, and I hope I can give it before long. I hope you'll wait."

Mary smiled the sweet smile that always tugged at his heartstrings as she set her empty glass down and placed her other hand on his.

Hand-in-hand. He wanted nothing more than to go through life hand-in-hand with Mary. They walked to the door together, and before she turned toward home, she reached out with a hug. Will was so happy over his realization that Mary really cared for him that he forgot about Fred.

That night, while he cleaned the calf pens, he couldn't keep his mind off his lovely lady from Hinton.

Will felt desperate. If he was to secure Mary's hand, he had to find a good job. For a few days Will had been working at the feed mill, helping Toonie Smith while he recovered from a bout with the gout, but Will knew it wouldn't last long. He needed to find other work.

Will pushed his way into Bennie's Bar. Bennie would know whether anyone needed a worker. Light from the single overhead bulb reflected off the counter, so bright that Will could read "In God We Trust" on the nickel he tossed onto the lacquered surface.

"What'll it be, Will?"

"Pour me a glass of our hometown brew."

"Mineral Springs?" Bennie tilted the schooner as he ran beer into it. Will watched the glass turn golden until it was almost full, then Bennie tipped it upright and added a fluffy white topper. "A beautiful brew and a bargain, too." He set the beer in front of Will and dropped two pennies alongside.

Will sipped the brew. "Tastes good." He drank longer.

"I see you in town a bit more often these days. What's up?"

"I'm working nights at the feed mill until Toonie Smith returns."

"I hear he's got the gout. Bad stuff when you're on your feet all day."

"It adds a few dollars to the fifteen a month Dad pays, but it won't last long."

"Got plans, have you?"

"I can't afford plans. Can't stay home much longer though."

"Your mother's a good cook, I hear. You can't beat a home-cooked meal. That's worth something, isn't it?"

"That, clean clothes, and a soft tick bed, but I … well, I'm not getting any younger, you know. I'll be twenty-five this winter."

"You're thinking about that school teacher, are you?"

Will felt himself blush. "It'll take more than fifteen dollars a month if I want her."

Bennie reached for a stack of glasses that had dried on a soiled wash cloth, but he remained silent.

"Then there's the other problem," Will said.

"Oh?"

"All I know is farming. All I've ever wanted is a farm."

"I know several farms on the market."

"Where'd I get that kind of money?"

"It's not so easy, I guess."

"Someday I'll have my own farm, Bennie."

"It's tough to get started these days. I've heard if you can afford to farm, you can afford not to."

"My teachers said I was smart enough. Maybe I can learn a new trade. You don't know of anyone looking for help, do you?"

Bennie shook his head. "Not right that Frank got your Grandpa's farm. I never see him. I guess he doesn't appreciate life's finer things."

"That's another reason Grandpa liked Frank. A teetotaler, you know." Will hoisted his half-full glass. "Grandpa thought I'd gone to hell when I left for school at Madison. He thought State Street was the devil's lair. Just one more reason for not liking me."

"I suppose some of my regulars got their initiation there. We should send more of our young to Madison." Bennie sloshed a glass in the sink's sudsy water, swiped it with a gray towel, and set it back on the shelf. "Problem is, most don't come back."

"Dad can't afford to pay the money I need. He could do better, but he's steeped in the old ways. Not open to new ideas." Will tipped the schooner, sipped long, and set the empty glass on the bar.

"So you've got your pants all tied in a knot over that school marm. Better get a move on. Lotsa fellas eyeing her." Bennie pushed Will's empty glass aside and leaned over the counter. "Now I think about it, I remember hearing that Patterson needs help." He lowered his voice. "His wife's in a terrible way. She's got consumption, you know."

"The Ford man? Sells those god-awful, smelly machines? Must be someone else needs help."

"I don't know anyone else."

"Beggars can't be choosy, I suppose. Cars? Not sure I can do it, Bennie."

Bennie snatched Will's glass off the bar and turned back toward the keg. "Another one?"

"No more, Bennie. Gotta go."

Will heard noises out back, so he moved in that direction. When he stuck his head through the garage door, he saw a pair of legs sticking out from under the Lizzie's running board. Banging and curses emerged from underneath. Will bent to see the legs' owner. "Is that you, Mr. Patterson?"

Will didn't know Patterson well, but knew he turned his bicycle and wagon shop toward automobiles when Henry brought out his Model T. He must be doing okay, Will thought. Beside Fred Schmidt's car, there must be a dozen Lizzies running around the county now. They scared the bejeebers outa his horses.

A small body twisted and turned as it squirmed from under the metal contraption. Will wasn't sure he could do this work. He'd rather shoe a kicking horse.

Patterson straightened and brushed grime off his coveralls. "I can't get that durned bearing off. Soaked it with oil. Maybe that'll loosen it." He threw a greasy rag into a barrel. "What can I do for you, young man? Looking to buy a new Lizzie?" He moved toward his office. "O'Shaughnessy, isn't it?"

"I'm looking for work, Mr. Patterson. It's Will. Will O'Shaughnessy."

"You farm, don't you?"

"Dad can't pay enough. Need more than fifteen dollars a month. I want to get married."

"Maybe you heard. My Matilda's real sick. Has TB. I may have to leave Ashley Springs. Doctor says she won't last much longer in this climate. He says I should go west to where the air is dry."

"That's awful. What'll you do with the business?"

"That's the problem. I should unload it. Too bad. I'm starting to do well. I can use a worker, but a buyer would be better."

Will shrugged and turned toward the door. "I sure hope your wife gets better. I've heard dry air does wonders. There was a professor at Madison who went to Twenty Nine Palms, in California, for his TB. I didn't know him, but Professor Babcock said he was doing real well. I hope you find someone." Will grasped the garage doorknob.

"Not so fast, young man. I said I need a worker."

Will avoided town for a week. He helped his father cut corn and haul the ears to the granary, but Jesse wasn't around much, and when he was, he slept late. Will knew it was a hangover. His father did, too, but he didn't say much. It wouldn't do no good.

Will was thankful for the late October warm spell. With the corn picked now, and most of the cows dried up and out to pasture, his father could handle the milking until spring when the cows freshened again. Will had been reluctant to tell his father about Patterson's offer so soon after Frank's leaving, but he'd decided to tell him tonight.

The six cows they still milked produced little, so milking didn't take long. Supper over, Will's mother went to bed early, sick with a headache, and Will sat alone with Thomas in the parlor.

Will licked his lips and stared at his boots. "Dad, we've gotta talk."

Thomas removed his wire-rimmed glasses and looked up from the Ashley Springs' *Weekly Democrat*. "Yes, son?"

"You know that I'm fond of Mary Tregonning." Will fidgeted in his chair.

"You're lucky to have so fine a lady, yes you are." He gazed at Will and smiled a broad smile. Small creases in his pudgy face danced between his upturned lips and eyes. "As pretty a lass as there is in the county. Smart, too, they say."

"That she is." Will leaned forward. "And I want—"

"It's getting serious, is it, now?" The smile faded. "You're thinking of marriage?"

Will's cheeks warmed. "I can't get married. Not yet. Not without money." He stood and faced his dad. "I know you can't afford more."

"More than fifteen dollars? Farm's not big enough. I can't get ahead as it is."

Will wanted to suggest they farm on shares, change some things, get modern, but he had preached modern for years and got nowhere.

The newspaper slid from Thomas's lap as he rose off his chair, stared across the room. "I wish I could help. You know I do."

Will noticed the tremor in his voice and felt sorry for him. He felt guilty that he thought to leave, but he had to tell him. "I have a chance to work for Mr. Patterson."

Thomas jerked his head toward Will. "You plan to leave? This soon? How can I get by? You'd leave me now?"

"Dad, there's no other way. You said you can't afford more money."

"But Frank's gone, too. Maybe you could bring your lady here. She could help mother. We'd give you both room and board."

"Dad. She's a teacher. Besides, it could never work out. You know that. She and mother—"

"S'pose not." Thomas slumped back into his chair. "Bound to happen sooner or later. But with Frank gone, and Jesse…"

"You don't need us through winter."

"But Fords?" Thomas frowned. "I thought you didn't like motor cars."

"It's opportunity. The only one I've got. Patterson wants to teach me the business. I hate to leave. I'd never do it at harvest time." Will stood over his dad and flashed a wan smile. "Besides, maybe this won't work out. Maybe I'm not cut out for it. Maybe I'll be back soon."

"Maybe Jesse'll have straightened out by spring," Thomas said.

"Little chance of that."

"Probably not." Thomas rose, walked to the secretary, and rolled the top up. "There are plenty of neighbor kids who'll work for a few dollars, so don't you worry 'bout that." He removed his pipe and a pouch of tobacco, slid the rolltop down, and leaned back against the desk.

"Are you sure you'll be okay, Dad?"

Thomas lit his pipe, took a long draw, and blew a puff of smoke toward the ceiling. "Son, you've dated a few fillies, so you know your way 'round the paddock. If you've decided on Mary, you'd better grab her. You know what Aunt Net said about her nephew Joe, don't you?"

"What was that?"

"'He jumped over many a pretty flower and landed on a pissablossom.' That's what she said. S'pose you better take Aunt Net's advice and pluck that pretty flower."

Will was excited but apprehensive, too. He didn't much like mechanical things, but this promised more income than he could ever make at home. Will was to report Monday morning. Patterson said he'd start him at twenty dollars but pay forty a month if he panned out. And he could stay in the spare room above the shop for free. Even though he didn't like cars, he was eager to begin.

Patterson started by teaching Will to service the cars and do the most common repair work. Then, after they closed the shop, he took Will out for driving lessons. Before month's end Will began to feel comfortable around the Tin Lizzies. How they ever got that name, he wasn't sure. Patterson couldn't help him there, but he helped with most everything else. He was a patient and fair man. And best of all, he said that Will had learned the repairs so fast that he paid him forty dollars the first month. But Will felt a sinking feeling when, at the end of the second month, Patterson handed him the paycheck and said, "I've decided to sell. I've gotta get my wife out West. But I'll give you the first chance."

He might as well be offered the Taj Mahal. How could he ever get that money? He wanted to save enough to get married and maybe return to the farm some day. But would a new boss keep him on? At first Will hesitated, but soon Patterson insisted.

"I've gotta move on this, Will. I hate to push, but see what you can do."

Will was excited but doubtful as he approached the bank. Would they give him the money? George Tyler, the bank president, had always loaned his dad money for seed and livestock.

"So you want to buy a business?" Tyler said. "That's pretty ambitious for a farm boy. What do you know about automobiles? I can't lend money unless there's reason to believe you'll succeed. The directors wouldn't approve, you know."

"I've learned a lot the last two months, and Patterson says I'm ready."

"How much does he want for the business?"

"Two thousand dollars, sir. I don't have anywhere near that." Will forced a smile. "The fact is, I don't have but a hundred dollars."

Tyler shook his head. "You must know that I can't loan it all. There'll have to be a down payment." He pressed his hands into his desk and leaned toward Will. "I want to help, Will. Your father's been a good customer. I know you're a good worker and that you were a good student, so I'm inclined to take a chance, but my directors will decide. And you'll have to find twenty percent." He folded his hands and sat back in his oversized chair. "I can't act with any less. See what you can do, then get back to me."

Will pained over it for a week. Four hundred dollars. He had two hundred dollars once, but he spent it on school. He thought short courses would help him become a better farmer. But where could he ever find another three hundred now?

Through the window he saw Patterson on the phone. Will hesitated with his hand on the knob. Patterson's face was drawn, and he paced back and forth at the end of the telephone cord like a tethered lamb. At first Will stayed outside because he didn't want to intrude, but Patterson lowered the phone and waved him in. Then he pointed to the hard backed chair beside his desk as he placed the phone back in its cradle. "I'm getting desperate. That was Dr. Ruggles. He says he'll have to put Matilda in the sanitarium until we go west. Have you decided, Will? Can you do it?"

Will explained the banker's requirements, and that he needed four hundred dollars but only had a hundred.

"I'd help, but every cent of profit goes to the doctor, and I'll need my savings to start out West. But I'll tell you what. If you'll agree to work for another two months while I get my affairs in order, I'll pay you the eighty dollars up front. You can apply that money to the down payment."

Will wanted to agree, but he would still be two hundred twenty short with nothing left to entertain Mary. He knew that Fred could smother her in dollar bills, and if given the opening, he'd do just that. Will was glad he hadn't been in this fix a year earlier, before he felt secure in his relationship with Mary. But he was still uneasy. And where could he get two hundred twenty dollars? Will could think of one possibility, but he was hesitant to do it.

Will wasn't sure where to turn. Then on Saturday afternoon, when he was replacing a broken board on his father's calf pen, Thomas called him to the house. "Telephone."

Will startled, and his misplaced swing sent the nail into the manager, but he was half way to the house before the thought struck him that he should look for it. A chunk of metal could kill a calf. He'd expected a return call from Mary, an answer to his request that she accompany him to the hay ride, so he stretched his stride and slammed into Thomas as he raced through the door. "Sorry, Dad."

"Whoa, son. In a mighty hurry to trade Fanny for that Lizzie, now aren't you? It's Patterson."

"Hello, Mr. Patterson?"

"Have you decided yet, Will? I need to know."

"Right now?"

"John Elder's son wants to buy. John has the money, but I don't want him."

"Serge?"

"I can't wait much longer. I've gotta know soon. Matilda's desperate to get outa that place."

"I understand."

Will walked toward the loft, to where his father pitched hay down the chute. "Dad," Will hollered through the dust. "Patterson says I've got to decide now. Serge Elder wants to buy the business. His father'll grubstake him."

"Serge Elder couldn't sell a two dollar gold piece for a plug nickel. He beats Jesse to the bars."

"Patterson doesn't like him either, but his wife's pushing hard to get out of that sanitarium." Will flopped onto a feed bag. "How'll I ever get enough money?"

"Did you try Frank?"

Will had considered Frank. He'd mulled it over every night since he talked to George Tyler. He didn't want to do it, but he had no choice. He would have to approach his brother.

Fanny nuzzled his shoulder and nickered when Will pulled her from the barn. He hadn't told her about his plan to leave the farm for good and supposed now was as good a time as any. "Fanny, I'm thinking about going to town."

When Fanny pulled away at the pronouncement, Will knew she understood. "Don't you worry now. You'll go along, too."

Fanny resisted his tugs on the halter.

"You don't want to leave. I understand. Not sure I do either, but it's the only way. You'll like Mary, yes you will."

But Fanny wasn't appeased. She continued to resist his urging.

"Now don't you worry, old girl. It probably won't even work out. I don't have the money yet."

Fanny refused to budge.

"It won't be forever. Only until I earn enough to get married. I promise, Fanny, I'll get you back to the farm before you grow old."

But what about Mary? Would she want to honor this promise? Will didn't mention these doubts to Fanny.

Fanny moved to the traces, but ever so slowly. Will knew she wasn't convinced either.

He hadn't been there since he pulled his grandpa from the hog pen, and he hadn't planned to return, not so soon anyway. He and Frank were never close. Even at school they had different friends, and Frank was never interested in books and new ideas. But he worked hard at home. Will had to give him that. They were both conscientious, but in their own ways. Life takes strange twists. Will had been closer to Jesse, even though Jesse didn't give a hoot about anything after he dropped out of school and ran with a bad crowd. He was always fond of liquor, but he fell off the edge when everyone around him boozed the night through. But Frank took Walter's ways from the time he was little. He never crossed Grandpa. That's why he had the farm now, Will supposed.

He heard Frank in the barn as he reined Fanny and tied her to his grandpa's cast-iron hitching post. Will looked across the farmstead. Walter Duffy may have been a hard man, but he earned his conceit. Not a rotted or loose board on any building, no mud holes in his yards. Will didn't know another farmer in the county who'd shoveled his barnyard so cows wouldn't wallow in muck and manure. Will supposed he shouldn't blame him for having been particular about its future.

Will avoided the hog pens as he made his way around the building toward the milk house. Frank saw him coming and lowered the pails he washed. "Hello, Will. I didn't expect to see you."

"I didn't expect to come."

"Well?" Frank said.

"Frank. Uh—" Will felt weak. "This is hard, but I have to ask a favor. I need money."

With no hint of his intent, Frank stared at Will as if he were sorting cows for keeping or market.

"I need two hundred twenty dollars. I don't even know if you have it, but I have no choice."

"I have the two twenty, but why should I give it to you?"

"I have a chance to buy Patterson's Ford dealership. I can have my own business." Will shifted his feet. "I'd rather be anywhere but here asking for money."

"Why do you think you're a businessman? Grandpa didn't think so."

"He wasn't fair." Will felt his neck warm. "You must know that." Will wanted to bash Frank, but he held back. "He had no reason. I always did well. I worked hard and was the top student in my class. Doesn't that count for something?"

"Maybe."

"But I've got to let the man know. He won't wait. I've gotta know now, Frank."

"Come back next week."

"I don't have a week."

Frank grinned but remained silent.

Will knew that Frank was extolling his pound of flesh. And there wasn't a thing he could do about it.

Frank turned toward the wash tub and grabbed a brush, but turned back before he touched it to the pail. "I've got the money, and I'll decide if and when it goes to work. I'll think about it."

W ill rushed straight to Patterson's garage. "Mr. Patterson, I might get the money, but I won't know until next week. Can you hold off until then?"

"Will, I want to. I think you'll uphold my reputation. But John Elder's put the squeeze on. He deposited the money at the bank with the order to put it in my account as soon as I've signed the agreement." Patterson pointed to his desk top. "There it is. Just waiting for my signature."

"I'll let you know as soon as I find out. It'll only be a week."

"There's a hitch, Will. Elder gave me two days. If I don't let him know in two days, says he'll pull the money."

"Can you get him to wait?"

"He's a slick operator, but I don't want to sell to him. I'd sure like you to have it, but Matilda's in a terrible way. Just stays in bed. Cries all the time. She won't even look at me. I don't know, Will. I'm in an awful fix."

Will felt caught between Frank's obstinacy and Elder's pressure, but all he could do was to keep busy and wait. He repaired fence. He trimmed trees. He hitched Fanny to the wagon, walked her up the lane and back again. He positioned grain bags so that his father would have little trouble pulling them out for feeding. When in the house, he stayed within hearing distance of the phone and waited for Frank's call, which he knew would come. Like his grandpa, Frank may be an SOB, but he was a dependable SOB. He prided himself on keeping his word.

But it had been seven days since he visited Frank and he still hadn't heard. Cold and snow came early, so Thomas decided to keep the cows in the barn. That meant shoveling gutters and hauling manure to the fields. Will was spreading manure in the far hay field when Frank's call came. Thomas rode out to tell him the news. "Frank called. He wants to see you."

Will hitched Fanny to the buggy and raced toward the old farm.

Frank strolled from the house when Will and Fanny slogged up the drive. Will could see he was expecting them. And Frank didn't waste any time. He grabbed Fanny's harness before Will got off the buggy.

"Have you decided?"

"Do you think Grandpa would have lent you the money?"

"Grandpa's dead." No wonder he got the farm. Why couldn't he be his own man? "What will you do?"

"Grandpa was a good judge of people. And I'm not sure he'd do it. He wouldn't put his money at risk."

"Frank, for heaven's sake, will you loan me the money?"

"I suppose I owe you a little. But business is business. I'll expect interest. And I'll want a security."

"You know I don't own anything. If I had collateral, I could get the money elsewhere." He reached toward Frank. "After I get on my feet, I'll make it worth your while. I'll give you a deal on a Lizzie."

"Why'd I want a Lizzie? No, I expect something now."

"But I don't have anything now." Will slumped.

"You do, Will. Grandmother's diamond wedding ring and her diamond brooch, too. You're the only one who got anything when she died. I expect the money to be repaid in a year, and I'll hold them until then, but no longer."

Grandmother's ring and brooch? Will hoped to propose, to give Doris's ring to Mary at Christmas. But he had no choice. Would Mary wait awhile longer? And then there was that more pressing matter: had Patterson waited?

W ill wasn't sure how to tell Mary that he couldn't afford to court her for a while because he would be spending even more time under the Tin Lizzies. Although most of the old farmers he knew were skeptical, Will felt certain the motor car business would thrive. His young friends were excited by anything that could go forty miles per hour. He was committed now, and Patterson expected him first thing Monday morning.

He thought about his agreement with Frank. His brother hadn't always held the upper hand. It wasn't that long ago that he'd challenged Will to a competition driving fence posts. They'd set and pounded posts from morning till night, agreed each day's winner would be exempt from helping Walter for a week. After being whipped four straight days, Frank quit the contest. Will smiled as he remembered Frank's chagrin when he had to do the milking all month. At the time Will felt so much pride in showing who was the better man that he decided he liked building fence lines. But maybe giving Frank that extra time with Grandpa wasn't so good an idea after all.

Will pushed the uneasiness from his mind and concentrated on the beauty around him. Fanny stepped quickly through the new snow. Her rhythmic hoof beats harmonized with the cutter blades' schuss across a white, velvet carpet that sparkled in the full-moon's light. Southwest Wisconsin was never more beautiful than on a night like this, a night when fresh falling snow fluttered onto the pastures, houses, and roadways, covering them with a coat of white. No grubby fields, no filthy rooftops, no muddy roads, no darkness—only light. This white wonderland lifted Will's spirits. All was right in his world. He would be with Mary tonight.

Although he knew that he wouldn't finish milking in time to attend, Will had arranged to meet Mary at the Granger's house party, and from there they would go to the hayride. Mary liked his little cutter, too. She said it looked like a Currier and Ives print. His friends said it was too small, but he thought it was perfect for courting. Will shivered at the thought of Mary pressed tightly against his side.

Mary paced the porch. She looked like a picture straight from a fashion magazine, in a red wool coat that was highlighted by floral embroidery down both sides of the button placket and her black high top boots. How could he deserve such a beauty? Could he afford to keep her in style? Will's spirits sagged at the thought, but rose again when she ran down the steps and past Fred Schmidt without even saying a word.

Will helped Mary into the cutter, returned to the driver's side, and pulled up beside her. When he clucked his tongue and flicked the reins, Fanny nickered softly and surged forward, moving as if she knew the importance of this night and wanted to do her part.

"I've never been on a hayride before, but my students talk about them all the time. Sometimes they whisper so I can't hear." Mary giggled. "Why'd they do that?"

"Gosh, I wouldn't know, but maybe we'll find out tonight." He jostled her side. "Do you think?"

"You're naughty."

Will's worries melted as the fluffy snow piled around them, and his spirits soared with Mary at his side.

Two teams of giant Belgians, hitched to sleighs so full that hay fell off the sides, stood alongside the Fitzsimmons's barn. When Mary saw them she dropped her blanket, stood, and clasped her hands to her face. "Will, they're beautiful. I've never seen such animals. They're so big." She reached out and touched the nose of the nearest one who responded with a head shake and a nicker. Mary pulled her hand back and laughed. "Whose are they?"

"William Fitzsimmons owns this farm. He loves matched pairs. Me, too, even if they aren't Belgians. Dad says he'll let me take his foil, Mabel, when she's old enough. She's a bookend to Fanny."

Fanny voiced her approval.

"Do we have to wait for the others?" Mary said. "Can we find a spot in the hay?"

"Go up front, near the middle. Everyone else will want to hang their feet off the sides—until they get cold." He handed Mary two wool blankets. "Take these. I'll unhitch Fanny and put her in the barn."

Mary climbed aboard, maneuvered around the bodies, and tiptoed toward the top of the wagon.

"I saw that," Will shouted from the barn door. "You're pretty agile for a town girl." He ran to the sleigh, climbed aboard, and sank deep into the hay when he dropped beside her.

"I have to be, chasing students all day. Besides, agility's in my genes. My ancestors were hard-rock miners. They had to snake through holes no bigger than those a badger would make."

"You don't look like a hard-rock miner," Will said as he snuggled tight to her side.

"I'm lucky that Mother insisted I have a vocation. Otherwise, I'd not be so prettily dressed, nor have hands so soft. She slaved like a mule all her life, most miners' wives do. I'll not do that." Will heard determination in her voice. "I'll never earn a living by the sweat of my brow."

Will's heart sank.

"But enough about me. Is your Patterson job going to work out?"

Will had hoped to enjoy the night together before telling her the news. He pulled the blankets over their legs. "It's getting chilly," he said. Then he sat quiet for a long spell.

"Did I say something I shouldn't?" Mary said.

"No, no, Mary, it's just that—"

"Hey, Will, got room up there?" a voice called from below.

Cutters, horses, and one Ford sedan filtered into the yard. Friends, acquaintances, and strangers scurried about tending their animals and filling the sleighs. People piled into the hay. Mostly they ignored everyone around them except the sweetheart they brought along. Like a church pew, the wagon's outside spaces filled first. Blanket-covered legs dangled over the sides and bodies snuggled for warmth. That was the excuse, but a good bit of canoodlin' put the lie to that claim. As stragglers pushed toward the wagon's interior, tempers flared and complaints were voiced, but no hostilities erupted. Love, not violence, permeated the air.

"Will, that you up there?" Bill Yahnke called out as he helped his wife onto the wagon. Bill owned the Ford sedan parked next to the machine shed. "Patterson tells me you're going to buy his business. Terrible 'bout his wife, isn't it?"

"You're buying the business?" Mary said. She flung the blanket aside and jumped up. Hands on her hips, she looked down at Will with a perplexed look on her face. "You didn't tell me."

"I was going to, but it's not so fine as you might think."

She cocked her head and wrinkled her brow. "Yes?"

He explained the terms, explained the demands it would make on his time and resources. "This may be our last night together for a while. Maybe for a long while. I'll hardly have a dime to my name until I take over the dealership, and I can't know what'll happen afterwards. I'm excited about getting my own business, but I'm bothered, too. I don't want to lose you."

Mary dropped next to him, snuggled close, and took his hand. "You won't lose me, Will. You're a silly man if you think your work can keep us apart forever. My father left and we waited and waited, but he never came home. But I'll know this time, you'll be near all along." She reached to him and turned his face to hers. "Besides, I have some money. And I can't think of a better way to use it. I won't let you spend all your time under an old Lizzie."

Love overwhelmed Will. He should have known that his Mary would be there for him. Will pulled her close and felt weak all over when she reached up and kissed his cheek. He snuggled into her and kissed back. It was a passionate kiss. This time on the lips.

Will felt warmed to his innermost fiber. He was excited to see his future prospects matching his heartfelt desires, but he knew time could change things.

7

Will fumbled with the key. It was his first day alone at the shop. He knew where to begin, but it wasn't the beginning that worried him. Patterson's words rang in his ears. "Now, Will, I expect you to uphold my standards."

Could he do it? It had been easy the first four months with Patterson by his side.

Patterson wouldn't leave until all the repair work was completed, so they had worked through the weekend. Late Sunday night, after scrubbing up, they walked out the door in silence. Patterson turned the key in the lock and handed it to Will. "It's all yours now, Will. Do your best." He shook Will's hand and said, "I think you're ready, and I wish you success."

"I hope so, Mr. Patterson, but I'll admit, I'm a bit nervous."

"Bound to be and that's okay. Keeps you on your toes. Remember, Will, always think of your customer. That's why I stayed until Sherman's repair was done. When he brought his Lizzie in, I told him I'd fix it, and I owed him that." Patterson's eyes met Will's, and Will saw sadness there. "I'm counting on you, Will."

When Patterson stepped into his Lizzie, he turned back, scanned the building, and sighed.

"Mr. Patterson. I'll do my best, I promise."

"I know you will, and you'll do okay. You've got the knack for it. But I'm nervous, too. I don't know 'bout this California place. I've never been past the Mississippi River."

Will took a rag off the rack and began polishing the big black sedan, the one car on a one-car showroom floor. It was delivered the past Friday, just in time for Patterson to see his last sale readied for the new owner, Lawyer Reed. Patterson didn't have time to finish the prep so he told Will, "First thing tomorrow morning, get that car ready. Reed will be here early, and he'll expect it tip top."

The shop didn't open until eight o'clock, but Will mopped dust off Reed's Lizzie at six. He had met Reed, but Will's family did their business with Attorney Brower.

By opening time, the car shined from Will's effort. He had scrubbed and waxed the outside, washed the windows, dusted the dash and steering wheel, and brushed the seat until his knuckles bled.

Reed marched into the showroom at eight o'clock, but he didn't say hello. He walked around his sedan, looked close at times, and paused every now and then to wipe his fingers across the metal. Reed opened the trunk and bent to look inside. When Will saw him nod, he hoped it was a sign of approval.

Reed slowly opened the driver side door, closed it, and then reopened it again and slid inside. He reached across to the passenger side and ran his gloved hand over the seat and across the dash. He inspected each finger, and then took the steering wheel in hand.

When he noticed Reed's lips curl into the slightest of smiles, Will began to feel better.

Reed sat behind the wheel and shifted his weight from side to side. Then he stepped out and approached Will, who, except for the apprehension, felt unconnected to this unfolding performance.

"Will O'Shaughnessy, isn't it? Patterson said you'd be here. Have we met?"

Will nodded.

Reed held out his hand and Will took it. A firm grasp, but not too tight. He released his grip and pointed at the sedan. "Seems to be in top shape."

Will exhaled. "I hope so, sir." He stepped toward the vehicle. "Would you like me to show you the controls?"

"No need." He waved Will away. "Patterson rode with me before I purchased. I didn't want to rush into anything so important as giving up my registered steed."

"No, sir, that wouldn't do."

"Just take it to the street and I'll be on my way. I paid Patterson the money."

"Yes, sir."

Will watched Reed drive away and hoped future clients would be friendlier.

Without a customer, a vehicle to repair, or paperwork to complete, Will ambled through the shop, dusted shelves, rearranged parts, and mopped the floor. He wouldn't make a living this way.

Then at noon hour, after he took a ham sandwich and a bottle of cold tea from his lunch pail, but before he took a bite, the door bell tinkled and Silas Murrish lumbered into the shop. Will had known Silas, a drinking buddy of his father, for about as long as he could remember.

"Hello, Silas. What can I do for you this fine day? Did you stop to wish me success in my new venture?"

"That I did, but I've been thinking."

Will had never seen Silas so nervous.

"Your father said you'd be here."

"I appreciate your stopping."

"You don't think I'm too old, do you?"

"Silas, are you thinking about buying a Lizzie? Why, you'd be my first customer. You'd sure look good sitting in one of these beauties." Will pulled the picture book from his desk drawer and handed it to Silas. "Look at these."

Silas leafed through the pages.

Will reached for the brochure and turned to a black, sleek convertible. "Driving one of those around town and flying cross the country like a bird on wing—why, you'll think you're a kid again. You'll never have felt so young."

Will smiled to himself while he wrote the order and stuffed the fifty dollar down payment into his desk drawer. Funny how profit makes you see the world differently.

"You think I'll be able to handle that speed?" Silas said.

"I'll give you lessons. We'll start slow. You won't have trouble, none at all. And you won't have to feed it, groom it, or rub it down. Just come back now and then for service. I'll see to that." Will patted Silas on his back as he walked from the showroom.

And the orders continued. By the end of the month, Will waited for four deliveries from Highland Park, Henry Ford's Michigan plant. In the meantime Patterson's customers returned for service and repairs. Maybe he could sell cars after all.

Six months later, with money in his pocket and his prospects looking bright, Will felt confident. He lay in bed, but he didn't sleep. It was one of those hot, sticky August nights when back home, his window wide open, he would hear the corn stretching upward as he lay naked on his sheet. He couldn't sleep, but it wasn't the heat. All he could think about was Mary.

The next morning, Will entered Luedke's Jewelry Store and looked at the many rings under the glass counter.

"Can I help you?" a man said in a pleasant voice.

"Oh, Mr. Luedke. I'm thinking—"

"Thinking 'bout that Tregonning girl, are you? Not only the prettiest girl in Iowa County, she may be the smartest, too. Best choice you'll ever make, young man. Lotsa guys are green with envy."

Will felt his face go warm. "Can you show me some rings?"

"We have all prices. How much do you want to spend?"

"I want one she'll be proud of. I saved my first Lizzie commission. About fifty dollars. Is that enough?"

"We have some nice ones for fifty, but for a bit more—" Luedke pulled a ring set from under the counter. "Here's a real beauty." He turned the engagement ring under the light bulb. "Full three-quarter carat."

Will saw a flash of sparkle as Luedke twisted it back and forth. "How much is it?"

"A hundred, but worth every penny."

"I don't know." Will looked into the display case. "Do you have one for a little less money?"

"Oh, sure." Luedke pulled out a smaller ring and handed it to Will. "Fifty, just the amount you wanted. A nice one, too."

But even Will could see that it didn't have the pizzazz of the larger setting. "That first one sure was nice."

"It is." Luedke slipped the inexpensive ring out of sight and flashed the larger beauty in front of Will.

Will felt like a little boy the night before Santa's visit. He told Mary he would pick her up at six o'clock and they would go to a movie at the new theatre. He wanted this to be the most romantic, most perfect night in Mary's life.

Dear Lord, don't let anything go wrong.

As always, his heart spun when he caught sight of Mary in her yellow, sheer chiffon dress. He'd never seen her more beautiful. The day was warm so she needed no jacket, and Will admired her figure as he helped her into the buggy. He tingled all over and wanted to cry out, will you marry me? To hand her the ring and blurt it out right there, with no ifs, ands, or buts. But he knew he couldn't. It had to be romantic, and at a place that melted any resistance she might have.

Will snapped the reins over Fanny's back. "Giddyap, old girl." He jostled the lines again to hurry her along.

"I love Mary Pickford," Mary said. "I used to pretend when I was little. I thought I was named after her."

"Were you?"

"With my mother a Mary? What do you think?"

"I've heard this isn't one of her best films."

"We'll not know, not until we've seen it, will we?"

"Guess not," Will said.

Two blocks above the theatre he turned down Pine Street.

"Will, where are you going? The theatre's behind us."

"It's a surprise, my dear."

"We're not going to the theatre?"

Will snapped the reins over Fanny's back but remained silent.

"Are we going to the Singletons? Did Penny invite us for the evening?"

"Not to the Singletons."

"Will, what is it?" She grabbed his arm, leaned toward him, and stared into his eyes. "Have you lost your senses?" She laughed, a strained laugh, one that left Will thinking she believed him daffy.

"Lost my senses? I hope not."

"Will! Tell me."

"It's okay, you'll see. You're not with a madman, my dear." He leaned over and kissed her cheek. "Just relax. You'll know soon enough."

Will guided Fanny into the ravine and down Valley Road. When he arrived at the park, he stepped from the buggy, walked to Mary's side, and gently lifted her down. He tied Fanny to a hitching post at the park entrance. Will was glad that no other vehicles were there. It appeared they'd have the park to themselves this night.

Iowa County had no lakes, but creeks carried runoff from the steep hills through its many valleys, and water that bubbled forth from its underground reservoirs created streams that were cold enough to support the German brown, rainbow, and Eastern brook trout which Will loved to fish for whenever he could find the time. But it wasn't fishing that rippled through his mind this night.

A small stream ran through Ashley Springs' bottom lands and filled an old limestone quarry, creating a pond the city fathers chose to make into a park. They cut a path around the pool, laid sawdust to keep it dry, and planted shrubs and pine trees down its perimeter. Along the way, they set out wooden benches, and at the path's far end, spring water, a hundred feet high, poured down a rock outcropping. Ashley Springs had its own Niagara Falls and lovers of all ages enjoyed its splendor. Here, at this magic spot, Will would ask Mary to be his bride.

Mary strolled the path a ways before turning back. "Tell me right now why we're here when we're supposed to be at the theatre." She took his hand. "You needn't have deceived me to bring me to this beautiful spot. But why now, why tonight?"

"There's an event tonight that will stop the stars in the sky, that will cause the moon to shine brighter. And it's ahead of us, at the falls."

"Then why isn't everyone else here, my dear?"

"No one else will know, no one but us." Will took Mary's hand, and she didn't resist but followed in silence. "It will be our secret tonight. Come, my dear." After a fifteen minute walk they arrived at the falls, which to Will looked to be dressed in its finest for this historic event. Now near dusk, the spray glimmered in the diminished sunlight, while water bounced off the protruding rock shelves, producing a mist that dampened Will and Mary as they stood before it. The low sun created countless spectrums of color as it shined through the vapor.

They watched in silence.

"This myriad of rainbows is God's work," Will said. "A grand presentation for this momentous night."

Mary sat on the bench and watched silently, her face cupped in her hands, a slight smile on her lips, and tears in her eyes.

Will waited. He wouldn't undo the magic of this moment that far exceeded his most optimistic vision for this earth-shattering night. He didn't dare break the spell by speaking.

The sun set, the rainbows vanished, and a full moon rose above the horizon. Will knelt in front of Mary and took her hand. "Mary, I love you. I want you to be my wife." He took the ring from his pocket and held it out. His heart almost burst through his vest. His fingers trembled, but he held the ring firm. "Will you marry me, my dear? I want that more than anything I've ever wanted in all my life. More than life itself."

Mary reached down and took his hand, lifted it and the ring to her lips, kissed them both. "I've wanted this, too, since the first day we met. I've always known you were meant for me. I love your wit, your intelligence, but most of all I love your gentleness and kindness. Yes, yes, yes! I'll be your wife!"

Will slipped the ring onto her finger, and she raised it into the moon's radiance. "Will, this is the ring I saw in Luedke's Jewelry the day I left a brooch for repair. It's beautiful. It's the one I wanted. How could you ever have known?"

"Fate, my dear. I couldn't have known the falls would provide this display tonight. I couldn't have planned it better. God must be with us."

"And I want you to be with me forever." She guided him to the seat beside her, and as the moon climbed high in the sky, their mouths met. But Will didn't notice the moon. Nature had provided the opening, but Will and Mary performed the night's main event.

Attorney Reed stormed into the garage and caught Will underneath a Lizzie. "That dad-blasted son of mine has no sense at all. He went and ran my car into a mud hole, and I can't get it out. Can you help me?"

Will found humor in that, but he kept his mouth shut. It was the third time, after the torrents last week, a customer came for help with a Lizzie stuck in the mud. The Lizzie was a hardy vehicle, but she couldn't wade through deep mud like a reliable horse. But then, a horse would have more sense than to get in too deep. He poked his head from under the car. "I'll get Fanny and come to your rescue. Can you wait until I close tonight?"

"Jigs won't keep his hands off my car, but he's too reckless to drive it. I need a lock to keep him out. He's not careful. What do you suggest, Will?"

"Buy him his own car."

"Are you crazy? He'll kill himself. Worse, he'll kill someone else. I don't want that kind of entanglement, not when I'm thinking about retirement. My wife wants to go back to New Hampshire, to be near her family. Don't need trouble, not now."

"Would you rather he killed someone in your car?"

"Of course not."

"I'll tell you what. Agree to buy him a car, and I'll give him lessons in yours until he drives safely, until you feel comfortable with it." Will scooted from under the Lizzie. "What's more, because it's your second purchase, I'll knock ten percent off the price."

"Let me think about it. It might free mine up."

A week later, Attorney Reed burst into Will's office. "He did it again, that hair brain. Can you bring your horse to Felp's Crossing? It's in so deep I can't see the headlights. And just when I planned to go to the state conference in Madison. I'll have to take the train, and it leaves in an hour."

"The deal still stands."

"Now, Jigs, this doesn't have to be difficult. Remember, just because it's fast doesn't mean it's sensible. It's not responsible like a horse. You'll have to supply the brains. Let's practice."

Will found Jigs Reed to be agreeable, but he was a bit uncoordinated. They practiced every night, and two weeks later, Will and Attorney Reed signed the invoice for a Ford Model T, two-door roadster.

"I hope this works out," Lawyer Reed said. "But it's worth the price to know that I'll have my Lizzie when I need it. I'm in your debt, Will O'Shaughnessy."

The man was a bit terse, but pleasant enough. Still, Will continued to feel apprehensive around him. It seemed to Will that people only needed an attorney when bad things happened. He wasn't eager to call this debt in.

"**M**aybe it was a mistake to have them as attendants," Will said. "I think so," Gertrude replied. "Too many hard feelings. It could mean trouble."

But Will wanted to bring them together, help patch the family woes. He didn't expect trouble, not today, not at his wedding. But he hoped they wouldn't be late. He wanted May 20, 1915, to be a new beginning for everyone in his family.

Charlie and Esther Nesbitt, longtime friends of Thomas and Gertrude, arrived early. Charlie hollered down from his buggy. "Hey, Will. So you're going through with it? Giving up the best years of your life." He winked at Esther, but turned back to Will. "Where's Thomas? I wanted to ask about the plow I bought at May's auction. Can't get it to scour."

"Did you steep the angle?"

"I tried everything. Thought Thomas might know."

"Dad's not back yet. He went to Hinton for Mary's mother." Will scratched the mare's nose. "Left early, should be back soon."

Charlie snapped the rein and clicked his tongue. His horse surged forward.

Will stepped away. "You don't seem to be the worse for marriage, Charlie. Of course, Esther may not see it that way."

"Whoa, Nellie." Charlie glanced toward Esther who grinned down on Will.

"I can't say that it's done him much good," she said. "But I'll not complain."

Charlie tapped Esther with his elbow and winked in her direction. "You didn't know me when I was young. We'll talk on it later, Will."

Charlie and Esther were the best testament for marriage that Will knew.

"Is it okay to put my horse in a stall?" Charlie said.

"Dad got it ready before he left. The bedding's down and fresh hay in the manger."

Charlie flipped the reins and turned toward the barn. "Get along, Nellie."

Will yelled after him, "Hey, Charlie, have you thought about trading that nag for a horseless carriage? I'll give you a deal on a Lizzie."

Charlie stepped off his buggy and opened the barn door, but he didn't look back.

The ceremony was set for three o'clock, and afterwards a full meal was to be served on the sunny side of the house. Chicken and ham sandwiches, milk, coffee, and lemonade were available in the kitchen all day, but his mother grabbed Will by the ear when he stepped through the door. "You stay out of here."

"You want me to starve? And on my wedding day?"

"No further than the kitchen. Bad luck to see the bride before the wedding."

After they unhitched their horses, the older men headed toward the hayloft, while their wives helped prepare food and decorate tables on the back lawn. Will's young friends weren't likely to show until just before the ceremony. With nothing else to do, he headed toward the older crowd. Charlie Nesbitt and half a dozen friends of Will's father passed a bottle while they lounged on feed bags in the loft.

"Will O'Shaughnessy," Silas Murrish, his father's favorite drinking buddy, called down to Will as he started up the ramp. "I remember the day you slipped and tumbled head over heels down that incline. Why, you couldn't have been more than three year's old, but you didn't cry, not one tear."

"He'll shed tears now," Dennis Newberry said. "Once she's hooked that ring in your nose." He spat a mouthful of tobacco juice into the hay. "Your life'll never be the same." Dennis removed a pack of Red Man from his vest pocket, dug out a chaw, and placed it under his lip. "'Fraid you're hooked, fella. 'Bout to be fried."

"He'll fry, okay," Rich Turner said.

The men laughed.

"Like that frog in the cooker when they turned up the heat," Silas Murrish said. "He smiles all the way to the hereafter. But what a way to go."

"Now don't be scaring the boy," Charlie Nesbitt said. "Will, you've got a bit to learn but a good woman to teach you. I hope you're as lucky as I am."

"Esther's a good woman, all right," Rich said. "You better keep a leash on her."

"Must be selling lots of Lizzies these days," Dennis said. "Sure lucked out when Grandpa snatched that farm away."

"I'll farm again, make no mistake about that. I won't sell Lizzies forever."

"You'll make too much money to leave for the farm," Dennis said.

Will stood and faced Dennis. "I tell you, I'll have my own farm someday. Just you wait and see."

"Money rules." Dennis snorted, a derisive laugh. "Besides, I doubt you could lift a full sack anymore."

Will reached toward Dennis, his elbow cocked and hand at ready to arm wrestle. "Try me."

"Hey, fellows, thought I'd find you up here, yes I did," Thomas O'Shaughnessy called as he scrambled up the ramp to the loft. "You don't have anything to warm the innards, now do you?" He rubbed his hands together and shuddered. "It's kinda cool for late May, 'tis. I hardly saw the sun all along the Hinton road."

Silas tossed the bottle in his direction, and Thomas snatched it from the air.

"Don't remember you being that handy with a kitten ball," Silas said.

"No loss there." He turned the bottle in his hands. "Old Crow? Shoulda dropped it." He tilted the bottle and frowned. "I expected a good Irish whiskey." Thomas took another mouthful, grimaced, and passed the bottle to Charlie. "S'pose I shouldn't look a gift horse in the mouth."

"Hey, Thomas? Will? You up there?" a voice called from below.

"In the loft," Will shouted back.

A small man shielded his eyes as he came in from the sunlight. "Thomas, did I see you unloading a cake when I drove up?" Bert Whitford said. "Biggest durn wedding cake I've ever seen."

"Will's new mother-in-law made that cake," Thomas said. "I brought her up from Hinton."

"Say," Whitford said, "when I drove through town I saw Jesse leaving Bennie's Bar. I hope you're not expecting him. He's not in any condition for a wedding."

Will's heart sank. Maybe his mother was right.

"Thomas, Will, come down here," Gertrude O'Shaughnessy called from below. "Frank and Jesse aren't here yet, and I need help getting the tables out so the ladies can decorate them."

"Come on, Will," Thomas said. He brushed the dust off as he got up from the feed sack. "I guess the fun's over." He tossed the empty bottle to Silas and started toward the open doors, but before he stepped onto the ramp, he turned back. "Look on the ledge back of the chute, Silas. You'll find a bottle of real whiskey there."

They rushed after Gertrude, who proclaimed their marching orders every step of the way.

When Gertrude reached the kitchen door, she turned back to Will and Thomas, who had followed her. She grabbed Will's arm when he tried to dodge around her. "And don't you go peeking in the back parlor." She hustled through the opening and slammed the door behind, but reopened it a crack and hollered out. "And when you're done with the tables, get the chairs out. But wash them before you set them up." Before she closed the door, she hollered once more, "And when that's done, I've got other things."

Thomas wiped the sweat from his brow. "That woman'll be the death of me yet."

By the time they got through Gertrude's to-do list, Will began to feel panicky. Where were Frank and Jesse? Maybe he would be better off without Jesse, but it wasn't like Frank to be late.

"Will, Thomas, you'd better get dressed for the ceremony," Gertrude called from the kitchen door. "I've hung your suits in my upstairs bedroom. You can dress up there. But go up the back stairs, and don't look into the parlor, Will."

Will motioned to his father. "Come along. I don't want to be late for my own wedding. What'll I do if Frank and Jesse don't show?"

"I asked Charlie Nesbitt to stand in. Thought we better be prepared. He's done it lots of times. Frank should be here though. It's not like him."

Will took a white, ruffled, starched shirt from the hanger and grabbed the pair of cuff links that his mother set on the dresser. After donning his shirt, he fumbled with the links. First, a cuff slipped from his fingers when he tried to hold them together. Then, as he held the cuff between his fourth and little finger and tried to manipulate the link with his thumb and index finger, the fastener snapped shut, and he couldn't fit it through the hole. He released the cuffs and used both hands to open the cuff link, but it slipped from his fingers and fell to the floor when he pulled the cuffs back together.

"Whatever Frenchman invented this shirt should be taken out and shot," Will said. "It's worse than threading a needle."

Thomas reached for the link. "Give me that." He turned the link in his fingers and rubbed the pearl inset. "Pretty. With these links and that starched, ruffled shirt, you look like a dandy I saw in a New Orleans bor—" He turned crimson, stifled a cough, and grabbed at Will. "Give me your arm."

Will finished dressing and looked in the mirror. With his tan, pin-striped suit, starched shirt, print tie, and polished brown boots, he looked okay. He felt uncomfortable as a pig in a boudoir, but looked pretty good. He held his arm up to where he could see the outer sleeve and link in the mirror. Nice. Maybe he could be stylish like his young wife, after all. He hoped she'd be proud of him.

"Frank's here," his mother called up the stairs. "He said he passed Jesse on the way. His wheel seized up, and Jesse was unhitching his horse. Frank said Jesse didn't look too steady on his legs."

"Didn't Frank offer a ride?" Thomas said.

"He offered but Jesse refused," Gertrude said.

Thomas, now dressed in his old gray suit, started down the stairs.

Will slowly turned in front of the mirror and looked himself over one more time. Nice. Fashionable wasn't so bad.

Jesse rode his dad's dapple gray workhorse into the yard minutes before the accordionist began "Here Comes the Bride." Thomas pulled Jesse off the horse and called at Charlie Nesbitt. "Looks like you won't be standin' in today. The groomsman is here. Sort of."

Thomas guided Jesse toward the wedding party. "Jesse, straighten up. Do you need some coffee?"

Jesse pushed his father away and staggered toward Will and Frank who, along with Mary's best friends, Jean Harvey and Penny Singleton, stood in front of Reverend Leonard.

Will wanted to protest, but he didn't want to attract attention, so he bit hard on his lower lip. Then the music began and Will forgot about Jesse. His eyes turned to Mary who strolled down a path that her friends had strewn with rose petals. Mary's father long gone, her older brother, Nicholas, gripped her arm.

Nicholas Tregonning was thought to be America's leading gold mining authority. European royalty and the wealthy employed him when they wanted expert advice. He left Europe ahead of his planned schedule so that he could fill in for his absent father.

Will's heart fluttered and his legs grew weak when he looked up at Mary. Her golden brown hair was pinned in a bun at the back, and it swept over her left eye in the front. Her white gown brushed the rose petals aside as she strolled toward him. The sweetheart neckline, lace bodice, and fitted silk skirt with ruffled trim accentuated a figure that Will already believed was the most tempting in Iowa County. How could he deserve such a beauty?

The music stopped and the minister said, "Who gives this woman in marriage?"

Nicholas Tregonning said, "I, her adoring brother, offer this woman in marriage."

Will stepped ahead and took Mary's arm, but as he looked up, he saw Jesse sway side to side, step forward, teeter back, and then regain his balance.

When Reverend Leonard called for the ring, Frank handed it to him. Jesse rocked but held his ground. But when Jean Harvey, the maid of honor, approached the reverend with Mary's ring, Will thought that Jesse was going to envelop her when he listed severely in her direction. Will knew that Jesse had been fond of Jean since grade school, but she had better prospects.

Reverend Leonard called the bride and groom forward, had them place the rings on their fingers, and proclaimed, "I now pronounce you man and wife. You may kiss the bride."

With his new bride beside him, Will heard nothing, saw nothing, felt nothing except his love for Mary. He reached and pulled her close, looked into her eyes, and lowered his mouth to hers. They kissed passionately, kissed long, kissed until he was jolted back to reality by applause and Jesse's slaps on his back, which stung. "You did it, Will," he said, slurring. He leered at Mary. "Now comes the fun part."

Will grabbed Mary's arm, pivoted away from his brother, and walked his bride up the path, through sunlight which immersed them when it slipped out from behind a cloud.

The crowd surged toward the party. Ladies circulated among the tables with pitchers of hot coffee, milk, and cold lemonade. They placed platters of pot roast surrounded by cooked carrots, browned potatoes, and boiled onions at the tables' ends. Bowls of fresh asparagus, snap peas, and last fall's creamed-corn and pole-beans filled empty spaces along the tables' interiors. And because no room was available on the big table, cherry, apple, rhubarb, and mincemeat pies filled a smaller table standing to the side. "Dish up your own pie when you're ready," Agnes Whitford called over the din. "And don't leave before we cut the cake. You'll not want to miss that."

The cake was something to behold. Will stared in amazement. If you tallied the bride and groom figurine on top, his mother-in-law had built it almost as tall as her daughter. White sculpted frosting draped like bunting around its perimeter, and was covered with mauve, red, and yellow roses, which looked so real that Will was certain he could smell their fragrance. And on the top tier, around the figurine, Mary's mother, Mary Tregonning, had written in yellow frosting script, "To my beloved Mary and Will. May they live a long and happy life together."

Mary Tregonning stood before Will's friends and neighbors. "Being from Hinton, I've not known most of you, but if you're Will's friends, you're my friends, too. I wanted to do something nice for his family and friends, so I made this cake." She fingered her apron and turned a bit red. "It kinda got outa hand."

The crowd laughed and Charlie Nesbitt said, "I've never seen one like it. It's way too pretty to eat."

"Well, it's for the eatin'," Mary Tregonning said. "And Gertrude asked me to cut the first piece for the bride and groom. So I'm 'bout to do that." She deftly wielded her knife and sliced one piece off the bottom tier, then placed it on a plate. She set the plate in front of Will and Mary and handed each a fork. "Now eat a forkful together."

And when they took cake in their mouths, Mary Tregonning said, "May your life together be as sweet as the cake you eat today."

Women cried and the men looked sober.

"Gertrude O'Shaughnessy will cut the rest of the cake, but the next pieces go to the Reverend and the attendants, then the ladies will bring yours 'round to your table."

Gertrude stepped forward and, without a word, cut into the cake. She handed the first slice to Reverend Leonard. The next slices went to the bridesmaids and then one to Frank and Nicholas. But as Frank walked away from the table, Jesse snatched the plate from his hand.

"Hey, give that back," Frank called after him. He looked over his shoulder at the cake that loomed large behind him and snickered. "Afraid there won't be enough? Go get your own." He grabbed at the plate.

But Jesse jerked the dish away. "What's the matter, Frank? Don't like somethin' of yours snatched from you?" He stepped around Frank but staggered as he neared Gertrude. When Frank grabbed for the dish again, Jesse stumbled, and fell face-first into that beautiful cake.

Will exploded, grabbed Jesse by his collar, and yanked him upright.

Mary and the nearest guests backed away.

Will grabbed Jesse's arm, spun him around, and like a full grain bag, he hoisted him overhead. His mom was right: it had been a terrible mistake to invite Jesse. But how could he not have wanted all his family here?

Jesse flailed as Will raced toward the water tank at the far end of the barn. "Put me down, you bastard! Let go of me!"

Will strode to the water tank and raised Jesse high overhead, then slammed him down so hard that water surged over the curved metal rim and drenched the both of them.

Jesse popped up with a gasp. "You bastard. I hope you'n' that bitch are miserable."

No one, not even a drunken brother, would slander his wife. Will grabbed Jesse's shoulders, pushed him deep into the water, and held him there while he watched the breath slip from Jesse's foul mouth and bubble to the surface. He'd never again call Mary a vile name.

But Jesse fought back with the strength of a man who knew he might die.

Thomas and Frank raced to catch up. Each grabbed an arm and pulled Will away. "For God's sake," Thomas said, "don't kill him!"

Now as soaked as Jesse, Will brushed water from his hair and eyes as he bent over to catch his breath.

Frank pulled Jesse from the tank. "One of these days your liquor'll get you killed."

Jesse gasped for air, tried to respond, but couldn't get the words out. He pushed Frank away, stared at his brothers the way a wild animal gapes at his tormentors, turned, and staggered down the road.

"I might have killed my own brother. And on our wedding day."

Mary leaned forward and kissed him ever so gently.

Will's anger and embarrassment subsided and he took her in his arms.

Eighteen-year-old Bernie Burns had driven them by car to the Walker House on the edge of Ashley Springs. Mayor Burns's only son was the spittin' image of his father, Tommy, and Will knew that his father shamefully spoiled him. A bit taller than Tommy, Bernie had the same freckles, carrot-colored hair, and an easy-going manner.

Bernie would come back in the morning and drive them to Madison, where they planned to honeymoon for the next three days. At first Will rejected Bernie's offer, but when Bernie said he was going anyhow, needing to pick up legal papers at the state capitol for his father, Will agreed.

They had cancelled the shivaree. Will's friends who attached tin cans to the Ford sedan's bumper and wrote "Just Married" on its back window wanted to go ahead with it, but Thomas O'Shaughnessy agreed with Charlie Nesbitt, who said, "There's been enough excitement already. They need some quiet time. It's a rough way to start life together."

Will sat in the big wingback chair, waiting while Mary busied herself in the bathroom. He remembered that Mary had said she loved his gentleness and kindness. He stood, walked to the window, and looked across the terrace, across a lawn of white trillium nestled under red oak and sugar maple trees, a tranquil scene that mocked his recent madness. And when she emerged with her hair pinned into a bun, he said, "I'm still embarrassed about my brutish behavior."

She walked to him and placed her arms around him. "It's over, and not much harm was done." She leaned back and flashed a wan smile. "Lucky it was a big cake. Mother salvaged enough to feed all the guests."

Will barely remembered that part. "I shouldn't have asked him there today." He took Mary in his arms. "Mom warned there'd be trouble, but I didn't listen. I wanted a new beginning, not just for us, but for Frank and Jesse, too. And I made it worse."

She reached up and gently stroked his cheek. Lifting his chin, and with a sparkle in her eye, she said, "Maybe there's more lion here than I know."

Without further words, she walked Will to the bed, sat him down, opened his suitcase, and removed his nightshirt. She tossed it to him, then turned to her valise. "I'm going to the powder room. When I come out, promise me that you won't look until I'm under the covers." She strode to the lavatory door. "And you'd better be ready, my fierce Celtic lion."

Will slipped between the fresh white sheets and fluffed Mary's down-filled pillow until it puffed up like a silken balloon. He thought about his young bride's body, a body that drove him wild every time he was with her. A slim and lithe body—but plump, too, in all the right places. The more he thought, the more excited he got, and the earlier events faded from his mind. He was about to explode by the time the light bulb darkened and he heard footsteps approach the bed.

"Are you in here?" Mary said as she lifted the top sheet.

Will raised the sheet all the way for Mary to slide in beside him. He reached for her and held her close. "You can't know how I've looked forward to this night," he said. "How I've wanted to touch and hold you. Wanted you next to me."

"You might be surprised at what I know, my dear." She touched her lips to his, and they kissed long and hard.

The night flowed toward morning. The wonder and excitement surpassed Will's greatest expectations for their first night together, exceeded his most passionate fantasies he had on those hot nights when he lay alone in his bed. They lay together, absorbing the warmth of the moment. They talked about their future, about children, about Mary's students and her hopes for their futures. They chatted about Will's business, its blossoming prospects, and his life on the farm. But not once did they say the names Frank or Jesse.

Bernie knocked on their door at ten o'clock. "I didn't want to come too early," he said, "didn't know what pool I'd wade into." He laughed.

Mary didn't bat an eye. Will knew she was accustomed to her student's wise cracks.

"And you can wade right back out," she said as she pointed to two fully-packed suitcases, "with those suitcases in hand."

The drive to Madison would take two hours, but there was no hurry. They couldn't check into their hotel until afternoon. Will felt like money, with a chauffer in front and Mary beside him in back. He described the farmland as they rode along. "Looks like a good year for corn," he said. "It'll be knee high by the Fourth for sure."

"By the Fourth of July?" Mary said.

"That's what they like now, but I tell you, the day will come when it'll be taller."

Bernie hollered back, "How so? Are they going to stretch the stalks? Besides, what difference does it make?"

"They'll not stretch anything, Bernie. You're taller than your dad. It's that food you stuff down your gullet."

"They'll push meat and potatoes up those stalks?" Bernie laughed. "I like mine mashed, with lots of butter."

"They'll add nutrients to the soil, more nitrogen and phosphorus, and other minerals, too. They're experimenting all the time over in Iowa."

"Oh, Will," Mary called out. "Look at those sheep. They all have jackets."

And they did. A hundred sheep in the field, all with cloaks tied around them.

"Why would they do that?" Mary said. "I've never seen them with jackets before."

"Farming practices are changing. It's still cool weather and sheep catch cold after they're sheared, but you don't see cloaks very often. Not many farmers change their ways."

"You sure know farming, Will," Bernie said. "Sounds like you miss it."

"Yeah," Will said as he turned away from the pastoral scene.

"I'm glad we don't have to go home for milking tonight," Mary said. "Most of my boys could be good students if they didn't miss so many days working in the fields. It's a pity to sell one's future so cheaply."

Will knew she was right. Farm boys missed far too much school, but he still felt like he'd been punched in the belly. He had never heard Mary talk this way before, but it didn't matter now. So he said nothing.

When they got near Madison, Will directed Bernie to the square, toward the Baldwin Hotel. It's on West Johnson, I think." He turned to Mary. "It's a small hotel, but the rooms are comfortable."

Mary raised an eyebrow.

Will felt his face warm. "That's what I'm told. Never been there though."

"I hope it's heated," Mary said. "I hope they'll keep it warm."

Will leaned toward her and whispered, "We'll provide our own heat." But he must have been too loud because he heard Bernie laugh.

"Mind your manners!" Will shouted forward.

Mary harrumphed and said, "I've slapped more than one ear that couldn't mind its own business."

"But, Miss, I was just sitting here," Bernie said, but his complaint went unanswered.

"Baldwin Hotel, 1902" was printed across the circular half-silo that seemed to hang unsupported above the entry door.

"How does that stay up?" Mary said as she stepped from the car. "I hope our rooms aren't in there."

Will was hesitant to tell her they were, that he had asked for the room that hung out front where they could look up West Johnson or down State Street.

"I'm sure it's safe enough," he said. "It's hung there thirteen years, so it won't fall now. It must be cantilevered or something. Looks strong enough to me. Doesn't it to you, Bernie?"

"I don't know," Bernie said. "It looks a bit shaky to me."

Mary shuddered and looked away.

"Bernie, whose side are you on?" Will said.

Bernie broke into a broad smile. "It's brick, Miss, and only two stories high. A Kansas twister won't shake your bed." He glanced toward Will. "You'll sleep like two bugs in a rug, and if you don't, it's not the building you'll be blamin'." He laughed again.

Bernie turned back to his car and Will and Mary walked through the lobby and up one flight to their room. "Oh, the view is wonderful," Mary said. "I can see Lake Mendota out one window and the capitol square out the other side." She turned to Will. "Can we walk around the capitol? I've ridden around the square, but I've never walked it. I've always wanted to look into the capitol rotunda. I've shown pictures to my students, and it looks beautiful, but I've never seen it. I can't wait to see it." She grabbed Will's hand and pulled him toward the door.

"Slow down, my dear. Let me get my coat, and you better take yours. The wind will be cold off the water."

They walked up State Street toward the capitol square. "Madison is set among four lakes," Will said. "Lake Mendota," he pointed, "off to your left, Lake Monona on the other side of the square, Lake Kegonsa, and Lake Waubesa. It's a beautiful city."

"Maybe so," Mary said, "but it's the capital city through subterfuge, you know."

"I know it could have been in Southwest Wisconsin, but it didn't pan out."

"Ha!" Mary said. "Our capital could have been Ashley Springs or maybe Hinton." She stomped hard on the pavement. "Why, in the early 1830s Ashley Springs and Hinton had populations greater than Milwaukee and Chicago combined."

Will hastened his pace to keep up.

"There wasn't even a village here at the time," Mary said, "not even a house when that scoundrel Doty made his move."

Will didn't answer. Their marriage had begun with enough conflict already, and Mary was even more adamant than when she stated her dislike for farming. She raced past the first capitol entrance, but Will knew there were three others.

"He gave land to enough representatives that they saw profit in voting the capital here. Probably plied them with alcohol, too. Crooked politicians, that's who did it." She picked up her pace. "But that's not new."

They approached the next entryway. Mary strode past.

"Do you plan to go in, my dear," Will called ahead, "or should we just continue our stroll around the square?" He quickened his pace to keep up.

Mary stopped and placed her hand at her mouth. "I get carried away, but it makes me so angry. Nicholas planned to run for a seat, but he went west instead, to the gold. Just as well, I think. He's far too honest to be a politician." She turned back toward the west entrance. "Let's go inside."

Sunlight sparkled off the marble pillars, and when they pushed through the doors, the setting sun followed them inside, casting its light across the hand-carved furniture and glass mosaics that graced the great rotunda.

Mary stood with her mouth unhinged, mesmerized by the rotunda's beauty. She leaned back and craned her neck to look more than two hundred feet above to where Edwin Blashfield's mural, "Resources of Wisconsin," decorated the huge circular ceiling. "Oh, Will, it's beautiful." She grasped his hand and squeezed tight. "I teach this to my students, but it's more breathtaking than I ever knew."

The room was bright with sunlight. They lay close, comforted by the warmth of each other. After years of greeting the sun's entrance into his world, Will smiled at the thought of lying in bed like this. But this morning, with Mary by his side, leaving his bed when the sun beckoned felt like a habit he could easily discard. He turned toward the half-awake Mary and touched her cheek. "Are you ready for an outing or should we just stay in bed all day?"

"Maybe just for a little while." She laughed and pulled him close.

At mid morning, Will and Mary took flight down State Street. Their destination: Agricultural Hall and the great Bascom Hall at the top of Bascom Hill, the buildings where Will took classes.

"It's a long walk. Are you sure you can keep up?" Will said. Then he remembered the last evening's outing. "I guess you'll do okay."

"You'd better have brought your running shoes along," Mary said, "because that's the only way you'll catch me." Mary laughed heartily. "Haven't you learned by now that I'm the runner in this partnership?" She scowled in his direction. "But I'll slow down, if I must."

They slowed when they reached the 100 block of State Street, walked past the Popcorn Shop and G. & A. Jewelers. "Can we stop for popcorn?" Mary said. "I love buttered popcorn."

"Let's cross the street." He pointed. "See down the block, Shiphe & Dorn grocers. We'll buy some bread, butter, and ham, then make sandwiches and eat them on Bascom Hill. We'll stop for popcorn on the way back. Is that okay? We'll be hungry by then."

"You're in an awful hurry to get to Bascom. You must have farming on your mind again," Mary said.

Will didn't answer.

"You seem right at home in Madison," Mary said. "Did you ever think of moving here? I always thought I'd like to teach in the city. They pay much better."

"Never! I'm a country boy through and through. My roots are in Iowa County." He leaned over and pulled Mary to him.

By the time they reached the 500 block, trees began to replace cement, and as they neared the university, elms overhung the curbs.

"You're sure in a rush to get to your classrooms," Mary said. "My students run from them every chance they get."

"I want you to see where I attended classes. I've not been back since I graduated."

When they got to the top, Mary looked across Lake Mendota and said, "How high are we, anyway?"

And Will knew the answer. Every student who trudged Bascom Hill more than once knew the answer. "It's eighty-six feet high and eight hundred fifty feet long."

After they had eaten their sandwiches, Will led Mary down the backside of the hill to Agricultural Hall on Linden Drive. He looked into each classroom, remembered his professors, and talked about things learned. After they climbed the great hill once more, he led her through Bascom Hall, and when they exited the building, he pointed up. "See that plaque?" he said. "See what it says?"

Mary read aloud, "Whatever may be the limitations which trample inquiry elsewhere, we believe that the great state University of Wisconsin should ever encourage that continued and fearless sifting and winnowing by which alone the truth can be found."

Will sat on the ground and looked up, reading and rereading his creed. "Farmers winnow grain from the chaff and sift to separate the fine from the coarse." He looked at his hands, at the grease he could never clean from his nails. "I learned that creed here, and Dr. Carver told how to apply it. 'We must find what works best,' he told me when I visited him at a conference in Illinois. 'There's a hungry world to feed out there.'"

"George Washington Carver?"

Will nodded. "A great man."

"You loved the farm, didn't you?"

Will looked toward the western horizon, toward a sun that now settled over his fields and pastures. "We better start back before it gets dark." He took Mary's hand, and they walked down the hill in silence.

10

When he walked through the door, he was greeted by, "Well, look what the dog dragged in. So I'm not the only O'Shaughnessy drunkard!"

Will wasn't surprised to see Jesse hanging over Bennie's bar. At first he stepped back, not wanting to confront his brother.

Jesse raced at him and grabbed his shoulder. "Cat got your tongue, brother? Too good for me now you've got that fine young bride?" Jesse pushed against Will, but he gave ground. "Kinda uppity for an O'Shaughnessy, aren't you?"

"We have no quarrel. I don't want trouble, Jess. It seems to me we're in the same bed."

"I'd like to get in your bed." Jesse made a crude gesture. "Maybe I'll come visit one of these nights."

"You stay away." Will grabbed at Jesse, but Bennie stepped between them.

"That's enough, boys. I can't have any fights. I don't want to lose my license." He guided Jesse toward the door. "Come back tonight, Jesse. I'll buy your first two drinks."

Will supposed that Bennie would profit before the night was over.

"He won't let go of it," Bennie said. "Feels sorry for himself. I feel bad for you."

"Bennie, if not for Jesse hanging 'round my neck like a millstone, I'd have nothing to complain about. If there wasn't a bump now and then, I'd never appreciate the smooth road I travel. I couldn't be happier."

"That new bride has you feeling pretty chipper."

"And the business, too. Henry Ford was right. Americans are trading their horses for wheels." He lifted the Mineral Springs that Bennie set in front of him. "Just two years and I've got my brother Frank paid off and money for a down payment on a new house. I never thought it possible." He took a long sip on the brew. "We're living high-on-the-hog nowadays, Bennie. Just hope it lasts." He pushed his glass toward Bennie. "One more, but make it a Jameson this time." Like the Mineral Springs beer, Grandpa's farm was relegated to a less prosperous past.

During the next two weeks they talked about it and Mary expressed interest in a small two-bedroom bungalow where the Ashley Springs working families lived, but she deserved better. Will had remembered that Lawyer Reed planned to retire and move back to New Hampshire. But his house wasn't yet on the market, so without a seller's fee, Will thought he might buy it for a good price. After all, he expected the lawyer to feel a bit beholden. And it seemed that he was.

That night, Will told Bennie, "Pour me a Jameson, and one for you, too. All the stars are aligned in the heavens."

"How's that?" Bennie said as he snatched the bottle of golden liquid off the top shelf.

"Reed said he wanted a quick sale. Tyler conditionally agreed to a loan, and with my down payment money and the house's excellent condition, I don't expect any problems."

"That's good." Bennie set two shot glasses on the bar and poured the elixir to the brim of each. "It looks like clear sailing, then."

"Well, there's maybe one problem."

"Oh, what's that?"

"It's Mary's frugality. Reed's house—with its four upstairs bedrooms, front and back parlor, indoor plumbing, central heat, cistern, and sink pump—may cost more than she'll want to pay."

"She'll be so overwhelmed by its grandeur, she'll probably not even ask. So don't tell her the price."

"Oh, she'll ask okay. And I wouldn't lie to her. But we can afford it now. I'm selling Lizzies as fast as Henry can ship them, and I'm making so much profit that we're able to save all of Mary's income, even more. Of course, Mary says that's for our children's education."

"Is there something I don't know?"

"Not yet, but I hope there'll be soon."

But Jesse continued to be a bur in his boot. On a Friday, the day he got paid, Jesse came to their house. Long after going to sleep, they were awakened by a pounding at the door and a slurred voice demanding entry. Will pulled on his trousers and rushed out the door, but slammed it shut before Jesse could slip past. "Oh, no, Jess. You'll not disrupt my happy life."

"You bastard. I need a place to sleep."

Will pulled two dollar bills from his pocket and reached them out. "Rent a room at the hotel."

Jesse grabbed the money and tottered off, but Will doubted it would ever reach the hotel cash register.

Two weeks later, when Will heard that Jesse was back in town, he waited up. When he heard footsteps and shouts outside, Will stepped out and grabbed his brother's arm. "Jess, keep quiet. Mary works tomorrow."

Jesse reached for the doorknob.

Will grabbed his shoulder. "Jess." He wanted to slap some sense into his numbed mind, but he knew it wouldn't help. "Jess, listen. You can't stay at my house. Mary needs her sleep." He shook Jesse, rattled his teeth. "Do you hear?"

"Yeah, yeah." He pushed his brother away.

Will handed him money again.

The next morning, after Mary had left for school, Jesse pounded on the door. When Will let him in, Jesse stumbled toward the kitchen. He sat head-in-hands, now and then sipping the black coffee Will had poured into his cup.

"I need money."

"You need to sober up."

"I'd not be here if Frank weren't so tight with his money. I asked for a loan, but he wouldn't give none." Jesse sloshed coffee onto the tablecloth when he raised the half-full cup to his lips. "Wouldn't even give his own brother money, the bastard. Ordered me off his property." Jesse sloshed his coffee again when he lowered the cup. "You'll give me money, won't you, Will?"

"Not if you'd throw it away on booze. No, I won't."

"You're a bastard, too. You're just like Frank."

Will thought it best to not mention Frank's loan for the business.

Saturday morning, Will said to Mary, "I've harnessed Fanny to the buggy. So get ready, we're going for a ride."

"In the buggy? Do we really need to keep horses now that we've got an automobile?"

Will took Mary's arm and helped her up. "It's a perfect buggy day. Warm sun and fluffy clouds in a pretty spring sky. No car roof to obscure our view." Will knew it was lavish to keep two horses and a buggy when he had the Model T, but it was his only remaining link to the farm. He thought that Fanny and his young horse, Mabel, would become a perfect team. And he'd always wanted a matched pair. Still, Mary's challenge caught him unexpectedly.

"Two horses are an extravagance. You'll have to admit that," she said.

"I couldn't sell Fanny."

"Don't people think it strange that you drive a buggy?"

"I s'pose so."

"You'd not have to giddyap Fanny anymore."

"I'd miss Fanny."

"Well, if it's a giddyap you want, I promise I'll not laugh if you giddyap our Tin Lizzie. But, if you must, I'll not say more."

Will was glad that Mary didn't press further. He picked up the reins. "Giddyap, Fanny," he said before he settled back in the seat and took his wife's hand.

"Oh, Will, I can hardly wait for summer. I'm so ready for warm weather and a rest from those heathen boys. Three of them are twenty years old, and let me tell you, Will, it's not history books that attract their attention. Why, I found a *Police Gazette* inside a desk yesterday."

"Boys will be boys, my dear. I remember——"

"It's a bit chilly." Mary pulled her shawl tight around her. "I don't want to catch a cold, not now. I've never seen a winter where I've been so healthy. The heavy snow's been a burden on the roads, but it's an ill wind that doesn't blow some good. That snow must have smothered all the germs."

"Mary, my dear, it's not the snow, it's me. You know what they say about a little lovin', how it's good for the complexion. I always figured if a little something's good, a whole lot must be better." He flicked the reins and clucked to Fanny. "And you thought it was the snow."

"Git on wit you, you old Irishman." She swiped at Will who sat smug in his seat.

Will turned up the lane toward Powell's Ridge. The flowering crabapple trees were in full bloom. "Oh, Will, I've never seen anything so beautiful. Why, when my soul leaves this body, I hope it takes Powell's ridge to heaven. It's like the the Aurora Borealis streaking across the sky in all it's splendor, except it's here on earth, here for us to enjoy each spring."

Amanza Powell loved beauty, so before he died, he planted scores of flowering crabapples along the rocky ridge that led to his house. He said it would be a fitting memorial for folks to remember him. Every May, when the flowers bloomed, dozens of cars and buggies drove the ridge, and their occupants enjoyed the beauty. Long before Amanza died, the trip became an annual passage into spring for many village residents. But when the cars and buggies turned for their return trip through Amanza's amazing trail, they dug ruts that slowed Amanza whenever he walked to the barn. So he hitched a horse to his Ball drag-scraper and carved a loop all the way back to the county road. Then he planted dozens more crabapple trees.

Will was sure that this excursion would put Mary in the right mood for his next surprise. Growing up in the neighboring town of Hinton, she hadn't known about Amanza's flowering trees until Will took her through the grove four years earlier. It was their first date, and she was so enthralled by the beauty that Will knew the buggy ride gave him a running start over his competition, that Amanza's flowers whetted her appetite for this O'Shaughnessy farm boy.

"God does wondrous things," Mary said as she absorbed the beauty. She nestled into Will's side.

Will took the reins in his left hand and pulled her close. He thought she should have given some credit to Amanza, but he said nothing. He didn't want to undo her heavenly moment. And he didn't want her to leave his side.

They made the circuit and returned to the county road. Will turned his buggy so they could look back toward Mary's Aurora Borealis.

"It's over so soon," Mary said. "They'll be gone by next weekend. Can't we go round again?"

Will flicked the reins across Fanny's back, and with no more direction, she moved to the trail's entrance. Will believed that Fanny knew his every wish. She walked slow, her favorite pace, and paused often. She had time to nibble tender young grass shoots as the young couple, captivated by the beauty around them, embraced. Will wished there wasn't so darned much traffic on the road.

Will felt as excited as a little kid in a candy store. He could see that Mary was pleased with their morning excursion, so he felt certain this next stop would delight her. They pulled up to Attorney Reed's house at eleven-thirty, the designated time. It was a huge house, one of the largest in Ashley Springs, and it had style, too. The roof flowed in all directions, valleys and eaves everywhere. Elaborate decorative trim intersected with the tassels and brackets which supported the eaves and anchored the porch posts to the roof. Visitors were greeted by side-by-side doors under a large fan window with an elaborate half-round sunburst overhead.

"It's a pretty house, isn't it, Mary?"

"Oh, yes." She sighed. "I hope we can afford one someday. I've never been inside, but I've heard it's gorgeous. Attorney Reed's niece Marge talks about it all the time. The other girls are jealous. She says they have central heat and indoor plumbing. Oh, how I wish we had indoor plumbing."

"I tried to get Atkins to install hinged seats in our outhouse, just like indoors, but he said that's too fancy for a rental property. He wouldn't even let me put them in."

"We'll get by. I'm sure we'll not rent forever."

"No, not forever."

"I love the wraparound porch," Mary said. "If we ever have a porch like that, we can sit on the swing and enjoy the warm summer evenings and the birds and the flowers, while waiting until the house cools off."

"Just like an old married couple."

Mary pointed to the border plantings. "Look, the crocuses are in full bloom, and the tulips are up. Marge says the gardens in back are filled with roses and lilies. I'd love to have gardens to tend during summer vacation. I have so much time on my hands—but that might change."

"I'd help. I've always loved flowers, just never had the time before. Why, if the business continues like it's been, I'll be able to afford a hired man, maybe two."

Will heard a car backfire behind him and turned to see Reed pull into the driveway. "Why, here's Attorney Reed now. Maybe he'll show us through."

"Will, that's not proper. Asking to see inside another's house. I'm surprised at you. He may agree, but his wife would be outraged. She'd not be prepared."

Attorney Reed approached their buggy and looked up at Mary. "Mary O'Shaughnessy," he said as he held out his hand, "I know you'll love it."

"What?" she said and pulled away.

Reed turned to Will. "Didn't you tell her?"

"I ... I wanted it to be a surprise."

"You made arrangements for me to see the house?" Mary said. "Mrs. Reed doesn't mind?"

"Mrs. Reed has gone to her sister's out East," Reed said. "I'll be joining her in a couple weeks."

"Well, I suppose. I'd heard that you're retiring, but I didn't know you were leaving." She took Reed's hand and stepped off the buggy. "It'll probably be my only chance. They say it's beautiful inside."

"I think you'll like it," Reed said.

Mary walked slowly through the rooms, admiring the maple wainscoting, the exquisitely flowered wallpaper with its vine-covered border, and the hand-carved rail with stag heads on each side of the landing where the stairs curved back on itself before continuing upward to the second floor. "It's a grand home."

Mary took Will's hand when they stepped into the master bedroom. "I never would have dreamed the day could turn out so beautiful." She squeezed tight. "First the rose-colored milky way and now a prince's castle. It's more than I can fathom. Maybe someday we can have a beautiful house, too."

"Look it over good, Mary. I expect to spend many joyous hours in this room. It's time we had those hinged seats you've wanted, the central heating, and the curved banister, too."

"Oh, Will, do you think we can ever afford something like this?"

"Not something like this, my dear. This is the one, and it's now. I'm going to buy it." He turned her to face him. "This will be your house. I've reached an agreement with Attorney Reed and the bank, too. We can move in by the end of the month. The bank has inspected our books and they agree: our income supports the payments. I may not be able to capture your milky way, but you'll have your castle. Grandpa was dead wrong when he doubted me."

Mary eased onto the red velvet love seat that nestled in the corner of the large bedroom. She looked across to the four-poster, double bed with the turned finials and carved headboard. She surveyed the over-stuffed chairs, the lamps, the lamp tables, and the drapes that were pulled aside with wide silk fabric. She looked toward Will who stood proud as an Irish landlord inspecting his dominion, her eyes full of tears. "My dear, I've never doubted you, but how—how—will we ever afford the furniture?"

That night, Will pulled Mary close. She eagerly snuggled into his warmth and turned her face upward to receive his kiss. "I've never been so happy," she said. "But can—"

"Shush, none of that." He fervently kissed her again. "I love you, my dear. A perfect ending to a perfect day."

"It couldn't be more wonderful. It was even more wonderful than you can possibly know." She leaned back, her questioning eyes held his gaze. "Will?"

"Not now, my dear. We'll talk about furniture later."

"But—"

"Shush."

They lay together. Will pulled Mary close and they kissed until he felt his whole body warm. He was ready and he knew by her intimate move-ments that she was ready, too. The bad times were behind, and they could look forward to a new beginning. The farm he dreamed about became a dimmer, more distant image, and he didn't know how he could be happier as they embraced and took pleasure in each other.

Mary pulled away and looked into his eyes, smiled, but didn't say a word, not for the longest time.

"Is there something wrong?" Will said. "Did I hurt you?"

"No, you silly, it was wonderful. But I got some interesting news when I visited Dr. Ruggles yesterday."

"**C**an we really afford it?"

Mary was still resistant when, after careful bargaining, Attorney Reed agreed to include the furniture, carpeting, and drapery in the sale price. He conceded that he could never get it back to New Hampshire anyhow.

"Mary, you're tight as an old Scotsman," Will said.

"You think so? Okay, you Irish spendthrift, if you want it so bad, then you figure out how to pay the mortgage." She whacked him on the rump with the *Ladies Home Journal* that she held in her hand. "Well, Mr. Rockefeller, while you're at it, find some money to furnish the nursery, too."

"We'll go to Samuels' this weekend. If he doesn't have what you want, he has pretty pictures you can order."

Mary smiled up at him.

Will knew that Mary was pleased. She hardly stopped talking about the new home—the mansion, she called it—and always with a smile as big as the pineapple on the headboard of their new, black walnut bed.

That night she drew an outline of the nursery she wanted and sketched furniture locations while Will watched. "Don't you think the south bedroom is best?" she said. "It'll get sun in winter when the leaves are off the maples." She drew a rectangle near the big front window. "That's a crib. Just in case you question my fine drawing."

"Well, of course," Will said. "Couldn't be anything else, now could it?"

"The windows are big, so it should always be bright and cheerful," Mary said.

"But you forget, my dear: this is Wisconsin, and it's cloudy much of the time. Why, I doubt if half our winter days have full sun."

"Don't be so gloomy. Half a loaf's better than none at all."

"I think the north bedroom's best," Will said. "With two heat ducts, it should be warmer."

"No, I want him next to our room, where I can hear when he cries at night. I wouldn't want him to be hurtin' and his mother not know."

"Him? Do you know something I don't know? What makes you think she'll be a he?"

"Mother's premonition." She looked up from her drawing. "Besides, I thought you'd want a boy."

"The O'Shaughnessies spent lots of nights praying for healthy young heifers. But a boy would be nice, too. Someone to help in the shop, and to take over the business."

"You don't think a heifer could help in the shop? You might be surprised, my dear, just what a girl can do."

"Well, I never had sisters, so I wouldn't know. Heifer or bull, just so he's healthy."

The news of their move spread through Ashley Springs. Their friends complimented them on their luck. Few people even knew it was for sale. "Why, it's the best house in town!" Esther Nesbitt said.

Jesse soon found them and continued his late night visits, but Will wouldn't let him in unless Mary was away.

One morning Jesse sat for coffee.

"Some house you've got here," Jesse said. He sipped at his coffee while he scanned the room. He tottered, regained his chair; then he glared at each kitchen convenience: the pump, the ice box, the laundry chute, the floor registers. "Pretty fancy for an O'Shaughnessy. Where'd you get the money?"

Will wanted to end it there, so he didn't answer.

"You rob the bank or something?"

Will gulped his coffee.

"Well?"

"You're almost right, Jess, but they gave it freely enough. My business is doing well."

"I always wondered how you got that business. The bank wouldn't give you money. Why, you weren't any more creditworthy than I am, and I can't get a dime. How'd you get started, Will? Who gave you your grubstake?"

"I worked for it. But it wasn't easy. I never knew if I could do it. Patterson helped. He gave me a start and down payment money, too."

"Don't give me that shit. I wasn't born yesterday. Patterson was drained by his wife's illness."

Jesse pushed off his chair and staggered toward Will.

"I don't believe for a minute that he gave you the down payment."

He grabbed Will's shoulder.

"How'd you get it?" He squeezed hard. "Tell your prodigal brother. How do you get that kind of money? Share your secret!"

Will pushed him away.

"Frank gave you the money, didn't he?"

"He loaned it, but not without interest. It was business."

"Bastard. Wouldn't give me a dime."

Jesse grabbed Will, turned him, and drove him into the kitchen counter. Will doubled over from the impact.

"And I'm beginning to think you're no better."

Jesse stepped back, but Will recovered and shot toward his brother. Jesse grabbed his neck, but Will seized his hand and jerked it away. Then with both hands, he drove Jesse down. Will cocked his right hand and started it toward Jesse's chin, but released his grip and stowed his fist before contact.

"I won't strike my own brother," he said. "Not even when you deserve a good whipping."

"And I thought you'd help," Jesse said. "You're no better than Frank. I hate you both."

"Straighten up, Jess. Get yourself together and I'll give you a job at the shop. I'll teach you the business."

"Go to hell. I'll get along fine without you or Frank."

The stacked dishes rattled when the door slammed against the jamb.

"You ingrate," Will hollered after him. "Good riddance. Don't come back."

Two nights later, Will awoke to a loud noise.

Startled by the sound, he sat up in bed, shook out the cobwebs, and rubbed his eyes. Was it a dream?

Mary sat up, too. "What was that?"

The wall shook as the front door rattled and a voice screamed, "Let me in, you bastard."

"It's your brother."

Will swung his leg off the feather tick and slid to the floor. "I told him not to come back."

The door rattled against its frame as if pounded by a violent windstorm, and the floor vibrated under his bare feet when he reached for his trousers and shoes. "Go back to sleep. I'll send him away." Will yanked his trousers on.

The noise grew louder as Will descended the stairs two steps at a time. He pulled the latch and yanked the door open. "I told you not to—"

Jesse grabbed his nightshirt and flung him sprawling into the yard. "Why won't you let me in?"

He stood over Will.

Will rose to one knee. "I told you not to come back. I won't have a drunk threatening my wife's health."

"The whore. This is her doings, isn't it?"

Will exploded upward. "If you weren't—"

Jesse wildly swung a looping right cross aimed at Will's chin.

Will turned his head away from the blow and grabbed Jesse's elbow. "Leave now, before I do something I'll regret."

"You're not man enough."

Jesse jerked his arm away.

"Grandpa was right. You're a wimp letting that whore run your life." He spat in Will's face. "Probably not even your baby. Probably a bastard like you and Frank. A real bastard, not just name only."

Will dropped his shoulder and drove into Jesse, knocking him to the ground.

Jesse rolled over, took a deep breath, and then lashed out at Will's knee with his foot, trying to leg-whip him down.

Will twisted and took the blow on his calf, on flesh instead of bone. Then before Jesse could get his feet under him, Will grabbed his raised leg and twisted hard, so hard that Jesse's body left the ground and turned a complete revolution—either that or his knee would have popped under the pressure.

Before Jesse's hips settled to the ground, Will slid his right leg underneath and clamped his left leg across Jesse's abdomen. As a youth, Will used this leg-scissors to squeeze his friends into submission. But Jesse was thin, wiry, and numbed by the liquor, so he didn't submit.

"Get off me, you bastard."

"Let's end this. Uncle?"

"To hell with you."

Will couldn't get enough purchase on Jesse's skinny frame to finish the fight with this wrestling move.

"That whore runs you now."

Will knew this confrontation would end with one of them bloodied. He could box with the best of them, but he hated fighting in anger.

Jesse went limp.

Will released his grip, but Jesse popped up as spry and feisty as a banty rooster.

Will wasn't surprised. He knew that Jesse was a street fighter who would use every trick in the book, but Will was ready.

Before Jesse could control his shaky legs, Will rose to face him. He learned the Marquis of Queensberry rules while at school in Madison, and felt at ease with his left foot comfortably ahead of his right, his body balanced, his left arm partly extended, and his right fist back. He held both hands high, his thumbs tucked under the knuckles. Will had done well with the gloves on. Only once had he been beaten, and that was by a far more experienced boxer. He practiced boxing like the school's fencers practiced swordplay: no malice intended. But he had never fought bare fisted, nor had he ever fought in anger.

Jesse tottered toward him and tried to gouge his eyes, but Will met him with a left jab on the nose that slowed his charge, and a quick, second jab that brought blood gushing down his face.

Jesse wiped gore from his mouth and staggered forward, this time to be met by a right hook that dropped him to one knee.

He shook his head, sprayed blood across Will's trousers, and then he dived at his brother's legs.

Will stepped back, grabbed Jesse's hair, jerked his head upright, and planted an uppercut under his jaw; a second one split his left eyebrow, and a third blow laid him flat.

By the time Mary rushed out the front door, Will had turned his brother onto his back and fanned his face with a large handkerchief that he pulled from his hip pocket.

"What happened? I heard a terrible commotion. Did he fall down in his drunkenness?"

"Yep, he fell."

Jesse groaned, stirred, and when he raised his head, blood trickled from his eye, mouth, and nostrils.

"Get some water." Will looked up sheepishly. "I think he cracked his noggin."

But Will worried. He hoped this feud would end without hurting Mary or the baby.

12

The baby's due date was more than a month away when Mary began labor. On November 10, 1916, she was home alone, having taken leave from teaching until January of the next year. She told Will, "At first I thought it was something I ate." But when her water broke, she called Will at work, urging him to get the doctor.

Will ran into the house on Dr. Ruggles' heels. He heard cries from upstairs and it scared him.

"Stay there. I'll call if I need anything," Dr. Ruggles said as he continued up from the first landing.

Will paced the hall floor but felt relieved when Dr. Ruggles called down, "She'll be okay, Will. But stay there for now."

Will sensed an edge in Dr. Ruggles' voice that was worrisome, but Will couldn't think how he might help. He continued to move but broadened his range through the kitchen and dining room. When he reached the far end of the house, he heard Dr. Ruggles' voice, raced for the stairs, and was at the landing when Ruggles called again. "Best you stay down, but you might want to call Mrs. Alderson. I may need her help."

Will rang Mrs. Alderson's telephone number, tried again, and when there was no answer the third time, he shouted up the stairs, "She doesn't answer her phone."

"She's probably out in her garden," Dr. Ruggles called back. "Spends most of her time out back. Run over and get her. It'll be a while here, and you might as well do something useful."

Will found Mrs. Alderson between the peas and the pole beans, shovel in hand, and sweat cutting a swath down her dust-covered face.

"Mrs. Alderson, quick! Mary's delivering and Dr. Ruggles needs help!"

Mrs. Alderson dropped her shovel and wiped her brow with a big yellow handkerchief which she pulled from between her ample breasts. "Why didn't you call me in the first place," she said. "That old fool's bound to make a mess of it. Why, I've delivered more babies than he's seen in his lifetime." She marched across her beans, potatoes, peas, and onions, stepping high to avoid disturbing the plants. "Get going now," she called back at Will as he stumbled along behind. "I'll be there as soon as I wash up."

"Hurry!" Will said. "The doctor needs you. Please hurry."

Mrs. Alderson was the most popular lady in Ashley Springs when baby time came. She arrived some twenty years before, yet no one knew where she was from. Some said she trained to be a doctor, but they wouldn't let a woman be an M.D. But she never mentioned it. And when a baby needed delivering, no one questioned her credentials. Most of the time, they called her before the doctor. Mrs. Alderson had never lost a baby, and that was more than Dr. Ruggles could claim.

Mrs. Alderson pushed past him when Will opened the door. He knew better than to follow her up the stairs, but he continued to pace and worry whenever he heard loud voices above. Eventually it was only Mrs. Alderson's voice he heard.

Will made a cold beef sandwich and poured a glass of milk, set them on the counter, and after the phone rang and he told his mother that nothing had happened yet, he resumed pacing and forgot his food. He read the headlines of the last *Weekly Democrat*, but he couldn't concentrate, so he threw it down. He left the house and walked around the block, then rushed back in and craned his neck up the stairs, but all was quiet. He was just about to call up to say he might as well go to the shop and get some work done, when he heard it. At first the cry was weak and Will wasn't sure what it was. But then it erupted into a full blown hurricane of a squall, and Will knew that he was a father. Mrs. Alderson motioned him upstairs.

His son was a robust baby, weighing five pounds, ten ounces. But Mary looked plumb tuckered out when she turned Will's way.

"See, I told you it would be a boy, and you doubted me."

"I'll never doubt you again, my dear," he proclaimed as he piled unneeded blankets beside her bed and continued to pester Mrs. Alderson with questions about Mary and the newborn.

Finally she said, "I've got work to do and you're in the way. Why don't you go to the pharmacy and buy more gauze and iodine." She took his arm and turned him toward the bedroom door. "Now, git!"

Will bought the medical supplies, but also a box of cigars that he handed out at Bennie's, a brief stop on his way back home. "It's a boy. I've got a new partner. Why, he'll be down at the shop before you know it."

Will resisted the congratulatory, "Drinks on me," and rushed home to his wife and newborn.

Mrs. Alderson didn't applaud his speedy return, but with a frown and a grumble, she accepted a cigar and stowed it within her ample cleavage.

"My dear, what'll we call the lad?" Will said. "Do you have a fine Cornish name in mind?"

"Oh, there's many a family name to choose from. Nicholas, Thomas, Joseph, and Sidney. But I rather like Charles. My Uncle Charles Tregonning died in the Civil War. At the battle of Perryville. In Kentucky. Lincoln said that he hoped God was on his side, but he absolutely must have Kentucky. And Charles did his part, a family hero. But I don't want him called Charlie. I'd rather it be the full name, a handsome name. Charles."

"Charles would be a fine name, but it sounds a bit Frenchy, now doesn't it?"

"Frenchy? You didn't know, Will. I wouldn't press your conceit by telling you, but my mother was a Collins and she named my brother after Uncle Charles, but he didn't make it." Mary sighed. "A lot of children died in those days."

"Your mother's Irish? You're Irish?"

"Well, just a little—maybe. But my Irish blood's diminished by my many Cornish ancestors. We'll just leave it at that."

"Collins? Might you be related to that Irish firebrand, Michael Collins?"

"We don't know. And I'm not about to inquire. I wish I hadn't brought it up."

"But Michael'd be a fine name, now wouldn't it? Michael O'Shaughnessy. Doesn't that sound just splendid?"

"It might do."

Mary's mother, the other Mary, the one with the Collins name, came to help for the rest of the semester, but she wanted to be home weekends, so Will drove her back to Hinton each Friday night.

Will loved spending Saturday with Michael. "He seldom cries," he said. "Why, I never saw a baby who didn't cry all the time," he told customers whenever he passed them on the street. They'd wink and nod, and they fawned over Michael as if they believed every word.

And Will also agreed to watch Michael Sunday afternoons, while Mary prepared work sheets for the coming semester. "Why, we get along just fine, yes we do." He turned to Michael. "Now don't we, my laddie?"

Michael cooed and smiled.

Will scooped baby Michael from the cradle and held him close as he whirled through the steps of a makeshift jig. "Have you ever seen a finer baby?" He danced past Mary. "You've given me a handsome lad, my darlin'."

Will returned from the barbershop, hair clipped to the noggin. When Mary chided him for going prematurely bald, he passed it off as a summer cut, short enough so he wouldn't have to pay again soon. "I read the *Journal* while I waited," he said. "Trouble's brewing in Europe. I can't see how they'll avoid war."

And he was right. Hostilities bristled into active conflict. At first America resisted entering the war, but Will knew they couldn't hold out long. He felt ambivalent about Europe's future.

When he stopped at Bennie's that night, the talk was all about Europe.

"I worry about this mess, Bennie. Life's been too comfortable for us here, but I think that'll change." Will lifted the shot glass that Bennie placed before him. "I'm not sure that Ireland won't enter on the Kaiser's side. I don't like the Kaiser, but Ireland's at odds with England, and if we enter the war, we'll be England's ally."

"So, who'll you defend?"

"I don't like it, but Ireland has as much right to be independent as our forefathers did. No country should be dominated by another."

"If we get in, there'll be a draft, you know," Bennie said. "What'll you do if you're called?"

What would he do if he was called to fight against his grandfather's country? It was out of his hands, so he shouldn't worry, but he couldn't help it. And Frank and Jesse? Just one more thing to tear his family apart.

On April 6, 1917, newspaper headlines and telegraphs trumpeted the news: America was finally in the Great War, as it came to be called.

Thousands of American men volunteered to enter the fray. Patriotic fervor surged through Will, too, but he was torn. How could he leave his family? Then he heard from his draft board. Because of wife and child, he received a deferral. Still, if the war's progress became grim, he knew that could change. His brother Frank received a farm deferment, but Jesse wasn't so lucky. Although he pleaded farm worker status, and his father supported that claim, too, many people saw him in town, knew his fondness for the taverns to take his claim seriously. The local draft board didn't. The military assigned him to the 85th Division, to be stationed at Camp Custer in Battle Creek, Michigan.

Before Jesse left, he stopped to see Will at his dealership, but he didn't come to say goodbye or to accept his brother's best wishes.

"I hope you and Frank are happy now. You've got me out of your hair."

"Can I get something for you?" Will clutched Jesse's shoulder. "I wish it hadn't turned out so."

Jesse jerked away.

"It didn't have to. If you had any guts and Frank any heart, I'd have my own farm now. I'd be at home, just like you."

He kicked Will's desk hard enough to slide it into Will and force him back.

"You better know, if something happens to me, it's on the both of you."

Jesse walked to the door and grabbed the knob; then, he turned back.

"Remember that while you enjoy your fine home and prosperity. I may see Hell in Europe, but you'll get yours. Sooner or later, you and Frank will get yours. I'll pray for that every day I'm gone."

Will pulled a bill from his wallet, held it out, but Jesse slapped it to the floor.

"Keep your money. A curse on the both of you." Jesse turned and strode out the door.

13

Will's sales dropped and his repair work slowed so much that he began to worry about mortgage payments. The war dampened most businesses' profits but none more than Will's. With the young men away, there were few buyers for his cars. He tried selling auto insurance, but paying good money for something not likely to happen wasn't very popular. Still, the insurance business provided a little income. He should have stayed on the farm. No matter how bad things got, they'd always have food. He was glad that Mary wanted to continue teaching.

With fewer customers he had more time, so on slack days he stopped at Bennie's Bar on the way home. He drank the cheap seven ounce beer and seldom took a refill. One day, when he stayed a bit longer than usual, Mary, Michael in her arms, waited at the door when he turned up his front walk. Will followed the sidewalk's crack to make sure he walked a straight line.

"Did you stop at Bennie's again?"

"I only had two beers." He held his hand over his heart. "Sober as a judge, I swear it."

"That's not much of a testament in this town," Mary said.

Will knew she was right. Tommy Burns liked his Scotch and ale. Will turned and walked back up the line. "Straight as an arrow, see." He pointed toward the crack.

"Will, I'm not going to complain if you stop at Bennie's now and then." She stood Michael down and he ran to his father. "Lord knows how I hate that wicked drink. But the vice runs through your family, so I suppose you can't help it. I don't know how your father manages. He always has a bottle. And Jesse." She took Michael from Will's arms. "But you've got this young one now. I'd think you'd want to set an example. You, better than anyone, should know the harm it does."

Will felt ashamed when his handsome little boy reached out to him and smiled as if he believed his dad could do no wrong. "I promise, Mary, I'll come straight home from now on. I'll close my eyes when I pass Bennie's."

For a while thereafter he looked the other way whenever he passed Bennie's, and thought ahead to his weekend with Michael.

And together, every Saturday and Sunday, they explored Ashley Springs. When snow was on the ground, they walked to Center Street and watched the big kids slide down the village's longest hill. "What fun," Will said. "Why, by this time next year I'll have made you a sled, and we'll race down the hills together. But you'd better hold tight, 'cause my sleds go fast."

Michael eyed the children whizzing by as if he believed Will's promise and could hardly wait his turn. When he wandered too close, Will called, "Come back to Daddy. Don't get so close."

But Daddy's voice emboldened Michael, and he darted toward the speeding projectiles. Will raced after him. "You little leprechaun," Will screamed as he ran, and when he caught him, Michael laughed uncontrollably while Will rolled him in the snow.

In spring they strolled to the village green where they watched boys play baseball. "I'll show you my slow pitch," Will said. "They'll have a terrible time trying to hit your fastball when you throw that changeup now and then."

Michael smiled, pointed toward the boys, and said, "my dada," as if he knew exactly what Will had in mind.

Sometimes, Will took Michael to the valley stream where they listened to the current sing its song and watched the birds at the water's edge. Will called out each bird that joined them.

"That's a brown-headed cowbird," he said. "A lazy bird she is. Must think she's well-to-do. Leaves her young with a nanny."

"Look over there," he pointed. "An indigo bunting. See the blue speck? See it move?" Will motioned across the stream. "You almost never see one. It stays hidden." He turned Michael's head toward the bird. "Behind that branch."

Michael looked to where Will pointed, but he lost interest, and instead clenched Will's fingers and stretched toward the water's edge.

When Will didn't move, Michael pulled and pointed at the flowing current. "Play water," he said and pulled harder.

"So my birds aren't so interesting after all?" Will sat Michael on his knee, took the boy's shoes off, and dangled his toes in the cold stream. Michael screamed and lifted his feet above the meandering rivulet.

"A little too cold for my laddie?" Will stepped away from the bank's edge, but Michael twisted his body and leaned back toward the flow. "Again," he said as he stretched toward the water.

"You want more, my brave little bear?" Will dangled Michael's feet over the water, and Michael dipped them, pulled back, then thrust deep and flailed the water until it splashed across the shoreline and drenched Will's trousers. Michael laughed when he saw his daddy soaked. "My dada wet," Michael said. "Again."

"Oh, no, my laddie. I'll not be taken in again." He set his boy down, took his hand, and started toward home.

At first, Michael resisted, but when his dad didn't slow, he trotted alongside all the way home.

"I wish I had your energy, my laddie. But you must use it to learn about your world. You can't just be a trickster."

Before they entered the house, Will pulled Michael close and hugged him tightly, and when Michael responded, "my dada," Will nuzzled his neck and said, "My son, I love you with all my heart. I don't know what I'd do if I ever lost you."

Will continued his quest to educate Michael. He identified rose-breasted grosbeaks, eastern bluebirds, cedar waxwings, and lots of robins. He expected Michael to be the best informed youngster in town.

But Will worried, too, and he still stopped at Bennie's now and then. "Business sure is slow these days," he said to Bennie. "I hope I can get by until this war is over."

"I don't think it'll last," Bennie said. "Now we're in it, won't be long till those Krauts are on the run."

"I hope so."

"You're a farmer at heart, Will. Maybe it's time to go back. Farmers are doing well. We gotta feed the world now."

"I think about it, I sure do, but I doubt Mary would want to leave our nice home. Farming's hard work, Bennie. I'm not sure I'd want to put her through it. Not sure she'd do it."

"Your dad's up in age. He can't farm forever. Why don't you buy his farm? Then he could afford a house in town." Bennie dipped a glass in hot, soapy water, swirled it, dipped it in a rinse, and held it up for inspection. "S'pose his farm's too small. Wouldn't support a family, not the way costs are rising these days."

"Not the way he farms, but I've got ideas to increase production. But Dad's not about to leave, not yet. Maybe someday."

On one balmy September Saturday Michael went to bed with the sniffles. By morning, his cough worsened, so Will walked to Dr. Ruggles' office, but when no one answered his knock, he left a message on the door: "Michael's ill. Please come as soon as possible."

Dr. Ruggles checked Michael thoroughly and assured Will and Mary the boy would be okay, that it was just a late summer cold, and after a few days he would be as good as new. It seemed that Michael's cough lessened when he was upright, so Will cradled him in his arms and walked the floor most of that day. He wiped his brow with cold washcloths and filled his bottle with a thin chicken broth that Michael seemed to like. When Will tried to put him down, he clung to his daddy and shook his head while pleading, "Dada, my dada."

Will pulled his son close, squeezed tight, nuzzled the boy's neck and whispered, "My son, I love you with all my heart."

But Dr. Ruggles was right. Will's worry lessened as Michael improved through the week.

In the evenings, to pass the time, Will fashioned a simple little ditty that he sang while he twirled Michael around the nursery:

Took my laddie out today, out today, out today.
Took my laddie out today, all the way to Downy.
Took my laddie out to play, out to play, out to play.
Took my laddie out to play, all the way to Downy.
Took my laddie in a sleigh, in a sleigh, in a sleigh.
Took my laddie in a sleigh, all the way to Downy.
Took my laddie far away, far away, far away.
Took my laddie far away, all the way to Downy.

Michael laughed and clapped his hands when Will dipped him toward the floor each time they arrived at Downy.

One evening, when Mary got home late, she found Michael and Will on the nursery rug, Michael snug in his blanket, his head on a pillow and fast asleep. Will sat beside him, like a shepherd caring for his littlest lamb. She kneeled by her husband, wrapped her arms around him, and cradled his head on her shoulder.

"I have no fears for Michael when you're with him, my dear. He couldn't have more loving care." She bent down and kissed her sleeping baby. "I know you'll never let anything happen to him. He'll always be safe with his daddy. I love the both of you with all my heart. The two princes in my life."

She took Will's head in her hands, pulled him close, and kissed his lips.

Although he lost more income than other merchants who didn't depend upon youth sales, Will continued to be confident that business would boom once the boys returned. He believed that nothing would deter their newfound enthusiasm for adventure and excitement.

But there were awful nightmares. Many nights Will awoke with visions of Jesse crumpled over, his face bloodied. Thomas called repeatedly to see if Will had heard anything, but there was no word, not a single letter from Jesse, and none from Frank, either. It felt as if the gods had swept his brothers away. How could they be so divided?

M ary took a strawberry cake from the oven and placed it out to cool.

Will eyed it hungrily. "It's been so long since I've seen a cake, my sweet tooth is plumb soured up."

"If you want frosting on this cake you'd better get movin' and bring that sugar back before supper. I don't have a bit left in the cupboard."

Will fingered through the pockets of his jacket. "Where'd I put that coupon?"

Hands on her hips and a smirk on her face, Mary let him struggle. After watching him assault each pocket for the third time, she took pity. "It'll be a miracle if this cake gets frosted today. Look in your pocketbook. You put it there less than five minutes ago."

He searched through his pocketbook and, to his surprise, found the coupon. "Mary, I don't know what I'd do without you."

"You'd be a whole lot thinner. Now get on with you. But come straight home. Don't you go stopping at Bennie's."

When Will turned his Model T onto High Street, he spotted kids playing mumblety-peg in the courthouse alley. He could see that Squeak McBride was having difficulties, so he parked the Lizzie, got out, and called, "You wanna see how that's done, Squeak?"

"Sure, Mr. O'Shaughnessy," Squeak said. "I can't get it to stick."

"You're throwing it too far out." He reached toward the small boy. "Give me that knife, I'll show you."

Will balanced the jackknife on his middle finger—but at a slight downward angle—paused for a moment, and then flipped it straight up. It turned once before sticking in the ground.

"Gee, Mr. O'Shaughnessy, I wish I could do that."

"You can, Squeak, just practice two things. Balance the knife on your finger, and flip it one turn. Practice, Squeak, practice. Remember, just one turn."

"Will you stay and play with us, Mr. O'Shaughnessy?" Squeak said.

"I can't today. Gotta get sugar back to Mary. Come over tomorrow and have some strawberry cake."

"Can I, Mr. O'Shaughnessy?" Squeak said. "You're sure good at mumblety-peg. You're better than the eighth-graders."

"You don't have to be big, no you don't. Just practice."

Will walked the three blocks to Sandby's grocery. "Mr. Sandby, I need my monthly sugar allotment. Mary says there'll be no frosting on the cake if I don't get it home by supper."

"Do you have your coupon this time?" He reached back to the shelf and removed a five pound cloth bag. "I'm tired of asking for coupons. I hope this darn war's over soon. I'd sell more sugar and you'd eat more cake."

"My sweet tooth's so deprived that it's all shriveled up," Will said as he dug through his pockets. "Where's that darn coupon?"

Mr. Sandby exchanged the sugar for the coupon and a dollar bill. Will walked back down High Street toward his car, but hadn't gone a block before he heard shouts and whistles from the bottom of the hill. People streamed from the telegraph office; then they ran toward him. Bert Whitford, who was in the lead, shouted, jumped, and flailed his arms in the air. "The war's over! An armistice has been signed! The boys are coming home!"

Before Bert reached Will, people rushed from the buildings and began an impromptu parade up the street. Some headed to the churches at the top of High Street, and others dropped out at the bars. Mayor Tommy Burns grabbed Will's arm. "Come on, Will, I'll buy you a drink."

"You're buying? That's a first," Will said.

"It's a great day. Bernie's coming home."

Will wondered if he'd see Jesse soon.

"Come along now, my man," Burns said.

Before Will could answer, someone shouted, "Everyone to Tony's Tavern! Tommy Burns is buying!"

Will didn't resist the crowd that flowed toward Tony's. As a young man he learned to not swim against the current, and he wasn't going to start now.

Burns shouted to the bartender, "Tony, I'll buy drinks this day, all that St. Louis brew you can pour!"

"You know I only serve Wisconsin beers."

"Ohhh, too bad. And I was going to buy for these good fellows. Sorry, men, no Bud tonight."

Hands grabbed Tommy and pushed him toward the door.

"Hold on. I was just joshin'. Fill 'em up, Tony. A pail or two to each table. And send the bill to the mayor's office."

The room reverberated with, "For he's a jolly good fellow," interspersed with, "You've got my vote, Tommy."

With a full glass thrust into his hand, what could Will do? He would be unpatriotic to refuse. After initial thirsts were quenched, the stories began. Not to be outdone by his constituents, Tommy shouted, "I've got a true story to tell, about a trip I took to the Black Hills. I was—"

"You suggesting that our stories aren't true?" Dennis Newberry said. "That Franz didn't wrestle a bear?"

"Of course not, Dennis. I know you're as honest as Father McCrery, and you know the good Father and I are close as Siamese twins."

"Why, you aren't even Catholic," Dennis muttered.

"No, but Father's working on him," Silas Murrish shouted. "Tell your story, Tommy."

"Last year when I drove west to see my invalid sister in the Montana wilds, I stopped for a night in Deadwood. Now, that's one scary town. Why—"

"Get on with it," someone shouted. "We know Deadwood. We threw those blokes outa the Springs."

A murmur of agreement filled the room.

"Yeah, they're rejects," shouted a reveler.

"Those who couldn't hack it here," chimed in another.

Tommy waived them down. "I stopped at a saloon, to inquire about lodging, you know."

"Sure, Tommy, sure."

"Of course, someone asked my name, and I said, 'Burns.' That guy looked me up one side and down the other, then he said, 'You aren't that Burns guy who won the world championship, are you?'"

"You never won any championship," Silas Murrish said.

"Of course not," the mayor said. "That was another Tommy Burns, heavyweight boxing champion. But I didn't let on. I said, 'Yes, I'm Tommy Burns.' I wouldn't lie, you know."

"Not you, Tommy. Like all the politicians, nothing but the truth outa that mouth."

"Now listen to Tommy, men," another shouted across the room. "He's an experienced man. Why, he's made the same mistakes dozens of times."

"Take that man's beer away," Burns shouted back.

"Get on with it, Tommy."

"Well, this fella looked me up one county and down the other and said, 'You're a heavyweight champion? Why, anyone in here could beat Billy blazes out of a wimpy guy like you.' He turned to his buddies and said, 'Isn't that right, fellas?'" Tommy swigged his drink. "I thought they were about to challenge me for the title right there. Never seen such a hullabaloo."

"Why, my old lady could beat the Billy blazes out of you," Dennis Newberry said.

Burns turned to Newberry. "I suppose she could. She practices on you every day. Fill 'em up again, Tony."

Will began to feel a bit wobbly, so he took a seat next to Rich Turner in the corner. "How're the Fords selling?" Rich said.

"A bit better. I expect it to boom when the boys get back, but the insurance business helps some."

"You're trying to sell insurance to these tight-fisted farmers? Sounds like a fool's errand to me."

"Maybe I should have stayed farming."

"Cheese and cash crops have been up. I never did so good as last year."

"The war's pushed prices higher," Will said, "but I'm not sure it'll last. I think about farming lots. There may be better ways."

"New ways?"

"With improved trucking, I think we could ship milk to Chicago and Minneapolis."

"Too chancy for me," Rich said. "Milk doesn't keep that well. Lot's of extra work and expense to meet Grade A standards, too. I'll stick to cheese."

"There's too much price fluctuation between spring and fall," Will said. "If we could just even it out."

"Farmers out East are dumping milk," Rich said.

"I'd hate to throw good milk," Will said. "I think cooperatives are a better way."

He'd pulled library materials about cooperatives every chance he got. He had even asked Mrs. Selkirk to search for any new articles that were published on the topic, and then he paid for them. He was excited to learn that Illinois and Minnesota farmers were beginning to talk cooperatives. Their idea was to bring farmers together as a group that could buy their supplies cheaper and sell milk for more money than they could negotiate as individuals. Will knew that someday he wanted to be part of that movement.

"Where's Will?" Tommy's voice floated across the room. "Will O'Shaughnessy, get up here and lead a song."

Tommy bought another pail of beer. "You're empty, my good man. Let me fill 'er up."

"No, Tommy, Mary's waiting for this sugar," Will said as he picked up the bag.

"Just one more." Tommy poured his glass full.

A voice hollered, "Take it easy, Tommy! Will gets tipsy on one drink."

"But he's not sure which one it is," Liam Shea shouted. "The tenth or eleventh!"

Tommy grabbed the bag from Will's hands and set it in the corner. Then he pulled him to the center of the room. "Come on, Will, just one song."

"We don't want another Irish song," Dobberstein shouted. "We've heard enough from those Kaiser lovers."

Rich Turner jumped at Herman Dobberstein. "Shut up, Herman. The war's over. Besides, you're half Kraut yourself. Go ahead, Will."

Glasses clanked and voices shouted, "Go ahead! Let 'er rip!"

In an acceptable tenor voice, Will sang his favorite Irish song, "Danny Boy."

The room was quiet as a cemetery at midnight by the time he finished.

"Oh, Will, why'd you go do that?" Tommy said as he wiped a tear from his eye.

Sniffles could be heard throughout the room, and several men pulled out hankies.

"Okay, fellas," Will said, "sing with me," and he turned the gloom to laughter when he belted out the bawdy lyrics of the "Irish Washer Woman."

Two hours later, Will threw the bag of sugar over his shoulder and staggered out of Tony's front door. There'd be heck to pay when he got home. He couldn't remember sugar so heavy or hills so steep. He was about to turn off High Street when he decided to rest against a telephone pole. Will hung on for dear life as it teetered to and fro. He'd have to tell Tommy about that wobbly pole. It wasn't safe.

After he supported the pole for fifteen minutes, Will wiped his brow and turned toward home, thankful that the bag seemed lighter now. As he walked up the path to his house, he noticed the shed door was open and his Model T was gone. Who'd have taken that? He entered the house and faced a more pressing problem.

"Where have you been? Give me that sugar."

Mary reached for the bag when Will struggled to unhitch it from his shoulder. He staggered against her from the effort.

She grabbed it from his hands. "You're drunk as a skunk. You'll not—" She turned the empty bag in her hands and pointed to a hole. "Why, you lost all the sugar. You threw our money away with your drunkenness."

Mary started up the stairs, then, she twisted around toward him. "You'll have to find your own dinner. I'm going to bed. My mother told me not to marry an Irishman."

Will banged around the kitchen while he boiled black coffee and sliced cold pork shoulder. He avoided going upstairs as diligently as he avoided the unfrosted strawberry cake, fodder for the guilt of a failed November day. America may have celebrated a victory, but Will felt the sting of defeat.

After four cups of coffee and a couple slices of the pork, his courage was sufficiently fortified to assault the ramparts and face the anger of a righteous wife. She complained a bit when he took a nip, but she'd never seen him tipsy before. He knew that this time, there would be a battle.

Will approached the bed cautiously. He hoped that Mary was asleep. He raised his leg, but when his toe hooked a sheet, he lost his balance and sat hard on the floor. "Mary, give mea hand. Can't you see I'm 'avin' trouble?" he slurred.

Will thought he heard a groan.

"You drank yourself into your problem. You can sleep your way out of it, right there on the floor."

"But don't ya know the war's over? Why, I was with the best people in town."

"Will, let this be a warning. I'll sleep on it, but don't be surprised if I'm not here in the morning."

15

Lungs filled with fluid, vessels hemorrhaged, and blood oozed from the nose and ears of the afflicted before they died. Others lingered with the fever, chills, and fatigue common to pneumonia. But they died, too.

War's curse ended November 11, 1918, but as the fighting wound down, a new scourge swept the land: Spanish flu. In the first year news trickled through the newspapers, but the boys returning home reported thousands ill and hundreds dying in the camps. During the winter of 1919 the usual head colds and flu prevailed, but by summer Ashley Springs felt the sting of this virulent disease. At first townsfolk expressed surprise that the flu extended into warm weather, but soon they panicked when the sickness worsened.

Harold Murrish was first. He fought through Europe's trenches, avoided the killing gasses, and escaped bayonet charges with no scars to brag about, but he bled profusely before succumbing to an organism that he couldn't even see. Then it was Rafe Turner and Frank Dobberstein, strong adults who never lost a day's work in their young lives. Stores closed, and people avoided friends and neighbors.

Mary rushed through the parlor door, almost knocked Will off the stick pony that he and Michael rode around the room. "I saw Agnes Sealy at the Post office. Her daughter Florence and their neighbor Jimmie Chappell are sick in bed. I knew we should have cancelled the school picnic." Mary threw the mail into the secretary without opening the envelopes.

Will noticed that several were bills. She always opened the bills. Said she wanted to get those behind her.

"We never should have brought those kids together. It's a shame."

"You wanted to cancel," Will said.

"I knew better, but I didn't insist. It's my fault."

Will dropped the stick and turned toward Mary, but when Michael protested, he took a horehound from his pocket, picked up the shaft, and handed both to his son. "Take Nellie to your room and put her in her stall, but groom and feed her before you eat your candy."

Michael rode his steed through the pocket doors and toward the stairway. Will turned back to Mary and embraced her. "It's not your fault. You tried to warn Gable about the danger, but he is the board president. You had no choice."

"I should have tried harder."

"Don't worry, Mary. The children will be okay."

But Will worried. With the scourge hard on the young, he knew that Mary was exposed daily. He hoped the Lord was with them.

Will stewed over having to close doors to his customers, but was thankful to have repair work. Then when Mary went to bed with a fever and the chills, he was glad he didn't need to work from eight to five. Will made tea, toast, and chicken broth and tried to keep Michael away from Mary, but he found that impossible, so he sent him to stay with his mother on the farm. Dr. Ruggles said to keep Mary in bed and make her drink plenty of liquids, and that there's little else he could do. "Besides, her symptoms seem mild," Dr. Ruggles said. "I have others who are so much worse."

"She's just plumb tuckered out," Will told Charlie Nesbitt when he passed him on the boardwalk the next morning. "I hate to leave her home alone, but she insists. She says someone's gotta work."

Mary's cough subsided, and she began to take solid food and to gain strength. Will thought he could call Michael home in a couple days, but he was haunted by other worries. He hadn't heard from Jesse since the war. He'd called his mother and Frank, and then contacted the Draft Board, but they knew nothing. Gertrude said that Thomas was drinking more these days. She said he was worried about Jesse. Now that most of the boys were home, Will expected to see Jesse or hear that he was in town, but he heard nothing. Then when he was most concerned about Mary, a letter arrived from the War Department, which was mailed nine months earlier and said that Jesse was missing in action. Will remembered Jesse's threat that if anything happened to him, Will would pay the price. Will remembered his nightmares.

Mary slowly improved. She washed clothes, dusted, and cooked, but she didn't start the flowerbeds that she had planned during the prior Easter vacation. She complained that she was just too tired to do more. It didn't help that Michael clung to her after his return from the farm.

Will was glad that Mary was on the road to recovery and that Michael remained healthy, even though more of his friends and neighbors took ill each week. Would this plague never end?

But as Ashley Springs' residents readied for winter—cut wood, chinked chimneys, filled root cellars, and hunkered down for the flu season's peak—the unexpected happened. Those who had survived the summer's assault improved, and the number of new cases declined to the year's lowest. It left as rapidly as it came. The worst was over. But that was when Michael showed the symptoms.

At first, it was a runny nose, a slight fever, and a mild cough. Then his dry cough turned to severe spells that lasted almost a minute, so severe that Dr. Ruggles thought Michael might have pertussis, but he never showed the characteristic whoop.

Mary and Will took turns walking the floor at night, and Michael seemed calmed by their presence. His severe coughing diminished when he was held upright, but the sleepless nights wore them down.

Now that Will could open his doors again, young veterans overwhelmed his office space, and the waiting list for new cars was six months out and increasing daily. Old cars that were stowed for the boys return home were brought in for repairs and tune-ups. Will couldn't keep up, so he hired two young fellows to help. But he had to stay longer to train and guide them as they learned the trade.

Mary couldn't find time to correct the papers that she brought home each night. "Will, I'm exhausted and getting further behind each day. Do you think your mother would come and help until Michael gets better?"

Will called home that night and caught Thomas in the house. "Dad, Michael's pretty bad with this flu and Mary needs help. Do you think Mother could come in for a few days?"

"Just a minute."

Will waited but not for long.

"I'll bring her in after milking tomorrow. Be glad to get some relief, myself. Tell the boy I'll bring him to see the new calf soon as he's up and about. Prettiest thing you ever did see."

Gertrude O'Shaughnessy arrived with a bag full of cures and a mouth full of advice. "I'll take care of him. I know what's best for that boy. He'll be better in no time once I get my tonic into him. You'll see." She pulled a garlic clove, a dried lemon, a cayenne pepper, bee pollen, and a bottle of peroxide from her satchel.

Mary gasped. "You're not going to give him that?"

"Calm down. This works wonders. Just two tablespoons each day and he'll be good as new. Tell her, Will."

"Your concoction tastes awful, Mother." Will picked up the peroxide. "Are you sure he needs this?"

"It's an old family recipe. It kept your grandpa Duffy on his feet, didn't it? He never went down."

Not until the hogs got him. "Maybe we should ask Dr. Ruggles."

Mary inspected each ingredient. "It shouldn't hurt him, I guess." She removed the peroxide bottle. "But no peroxide. I'll not let him drink this."

"A little won't hurt him," Gertrude said.

But Mary placed the bottle in the medicine chest. "He'll not take peroxide, not even a little."

"I'll put some behind his ear."

Mary shook her head and planted her feet between Gertrude O'Shaughnessy and the medicine cabinet.

Gertrude fumed, but began to chop a garlic clove. "Will, go get some fresh water. This needs to be mixed in clean spring water."

Michael continued to languish. The only time he showed spunk was each morning and night when Gertrude O'Shaughnessy poured a spoonful of tonic into his mouth. "See how it perks him up," she said.

But Will knew it was his laddie's protest against that awful concoction.

"It can't be much worse than the cod liver oil he takes," Mary said.

"He hates that, too," Will said. "I don't blame him, do you?"

They called Dr. Ruggles back, and he said to pour as much liquid into the boy as he could take. Plenty of clear, cool water, and juices, too.

But Gertrude O'Shaughnessy didn't stop at water and juice. She tried chicken soup, onion syrup, bitter teas, and apple vinegar mixed with honey, but Michael didn't improve. She bathed him with Epsom salts, rubbed oil of oregano on his chest, hung a sack of cloves around his neck, and bathed his feet with eucalyptus oil, but Michael's cough persisted and his body temperature climbed. They called the doctor again, and he tended Michael overnight while Grandma swabbed the boy's chest with cold water which Will pumped from the well.

Christmas 1919 was one week away, and they hadn't even raised a tree. No candles, no tinsel, and no colored balls. Will was so busy at his shop that he hadn't noticed the season, not until he saw lights in the windows as he walked home that Friday night. When he noticed the candle-shrouded star through the glass, Will thought about the Christ child, silently prayed for his intervention in curing Michael's disease. He dropped onto the snow and whispered a simple prayer. "Dear Lord, take care of my laddie. Don't let him die. Please, don't let him die. Let him live a full life." He followed the star's light downward across the decorated tree. "Your will be done, O Lord."

Will rushed into the house. "Mary," he shouted, "it's almost Christmas and we don't have a tree! How will Michael know it's Christmas without a tree?"

"Shush," his mother hissed down the stairway. "Michael's sleeping."

He raced to the kitchen to find his wife. "Mary, get out the decorations. I'll take Fanny to the farm and cut a fir. We'll put it up tonight."

"Slow down, my dear. Dinner's almost ready. We'll eat, then we'll pull out the decorations. The tree'll wait until morning. While you get it, I'll clear a space in Michael's room. We'll put it where he can watch while we decorate. But he's asleep right now."

Will slumped into his chair. "I so wanted to take him along this year. I wanted him to pick the tree."

"This will pass, my dear. He'll not only select one, but he'll help you cut it next year."

But it didn't pass. Michael weakened each day, and on Christmas morning his breath came in short shallow gasps, and his skin turned blue. Will raced to get Dr. Ruggles.

Dr. Ruggles worked over his laddie throughout the morning.

Will wanted to run from the room when Michael screamed with pain and his body shook so hard that his teeth chattered. But he couldn't leave his son in this moment of darkness.

Dr. Ruggles called out, "Will, get more blankets."

Will was glad to leave for a moment, but he rushed back immediately with his arms full.

Michael continued to gasp for air and he coughed and spit phlegm. Will cringed while the doctor tilted Michael's head to the side and wiped the greenish, foul smelling mucus from his lips. Sweat wound down Michael's brow and his chest heaved as his breathing rapidly increased. Even Michael's fingernails were turning blue.

Will felt helpless as he saw his child slowly slip away. He knew there was little hope. Why was this happening to them? Had he not bundled Michael adequately against the cold? Had he offended God? Life had been easy these last years, and although he'd given money, he hadn't furthered God's work like he should. Was it that? But Mary was fervent about doing God's work. She couldn't deserve retribution.

The boy lapsed into a coma and stopped breathing by noon. Sweat pouring from his brow, Dr. Ruggles turned to Will. "I did all I could, Will, but it turned to pneumonia, and pneumonia's a deadly disease."

Will slumped on Michael's bed. "My baby. Why? Why did God need him? Didn't He call enough children home this year?" He pulled Mary to him. "Did we do something wrong? Was it Mother's tonic? Should we not have given him that horrible medicine?" Will slumped on the bed and sat with his head in his hands. "Why?"

"No, the tonic didn't hurt him, but it didn't help either," Dr. Ruggles said. "If we only had more tools. I'm sorry, Will, Mary." Dr Ruggles' shoulders drooped as he stepped away from Michael's side, then he turned back and pulled the blanket over the child's still head. "You can't know how sorry I am that I couldn't save your little boy."

Most everyone in town attended Michael's funeral. Family, friends, neighbors, and customers stumbled through the service and burial as if they were everyday occurrences. And they were. No Ashley Springs' family went untouched by the scourge of war or the curse of illness during those years.

The minister recited the Twenty-third Psalm from memory. Annabelle Murrish sang "Blest be the Tie That Binds" as discordant as ever, but with only half her usual enthusiasm. The pall bearers stumbled, although the casket was light.

Mary wept inconsolably, clung to Michael's casket, and refused to leave the gravesite, but nobody pressed her. They had seen too many mothers cry by their child's grave, and everyone there felt death's sting.

Will wouldn't sit up front near the casket, wouldn't console Mary, and stayed as far back in the burial tent as was possible. Thomas and

Frank urged him forward, told him that Mary needed his support, and Will tried. He started up the aisle, but after two steps, he retreated to the back and ran from the cemetery at the last amen.

Mary slowly recovered, but Will stayed nights at the shop, and he spent Saturday there, too. He came home Sunday, but spent the day stacking firewood in the garage.

"I know you're busy," Mary said, "and I hate to push you, my dear, but I asked you last week to remove the tree and crib from Michael's room."

"I'll get to it."

But Will didn't get to it that week either. He continued to stay at his shop, and when he did come home, it was late, and he went straight to bed with little or nothing to eat.

When Mary pressed him, he growled, "Mary! You don't understand how much business I've got now the boys are home from the war. I can't keep up."

On the third Sunday morning after Michael's funeral, Mary pleaded, "You haven't been to church since Michael's death. Please come with me this morning."

"You go," Will said. "I'll do some of those things you've wanted me to finish."

Will removed the wreath from over the fireplace. He took the Christmas candles from the parlor writing stand. He stowed the tinsel, balls, and beads that decorated the kitchen, hall, and their bedroom. But he rushed past Michael's room without looking through the door.

When Mary arrived home she found Will in the basement boxing the decorations he had taken down. "Oh, Will, I do appreciate all the work you're doing, but please remove the tree and take Michael's crib down."

"I'll do it, but first I've got walks to shovel."

"You can't pretend that Michael's room isn't there, Will. We must get on with our lives. You'll make yourself sick over this. You've hardly eaten a thing these past weeks. Please, take the tree and the crib out. Then I'll clean the carpet."

"Mary, get off my back!" Will snarled. "I'm fine. I got so far behind when Michael was ill."

He rushed from the house into the garage and grabbed his snow shovel as he hurried through.

Michael's tree shed its needles until the carpet looked like an untended autumn lawn, but Will didn't care. Michael's room had become enemy territory, as unapproachable as Grandpa's hog pen.

Three nights later, Mary waited up until he got home. "You must face it, Will. You've got to realize that Michael's gone."

"Of course I know he's gone," Will snapped. What kind of dunce does she take him for? He turned and rushed from the house, running to the shop, where he worked throughout the night, through the following day, and into that night.

The next morning, Mary traced brown needles through the upper hallway, down the stairs, and out the back door. She found Will asleep in his parlor chair, cheeks tear-stained, and his head scrunched against the large side wing.

Early in 1919, prohibition against the sale of liquor had been ratified by the U.S. Congress, but with the onset of the Spanish Flu, Ashley Springs had more pressing problems. Beset by her family's illnesses, Mary hardly noticed. But when the 18th Amendment went into effect on January 17, 1920, Bennie's customers took notice. With Prohibition the law of the land now, Bennie had boarded up his bar and moved to an old house near Will's business on the east edge of town. It had all the trappings of a country residence—until you walked through the front door. It may be illegal, but Bennie's clientele didn't complain.

Will passed through the entryway, but when he looked inside, he thought that he'd stepped into the wrong building. The room was filled with showcases of tobacco products and shaving paraphernalia. But the man behind the counter, Dennis Newberry's son, Wilmer, beckoned and pointed to a nondescript wood paneled door. "Bennie's in the back. Through that door."

Not knowing what to expect, Will cautiously edged through the opening, but was immediately greeted by a familiar voice. "Come right in, Will," Bennie called. "How do you like my new establishment?"

Will scanned the room. Except for a short bar that looked like an elongated kitchen table and booze bottles aligned on a shelf behind, it looked like anyone's dining room—a side table, wooden chairs all around, a china cupboard, and a corner curio cabinet.

"You've gone to a lot of work, but didn't you forget something?" Will pointed to the shelf lined with bottles. "The evidence is indisputable. But I suppose Tommy looks the other way."

"Tommy's not my worry. It's those damn feds. But I doubt they'll come up here. Chicago keeps them busy enough. But I'm prepared if they do."

"Wilmer'll hold their attention out front?"

"Just long enough for me to dispose of the evidence. By the time they come through that door, all they'll see is my sparse dining room."

"How will you know?"

"Know they're out there? Wilmer has a buzzer behind the counter that alerts me, and when I press on this section," he pointed to a wood strip embedded into the bar's side panels, "the liquor shelf tips back and drops those bottles into a pillow lined bin. Then it becomes a plain old wall shelf again."

"You don't think a room full of people holding half-full glasses will draw their attention?"

"By the time Wilmer lets them in, the room will be empty. The back door opens to a blind ally."

"You're prepared. I'll give you that. What're you serving?"

"Not much variety these days, but I've got some hooch and homebrew."

"I'll take a brew, Bennie."

16

ummer 1920 arrived, but memories and work weighed heavy on Will's mind. He turned his head whenever he passed Michael's room. He didn't need reminders that his son was gone. He thought about their strolls through town, about the baseball games and sleigh rides that Michael would never know. He thought about the valley road, the stream, and the indigo bunting that Michael couldn't see.

One night he sat past midnight and thumbed through the pages of his new *Farm Journal*, but he couldn't concentrate on it. He couldn't sleep and he couldn't read, so he got off his chair and shuffled toward the kitchen. Maybe a cup of hot tea would hit the spot. Will reached for the light cord, but before he grasped it he thought he heard a noise outside and looked toward the big window, the one that Mary enjoyed while she did her kitchen chores. A face looked back. But it was a strange face, a face unlike any he had seen before. Not quite human, it was like a poorly made puppet, all wood and metal. Will rushed to the back door, but when he stepped out no one was there. He locked the doors before turning to bed for a restless night's sleep. The next morning Will didn't mention the ghoul to Mary as she prepared for school.

On the way home from work that night, Will stopped at Bennie's. "Hey, Bennie, is there any word about spirits haunting the neighborhood?"

"Only those I sell."

"Peered in my window last night. It wasn't even human."

Bennie shrugged. "I haven't seen you for a while. Must be busy."

"Sales are soaring. I can't get outa the office. Lucky to have Ed Spencer and Ray Fitzgerald."

"Help is just a headache," Bennie said. "An irate employee complaining nowadays could mean trouble, but Wilmer's no threat."

"I don't have that problem. Ed and Ray are good workers, but I'm so busy I don't have the time to teach them the finer points. I have to stay most evenings and Saturdays, but they're willing. I'm just lucky, I guess."

Will did consider himself lucky. He was glad that he scarcely had time to think about Michael, but there was little time for Mary as well. Still, the hours away from home weren't for naught. He happily watched their debt diminish. It was a blessing and a curse to have the only car dealership in town.

When Sunday arrived, despite unfinished car repairs, Will spent the day with Mary. They began the morning with a hearty breakfast. Will had few kitchen credentials, but he could scramble eggs, fry bacon, and cook last night's baked potatoes into a heaping plate of cold fries. He wasn't sure why, but those cold, leftover potatoes tasted better than the fries he cut from raw spuds. Will insisted that Mary stay upstairs until the table was set and the skillet heated, just enough time to pretty herself for their Sunday breakfast.

After they finished their meal and drank a second cup of coffee, they retreated to their bedroom to dress for church. Will knew that Mary appreciated his efforts, so he cozied up to his pleasing, attractive wife.

"None of that, not now. We barely have enough time to make the first service."

"We could go to second service, couldn't we?"

"But you promised we'd go to Hinton today. You wouldn't renege on that, would you?"

"No, I wouldn't renege on that. But we have so little time together." Will lifted his pants and buttoned his fly. His work left so little time for life's important things. Maybe prosperity wasn't so attractive after all.

W ill felt uneasy about going to Hinton. He'd faced many barns filled with cows but never a room full of rambunctious boys. He hadn't wanted on do it, but when Mary came down with a cold and hoarse throat, she could only whisper. "Will, you'll just have to substitute for me. I told mother I'd do it, and I can't leave them in the lurch."

"But, Mary, I'm no teacher."

"You know our history. You'll just have to go."

He knew that Mary would help him in a pinch, so he hitched Fanny and drove to the 4H meeting at the Hinton Town Hall.

"Boys, my wife—your parents knew her as Mary Tregonning—is sick, and she asked me to substitute."

"Mr. O'Shaughnessy," a tall boy called from the back. "No disrespect, but what can you know about mining? You're Irish."

"What's your name, young man?"

"Bob Tredinnick."

Will groaned under his breath—another Cornishman. What could he expect in Hinton? A room full of boys with parents straight from Kernow. "Well, young man, the Irish mined, too. A few of them did."

"Just to haul slag," another voice called. "They didn't go deep."

Will wanted to whack him, but he smiled instead. "Regardless, I can tell you about the history. I have a history minor from the University of Wisconsin."

"You went to Madison?" the first boy said.

Will supposed that he'd established his credentials. "Do you know why we're called the Badger State?"

"Well, of course," the first boy said. "It was those Irish miners who dug shallow holes like the badgers who gave us that name. They didn't know nothin' 'bout mining."

Laughter assaulted Will's ears.

"Not just the Irish, my son. But many people think our state's named for the animal."

"How many badgers you see 'round here?" shouted a third boy.

"I agree with you. The Cornish made it professional, but let me tell you a bit more about our history. A hundred years ago, Hinton and Ashley Springs were the two largest cities in Wisconsin. Eight miles separated the two villages, eight miles of tree-covered hills, intimidating limestone outcroppings, a sharp valley with a stream so small it could be stepped over in the dry season but became a raging river during spring downpours."

But Will knew that geography wasn't the only divide between them. The more snobbish of Ashley Springs said the two villages were separated by eight miles of geography and a hundred miles of culture, but Will decided that was best unsaid.

"There was a time when the two vied for the region's leadership and times when Hinton seemed to be winning."

Shouts of "Hinton, Hinton" filled the room, but Will waved them silent.

"Although lead had been extracted here since before white men came to the region, the diggings were shallow openings in the ground that exposed surface lead. The early European miners—such as they were—the Irish and others, lived in the holes they dug into the hillsides. Although few of the animals were ever seen in the state, those miners who dug like the badgers that people had seen farther west came to be called by that name. Ever since, Wisconsin has been known as the Badger State.

As you well know, that all changed when Cornish miners trickled into Southwest Wisconsin during the early 1830s. You Cornishmen were professionals who braved deep underground shafts to extract the treasure that awaited your picks and shovels."

The room erupted with whistles and applause.

Will bowed to the left, to the right, and at last, to the center. He had their attention now. "Well, these miners, these Cornish miners," he held up his hand to still the outburst, "flooded the area as demand increased. And the Cornish immigration flow reached its peak when the price of lead exploded through the Civil War years and during America's expansion westward. But after gold beckoned the miners elsewhere, the communities faded into off-the-map hamlets inhabited by retired farmers."

"I bet they were Irish farmers," the tall boy called.

"Yes, the Irish often farmed. My grandfather was a farmer. But unlike Ashley Springs whose economy revived when the zinc mines opened early in the 1900s, Hinton died under its rubble."

A chorus of boos enveloped Will.

He'd planned to tell them that Hinton couldn't afford the amenities that its neighbor to the east provided its youth; that Hinton only had a small three-shelf library, but no opera house, and they couldn't attract an annual Chautauqua. But he decided to let discretion be the better part of valor and instead said, "But Hinton is on the rebound. I heard that your grocer, dry goods operator, and Chevrolet dealer have pooled their money and are looking for entertainment they can bring to your village. They want to make life more interesting for you and your friends."

When the boys stood and cheered, Will knew it was a good time to end his history lesson.

18

Until he stopped at Bennie's on the way home from work one evening, the face in the window had faded from Will's memory. "Hey, Bennie, a shot of liquor if you will, my man."

"It's not Jameson, but it's the best I can get."

"They got guns past the English. You'd think Irishmen could get a good whiskey over here."

"Thought this prohibition might slow my business, but I've never done so good. Kinda late for leaving work, isn't it?"

"Lots of late nights these days. Besides, Mary's not home tonight. She's interviewing for the principal's job at her school."

"That's man's work."

"Usually, but they like her. She's got a good head on her shoulders. Of course, she may not get it."

"Been a little excitement around. Did you hear a vagrant's been hustling folks for money? He comes to their houses at night. Scares them." A customer called for a beer. "Hold on. I'll be right back." Bennie walked down the bar to serve the man.

Will sipped on his whiskey. Not smooth like a Jameson, he thought.

Bennie set a beer on the bar and served two shots of whiskey on his way back toward Will. "Well, this guy came in the other day and bought a bottle of rotgut. He scared Simon Pettigrew sober. Simon thought the guy was an apparition, that the guy came to haunt him. Why, I haven't seen Simon without a bottle since I came to town. The guy is ghastly. Has no face."

Will knocked his drink over when he grabbed for Bennie's arm. "Whatta you mean?"

"He's repulsive. A wounded vet, I'd guess. Lots are coming back maimed. Must have been terrible over there."

For the rest of the week, Will couldn't keep the face from his mind. Then he was startled to see it again at his window late one night, after Mary had gone to bed. This time Will didn't go out the back door but sneaked around from the front and caught the intruder as he slithered around the house. When he tried to avoid him, Will grabbed his arm. "Who are you? What do you want?"

The man pulled, but Will didn't release his grip.

"Let me go. I'm not hurting anyone."

"You're trespassing. I could call an officer."

"Please don't," he whimpered. "Don't want trouble. I need money—for food."

The moon broke from behind a cloud, and Will cringed when he saw the emaciated and broken figure before him, the left side of his face little more than a tin can with a painted eye overlay. And his right side had skin flaps protruding from a sunken cheek and a depressed jawbone. Will looked away. "Are you back from the Great War?"

"Not so great. You can see that."

"Why'd you come here? I saw you the other night."

"Are you O'Shaughnessy? Jesse's brother?"

"You knew Jesse?"

"I was in the 85th Division. He was captured. I never saw him again."

"Come in the house. Tell me everything."

"Not now. I need money."

Will released the stranger's arm and turned toward the front door. "Wait here. I'll get some food."

But when he returned, the creature was gone.

Will didn't hear more from the stranger, but he wondered and worried. What did he know about Jesse? How could he make it through the winter?

And winter arrived early that year. A January blizzard hammered Southwest Wisconsin on November 1, 1920. Will struggled home through the snow, glad that Mary had decided to stay at the school superintendent's house for the night. His mind was on Michael, how they had built snowmen and dug tunnels through deep snow like this. By the time Will got to Bennie's, he was plumb tuckered out, but it wasn't just the strenuous walk that weighed heavy on his soul. He needed a drink. The room was full. "Bennie, pour me a whiskey. I've got a terrible thirst." He pulled off the scarf that Mary gave him last Christmas and tossed his mackinaw on the side table. "I must be outa shape. Trudging through this snow is worse than pitching hay in a hot loft. My body's not ready for this weather."

Bennie poured a shot of whiskey.

"Have you heard more from that vagrant?" Will said.

"I haven't seen him, but there are rumors. Don't know though."

Rich Turner straddled a chair alongside Will. "You talking about that war beggar? Poor bugger. I heard you saw him."

"Not lately," Will said. "He came to the house this summer. Wanted food and money but left before—"

"You didn't recognize him?" Bennie said.

"Should I have?"

"Some say he's Jesse. Your brother Jesse."

"No." Will reached for his coat. "He said that he knew Jesse though."

"What does your dad say?"

"He's worried about Jesse, but he hasn't mentioned a maimed vagrant."

"I've heard he's living in an old miner's shack down by Barreltown," Rich Turner said.

"It'd be a terrible place now," Bennie said. "He can't possibly survive for long, not in this weather."

Will knew there was no way he could get through the narrow roads to Barreltown in this deep, drifted snow, especially not in the dark without a sleigh. And his set in his garage with a bent runner.

At sunrise the next day, Will pounded metal. Not needing his sleigh to get around town, he had put off working on it's broken runner, but now he felt desperate. Cold as it was, he was glad to have a wood fire heating the large room, but his mind was elsewhere as he worked. He wasn't sure why he should worry about this man. He probably wasn't even Jesse. Lots of maimed and dispirited veterans wandered the roads and looked for handouts these days. He could be anyone.

But what if he was Jesse? Will knew that he had to get out there, that he had to help if he could. He pounded on the metal with his sledge, but it bounced off the hardened steel. He had to calm down and get this runner straightened so he could to get it back in its frame. Why hadn't he done this before?

While Will pounded, Mary stacked plant flats on the garage shelves. Will mumbled about the man as he pounded the bent runner, said that some thought he was Jesse. "But he couldn't have been. I looked him straight in the face." Still, the night was dark and the face grotesque. "How could I not recognize my own brother?"

"Why don't you go get Frank and his sleigh?" Mary said, but she didn't press when Will didn't answer. Instead, she continued organizing the empty flats.

Will hoped he could repair the sleigh and get to Barreltown by noon. That would give him plenty of time to bring the man back to town before dark. "Doggone it, I can't get this runner straight." Will banged his sledge off the inflexible steel, sighted down its length, and banged some more. He looked again. "I should have taken it to the forge."

Will worked and cussed under his breath for half an hour, and then he tightened the resistant runner in his vise, and pushed his weight against it. "There, maybe that will do it."

He called to Mary who now busied herself outside the garage door. "You don't really think it could be Jesse, do you?"

When she didn't answer, Will supposed she hadn't heard. "Mary," he shouted, "this may be serious." The sun climbed in the sky, but it seemed to be getting colder. Maybe a front was moving in. No one could survive long in this cold without a warm shelter. He took the runner from the vice and sighted down it again, but it still didn't seem straight enough. He picked his sledge off the floor and was about to pound the runner some more when Mary snatched the raised sledge from his hand.

"Will, stop your fuming and go get Frank to take you to Barreltown. He's Jesse's brother, too." She set the sledge on a shelf. "Even if the man's not Jesse, he's probably a veteran. We owe him something. The least you can do is help the poor man. The road to Frank's should be open. The wind usually blows that clear."

Will hadn't seen Frank since Michael's funeral, and not for long then. He wasn't keen on asking his brother for help when he was not likely to get it anyway. But maybe Frank knew something that he didn't.

As Will approached Frank's barn he heard a frantic grunting and squealing. He supposed his brother was separating piglets from their mothers. The noise was almost as frightening as it was the day he tried to chase the hogs off Grandpa. Will backed away and waited until Frank ran the piglets into the shelter.

Frank set his pitchfork inside the barn and strolled toward Will. "Surprised to see you here. Did you come for another loan?" He smirked, but Will shook his head.

"I won't be needing money anymore, not from you or anyone. I took more profit this summer than you'll take all year." Will strained to hold his broad smile beyond his comfort level. "Why, Grandpa'd be delighted to hear I'm doing so well." He glared at Frank and directed a stream of spit toward his boots. "Maybe he wasn't so good a judge after all. But that's not why I'm here. It's Jesse. He may be down at Barreltown. He might need help."

"I saw him a week ago, before the storm hit."

"He's here?"

"Some of him is. Left a good part of his face in France."

"You're sure it was Jesse? Where'd you see him?"

"Here in my barn. My cows were restless at night, so I started looking around. I found a whiskey bottle and cigarette butts in the hayloft."

"You're sure he was Jesse?"

"I waited that night to see if someone might come back. Can't have smokers in the loft. Only a fool'd allow that. Scared the daylights out of me when I saw him." Frank shook his head and shuddered. "Looked unearthly. Never seen such a face."

"Did he say he was Jesse?"

"Not until I leveled my shotgun at him. He shrieked like a stuck hog. I thought he'd collapse at my feet. He screamed, 'Don't shoot. I'm your brother. I'm Jesse.'"

"And you didn't let him stay?"

"I couldn't chance he'd burn the buildings in his drunkenness. Grandpa said he was no good."

"Frank, he's our brother. He fought for our country, for us."

"I gave him a bucket of food and a ten dollar bill, but I suppose he drank it away. I said if he didn't get off the farm, I'd fill his bottom with buckshot. Haven't seen him since. Why'd he come here?"

"For God's sake, Frank, he came home. I heard that he's down by the creek near Barreltown, in Chandler's old mining shack. It's half collapsed. It can't provide much shelter. He'll never survive." Will grabbed Frank's arm. "We've gotta help him."

Frank jerked away. "I don't gotta do nothin'."

"Even Grandpa would have helped a wounded veteran."

"I'll help, but don't expect to bring him back here. Grandpa wouldn't want that."

"You'll not have to keep him." Will cringed at his brother's callousness. "Hurry, I'll help you hook your horses to the sleigh." He knew that Frank wasn't about to worry over his brothers. He followed Frank to his carriage house. "There's an empty room over my shop. I'll house him there."

They pulled the sleigh into the yard and hitched Frank's horses. Will tied Fanny to the sleigh, hopped aboard, and helped Frank up.

Will saw no sign of life as they approached Chandler's shack. The deep snow between the roadway and hut was unmarred by footprints. "Maybe he's not here after all," Frank said. "Maybe you're wrong."

"I hope he's some place warmer," Will said as he trudged through the snow.

Frank followed.

Will yanked on the knob, but the door didn't budge. On his second tug, the knob broke away from the lockset, and he flew backward into a drift. Will thrashed about in the deep snow. "Frank, give me a hand." He reached out.

After Frank pulled and Will struggled to get upright, they kicked snow away from the sill and off the step, grabbed the door, and slammed it back and forth until it shoved the hardened pile aside. At first Will couldn't see anything inside the shack, but when he shielded his eyes, he noticed an ember in the potbelly stove that cast a glow through the room. It was then he saw him, Jesse, collapsed across a broken cot. Will rushed to him while Frank inspected the room's lone cupboard. "No food in here. I saw the spring running when we came in, so he has water." He lifted a mostly empty bottle of rotgut off the shelf. "But it's not water he's been drinking."

"Get the blankets from the sled," Will said. "He's cold as an iceberg. Hurry, Frank. We've gotta get him back."

"Probably drunk."

"Bring the blankets, Frank. His arms are blue."

Frank tossed the whiskey bottle toward Will. "This'll get a rise outa him."

"You may be right. If we can get him moving, a little whiskey will warm his insides."

They worked Jesse's arms and legs and rubbed until the limbs showed color, but he remained unresponsive.

"We gotta get him to Dr. Ruggles." Will worried that it may already be too late. He lifted Jesse off the cot and swung underneath his right arm. "Hurry up, get under his other arm." Will remembered Jesse's parting words the day he left for war, and he hated the thought that Frank's heart seemed as cold as Jesse's body. "Help me out, Frank."

Three days later, after Dr. Ruggles said Jesse was well enough to leave the hospital, Will took him to the room over his shop. He brought linens, blankets, and towels from home and food enough to last the day.

The first evening Jesse was there, Will said, "It must have been awful over there."

"It was Hell. I should never have been there."

Will nodded toward Jesse's face. "What happened?"

"We'd been shelled all day. Guys on both sides of me were lying in the mud—screaming and bleeding. I was scared." Jesse's brow creased, his lips tightened, and his voice wavered. Will could see the fear mount as his brother remembered. "We kept our heads down. Then they were in our trench."

"Didn't you have a weapon?"

"My rifle jammed." Jesse grabbed Will's shoulder. "My friends ran. I looked down the trench, and I was all alone. Like when I was shipped away. You and Frank shoulda stood up for me."

Will winced.

"A Kraut stood there and laughed. Then he pushed his rifle in my face and fired. A week later I found myself in the Kaiser's field hospital. They did what they could."

"I'll do what I can now," Will said.

"Like always?" Jesse laughed. "I don't need that kinda help."

But when Will had promised shelter, heat, and food, Jesse wavered. And when Will said he'd furnish booze money, Jesse decided to stay. "But you'd better not tell anyone," Will said. "And except for the privy out back, stay in your room. It pains me to say this, but I can't have you in my showroom."

People'd think him wrong for doing it, but Will knew that if he didn't give him money, Jesse would find other ways to get his booze. And that might cause more problems. Maybe he could control Jesse's drinking with a few handouts. But he never discussed their agreement with anyone, certainly not Mary.

Throughout the winter, Jesse stayed in his room and away from Will's customers. Will told himself their arrangement was working, that Jesse was safe and comfortable, and all was well. But he knew the cold weather was his ally.

As the weather warmed, Jesse strayed, but at first it was only at night after the shop was closed. Then Will's worst nightmare struck like a summer storm which raced over the horizon. Mrs. Vanevenhoven sat in Will's office waiting with her husband for Ed Spencer to change the oil in their big Ford Sedan. Will thought she was a prude and knew she was the town gossip, but Mary said to be nice. "After all, her husband's a good customer, and she's on my school board. We can't afford trouble."

Will didn't want trouble either, so he talked about pleasant things: the warm weather, Mrs. Vanevenhoven's spring operetta, the merits of their sedan. Then the storm struck. Jesse staggered into the room. Mrs. Vanevenhoven screamed. Jesse panicked, and in his stupor he stumbled toward the front door, right into Mrs. Vanevenhoven, who, in her fright, fell across her chair and sliced her head so severely that blood gushed over the floor.

Will grabbed a clean cloth, ran to Mrs. Vanevenhoven, pressed the fabric against her bleeding forehead, told her husband to get Dr. Ruggles, and screamed at Jesse to get the hell out.

The next day Mrs. Vanevenhoven and her husband drove to Hinton and traded their Ford for a Chevrolet Touring Car. Jesse never returned to the shop and wasn't seen in town, and before the week was over, Board President Gable informed Mary that the principal position was awarded to an out-of-towner, a Mr. Hiram A. Smithers.

Will paced the floor. It wasn't the car, but Mary's lost opportunity. "It's all my fault," he said after he calmed down. Then he told Mary about his arrangement with Jesse, how that probably led to his drunken episode.

"I felt so sorry for him," Will said. "To be alone with that terrible injury. And now he's alone again, and I've cost you your promotion."

"It's okay, Will. You tried to help." She lifted his face and gave him a smile that was like sunshine on a frigid day. "I wasn't going to get that job anyway. You know that. They were doing me a courtesy by considering me, but they weren't going to give the principal job to a woman. I knew that all along."

Will wasn't so sure.

Will headed for the Ashley Springs Community Bank with a bag full of money in hand. Business boomed all summer and his bank account grew each day. When he stepped through the door, George Tyler caught his eye and beckoned to him. "Will, come on over and step in my office a minute."

Will followed George into the sparsely furnished room. "What's the problem, my friend? You can't handle all the money I'm bringing?"

"It seems you're doing well." George guffawed. "You didn't rob a bank, now did you?"

Will shoved the money bag at George. "As honest a dollar as you'll find in town. What do you have in mind?"

"I thought you'd like to know. We had to foreclose a small farm out on Hinton road. I'll sell it cheap. Thought you might be interested. I know you'd like to return to farming."

Will sat down. He hadn't expected a chance to buy a farm, nor had he thought about it in a while. "I don't know. It would get Mary closer to her home." He considered it for a moment. "I don't think I can. But keep me in mind, George. I'm going back someday."

Will hoped that he hadn't missed his opportunity. Every time he got near the country he felt farm life's irresistible tug on his psyche. But he was beginning to realize that it's more difficult to return to farming than to have stayed there in the first place. He'd never have known the attraction of wealth if he'd stayed home. But he wouldn't have known the comfort of his good wife, either.

19

Christmas 1920 neared, and Will couldn't wait for the day. In the past they'd exchanged gifts on Christmas morning, but this year Will badgered Mary to change their custom to giving their gifts on the Eve.

"What do you think I bought you?" Mary said. "I hope you're not expecting one of those new Cadillacs that people say outshine Henry's cars."

"You wouldn't."

"No, I wouldn't." She shook her head and laughed. "Why, I think it's even better."

"Well, I'm glad you've got some sense, but it wouldn't take much intelligence to refuse a Cadillac."

"You'll like it. You'll see."

"I think you'll love mine. It took me all summer to find the perfect gift for the prettiest woman in town."

By the time they'd dropped their hints and promised the best gifts ever, they were both ready to celebrate on Christmas Eve. "Okay, we'll open gifts tonight," Mary said, "but not until after Church."

"Do we have to?"

"Will!"

"Just kidding."

They returned home at eight-thirty. Will scrambled to grab Mary's present from under the tree.

"Whoa, slow down," Mary said. "Give me a minute to get out of my clothes, into something more comfortable."

"No, I want you just like you are. I want you dressed in your best when I give you your gift. I want the prettiest girl in town to get even prettier—if that's possible."

"Oh, Will. Whatever could it be?"

"You'll see." Will lifted a package from under the tree, a package wrapped in gold paper with so much ribbon that the gold looked like gilt along the blue ribbon's edge.

"You didn't wrap that, did you, Will?"

"I confess. Mrs. James did it. They say she's the best wrapper in town."

"It's beautiful."

"Well, open it."

Mary opened the package without tearing the paper or breaking the ribbon.

"Hurry up, Mary. I can't wait to see your face."

After the ribbons and the paper were removed, and the box was opened, Will received his reward. He had never seen so bright a smile or so much sparkle in Mary's eyes. She looked at the gift, then back at Will with her mouth agape, and although her lips moved, no words emerged. She tried again, but once more she remained silent as tears streamed down her flushed cheeks. Mary reached for him and pulled him close while she whispered in his ear, "My dear. It's fit for a queen." She lifted the diamond brooch until the tree's candlelight reflected its thousand facets across the room. "I never dreamed I would ever have such a treasure."

They embraced, and then Mary regained her composure. "But now it's your turn. Maybe I can match your gift this time." She handed him a big package, and when he quickly opened it, he was rewarded with a gold, silk smoker's jacket. "It's for you when you get that Meerschaum pipe you've always wanted. I tried to find that, too, but with the war and all—"

"It's beautiful. Why, we'll be the exquisite couple, you in your diamond brooch and me in my silk jacket. We'll wear them when we go to Highland Park, to Henry's conference."

Mary squealed. "Conference?" She clasped her hands to her face. "We're going on vacation to Michigan?"

"Yes we are. It's next July, right after your school is out. I'll be so proud to show you off. You'll be the belle of their grand ball. And I'll take my jacket. Why, maybe I'll wear it to the ball."

Mary leaned back and clutched the brooch to her chest. "I don't think I can go."

"What? Why can't I escort the most beautiful lady in Wisconsin across Lake Michigan? Tell me why."

"I wanted it to be a surprise. I wanted you to be happy. And it's not so happy after all."

"Whoa. What are you talking about?" He brushed her tears away. "It can't be that bad!"

"I thought it was good." Mary continued to cry. "I thought it was the best present I could give you. But maybe it's not so good. I'll not be able to go to the ball. We're going to have a baby in July. I'll have to stop teaching soon."

Will took her in his arms. "It's the best gift ever."

"It's okay if I can't go to Michigan? But you can go. You don't have to stay home."

"Do you think I'd leave when you're about to have a baby? How'd Mrs. Alderson get by without my help?"

Mary laughed.

"Why, we can go to Highland Park any old time. Henry'll wait."

"What should we call him?" Mary said. "Can we call him Charles this time?"

"And what makes you so sure it'll be a boy? What if he's a she?"

"I rather like Sharon. That was my grandmother's name, and I'd like to honor her."

"Then that's what it'll be. Charles if he's a boy, Sharon if a girl. Sharon's a good name. Why, it's not only your grandmother's name, but it's a biblical name and one of my favorite flowers, too. Yes, we'll name her Sharon."

Although the thought of another child thrilled him, Will couldn't help but feel a bit apprehensive, too.

—•—o—O—o—•—

And Sharon arrived on July 21, 1921, a healthy and plump nine pounds, ten ounces. Dr. Ruggles and Mrs. Alderson had arrived, but her birth was so fast and easy that Mrs. Alderson didn't have time or reason to hassle the doctor or push Will from the house. And Mary was so captivated and attentive to their new family member that Will felt unneeded, like another finger on an already full hand. But he felt a sense of relief, too. Maybe this peaceful occasion and happy, healthy baby were signs of good things to come.

S ome townsfolk thought Tate, the village stockbroker, an opportunist. But Will liked David Tate not because he owned a Model T Ford, but because he was a genuinely good fellow. They served as church trustees, and Will knew that David was keen on volunteerism, and that David could be counted on whenever there was a need. And now, in late 1922, the market moved upward and David began to prosper. Will was happy for his friend's good fortune, but some people thought Tate's wealth was the Devil's money.

One day Will heard, "Hey, Will, you in here?" float through the office and into the garage, where he was working. He slid from under a Lizzie. "Hold on, I'll be right there."

Will rubbed grime off his hands and tossed the soiled cloth into the steel barrel that he kept for greasy rags. "Can't be too careful about fires," he'd say.

"Is that you, David?" he called through the door as he walked into his office and showroom. "I kinda expected to see your face today. I heard the markets are up."

"Now's the time to buy, Will. Coolidge says the business of America is business, and he's right on that score. Cal doesn't speak often, but when he does, you better listen. Our country's booming and it's time to get your share." David paused "It's time to expand your horizons. Time to put your money to work. You can never earn by the sweat of your brow what your money will earn for you."

"Maybe you're right. But I don't know. You saw what happened in '07."

"It's different this time. You know that. Just look how your business has grown. The Doughboys are back. Everything's booming, everyone's buying. Best to make hay while the sun shines."

"I could always sell the hay. But I don't think so." He grabbed a handful of clean rags from his desk drawer and stepped toward the garage. "I've gotta get Dobberstein's Lizzie out. He'll be here at noon."

"Think about it. You can make money." Tate started for the door but turned back. "Oh, I almost forgot what I stopped for. I'm glazing Mrs. Fransen's windows this Saturday. A good wind'll drop that glass on the ground. Can you help? Shouldn't take but half the morning."

"Poor lady. Mary says she's having a terrible time getting by."

Tate shook his head. "Sad. Some people won't have anything to do with her. They say it's her fault. That God's punished her for allowing those Mormons in her house. I think it's poppycock."

"It's a wrathful God who'd take her husband and son because she befriended two strangers. They seemed like nice young fellas to me." Will hollered back as he stepped into the garage. "I'll be there Saturday."

Will knew everyone was doing it, and everyone made money—so they said—but it didn't feel safe to speculate on the market's whims. The only money he'd ever made was by the sweat of his own brow. He was glad that Mary had sensible attitudes toward money, too.

When Will got home, one-year-old Sharon waited at the door. "Mamma's home," she called to Mary who set a dish of steaming peas on the dining room table.

"You can see who's important in this house," Will said as he swept his daughter into his arms. "What'll she do when she has a brother to confuse her?"

"What makes you so sure it'll be a brother?"

"Law of averages. A fifty-fifty chance and the first fifty went to our girly here."

"I don't think it works that way."

"I can dream, can't I?"

"You just want help at the shop. Cheap labor."

"I'm busy enough. I could use some help." Will sat by the table while Sharon pulled on his watch fob. "David Tate was in today."

"He wants you to invest?"

"He's convinced it's time to buy. Says the market's going up."

"Mr. Gable says the same." Mary placed a pork chop on Will's plate. "He wants me to teach again next year."

"Our business is booming, so if you want to stay home, I'll not stand in your way."

"I hope I can get to the end of this term before I show. It'll be close." Mary ladled gravy onto Will's mashed potatoes. "Do you think your mother can handle two? I'm not ready to hang my ruler up just yet."

"She handled the three of us, didn't she?"

"Can your dad get along without her?"

"He won't object."

Summer 1923 was almost over when Mary called Will at the shop. "I think it's time. I called Mrs. Alderson. You better get Dr. Ruggles."

Will dropped his ledger onto the desk, stumbled over the chair on his way to the coat rack, grabbed his cap, and rushed out the door.

Ten seconds later Will ran back in, grabbed the dangling phone, and whirled the crank one long twirl, the operator's signal. "Marge, get Dr. Ruggles to our house. Mary's having a baby. Hurry, Marge."

He was half way home before he remembered that he hadn't told Ed and Ray that Rocco Mangardi would be there at noon for his car. When he burst through the door, he almost knocked Mrs. Alderson to the floor.

"Calm down, Will. It's under control. Just boil a kettle of water."

She was half way up the stairs before Will hung his hat on the rack. At the top of the stairs, she shouted down, "And send Dr. Ruggles to your bedroom when he gets here, but you stay there. I'll come for the water."

Will paced the kitchen floor while he waited for the water to boil.

Dr. Ruggles didn't bother to knock, but rushed through the entryway and caught Will leaning across the railing and craning his head up the stairs. Will pointed up, but before he could say anything, Dr. Ruggles was at the landing. "In your bedroom?" he said.

Will nodded, and started to follow, but Dr. Ruggles waved him back. "Better stay there. Don't want you to get on Alderson's bad side."

Will knew that Ruggles wasn't thinking about him. No one, not even the doctor, crossed Mrs. Alderson at times like this. But no one complained either. She still had never lost a baby.

Will waited for the sound of bubbling water and steam. And he continued to pace, but that didn't help. What did they say about a watched pot? He was sure he could have returned to the office and told Ed about Mangardi and still been back before the water sang its song. He paced some more.

Mrs. Alderson tromped down the stairs. "Is that water ready?" she called.

Will handed her the kettle.

"Now stay right there. Mary's doing fine. It won't be long now."

Fifteen minutes later, Will heard a weak cry, a couple gasps, then a wail from the room above. He took two steps at a time, but ran into Mrs. Alderson at the top step, a pan of rosy water in her hands. "Hold on, Will." But he brushed past her and rushed into his bedroom.

Mary looked exhausted, and Dr. Ruggles scrubbed the baby, which screamed bloody murder. She wasn't very happy in her new world. Well, it wasn't always a comfortable place, Will knew.

He turned to their bed and knelt beside Mary. "Are you okay?" he said as he took her hand. "You look plumb tuckered out."

She smiled up to him. "Tired like a runner who just won the Olympic mile." She looked toward her screaming baby, then back to Will and flashed a weak smile. "Dr. Ruggles says she's hardy as a range colt." Mary cocked her head and listened to the noise. "She does have a voice, doesn't she? Must be an O'Shaughnessy?"

Dr. Ruggles handed the squalling baby girl to Will who cradled her in his arms before handing her to Mary. "She sure knows how to complain," he said. "What should we call her? Do you have a family name in mind?"

Mary took Will's hand. "I'm sorry, my dear. I know you wanted a boy, someone to help at the shop."

"The thought never crossed my mind." When he patted baby O'Shaughnessy on the head, she stilled her screaming for a moment, and Will was sure she tried to smile. "She's a real gem. You couldn't have done better." He leaned down and kissed Mary's lips. "I love you, my dear."

Baby O'Shaughnessy began screaming again.

"Maybe that's it," Mary said. "Maybe she's telling us something. Why, she's ruby red. Maybe we should call her Ruby."

"Ruby O'Shaughnessy. I like that. Bold and vibrant."

Mary scowled.

Will pounded on his chest. "A warrior. Let's call her Ruby. With that voice, she'll be another Boudica."

"Boudica was Welsh, Will."

"Boudica was Celtic. A fire burns in that girl. She'll surely live up to that moniker."

21

Will hadn't expected this evening to be different from any other. Mary placed supper on the table by six and the babies in bed by eight. When Ruby, almost one year old and already living up to her name, lingered, or Sharon, now three years old, protested that she wanted time with her father, Mary resisted their complaints. Even when Will pleaded their case, Mary was resolute. "I told you when we married that we must have time alone each evening. It's the glue that'll hold our marriage together."

Will couldn't argue with Mary's reasoning. But she seemed so intent tonight. The girls didn't resist for long. After a day of play and a strenuous hour with Will, their tired bodies aligned with Mary's demands, even though they protested all the way to their beds. Will didn't remember Michael raising such a fuss. But then he didn't have a sister to impress by showing his resistance.

Will knew that Mary had something on her mind, but instead of saying anything, she busied herself in the kitchen. He heard the kettle sing and knew she was busy making, in her Cornish parlance, "a dish of tae."

He approached as she reached high into the cupboard for the can of tea leaves and couldn't help but notice that her waist had returned to her pre-birth size and her rear was as pleasing as ever. He put his arms around her and whispered into her ear, "Don't you think it's about time for bed?" He nuzzled the soft of her neck.

"None of that." She pulled away. "I want to talk. Just as soon as I get this tea made." She pushed him toward the doorway. "Go into the parlor and wait."

Will knew it must be serious, but not so serious that she couldn't stop to make her "dish of tae." Will supposed she wanted to soften him for the kill.

Mary approached carrying her best tray, on which were properly positioned the two cups, the tea tin, creamer, sugar bowl, and pot of boiling water. She moved the coffee table with her foot until it rested in front of Will and lowered the tray to its surface. Silently she spooned tea leaves into his cup, poured hot water, and offered him the creamer. Then she prepared her own cup and sat on the divan to face him, while he dropped two spoonfuls of sugar into the simmering liquid. And she didn't say a word, not one word about his waistline.

Mary sipped her tea, then placed her cup on its saucer and lowered it to her side of the coffee table. "Will, I was in the beauty parlor today and Miss Fontenot was excited about a new investment opportunity."

Will frowned.

"I know, you're not keen on the stock market, but I think you should listen." She leaned toward him and lowered her voice. "Miss Fontenot has an uncle who buys gold mines, he and a group of investors. To raise cash, they're going public soon. She says now's the time to buy. He'll let her buy in before they offer the stock. Then when it goes public and the price goes up, she'll make a quick profit."

"May be illegal. But what does it have to do with us?"

"She said if I'll give her a thousand dollars, she'll buy for me, too."

Will had plans for that money—although he needed more. If he could save enough before his father decided to retire … but that would be a while. "That's a big chunk of what we've got in our savings."

"I know, but we can increase our savings, increase it fast this way."

"It sounds a bit chancy."

"Nick made his fortune in gold."

"And your brother's on his deathbed while we talk. What good does his fortune do him now? It's not for me."

"Will O'Shaughnessy, that's my money, too. I can't swing a pick or a maul, but I can put my money to work, and I will."

"I won't."

"Then you can sleep on the sofa." Mary turned and bounded up the stairs.

Will hadn't yet taken a sip from his cup. What was that all about? He didn't know that Mary had enthusiasm for investments. She always said he should do as he saw fit, and a safe bank account fit him. This mania about buying stocks was beyond his understanding, but everyone was doing it, that's for sure. Will pulled a blanket and a pillow from the back room and curled up on the couch. He'd let Mary sleep on it. She'd probably come to her senses by morning.

But she didn't. All the next week, Will slept alone on the sofa. And the evenings before bedtime were tense. This wasn't like Mary. Just like everyone else, she'd lost her wits over this investment obsession.

Finally, Will decided to settle the matter. It was apparent that their nighttime glue had lost its adhesiveness. The girls were off to bed, and as usual, they protested all the way. Mary busied herself in the kitchen, but Will was determined to get her attention. "Mary, we need to talk. We need to get past this dispute. Come, let's sit in the parlor." He took her arm and she hesitantly followed. "Are you still intent on those gold stocks?"

"They're not stocks, not yet. That's the beauty in it. We can get in before they go public and the market drives the price up."

"Miss Fontenot says?"

"Well, yes. It's her uncle. Her uncle wouldn't cheat her."

"I suppose her uncle's honest. I suppose he knows mining. But it's what he doesn't know that worries me. If we only knew what we don't know, a lot more fortunes would be made, and lots of disasters avoided."

"It's an opportunity. I want my girls to go to college, to be someone, and I can secure it with this money."

"My dearest Mary, I don't want to fight over this. Why, we've never had a serious argument, not until now."

"You forget that Armistice Day night."

"That memory isn't too clear."

They laughed together.

"Let's find a way to resolve this," Will said. "Let's find a compromise. I can't take many more nights on the couch."

"I want to feel confident that our girls will be self-sufficient, not dependent on a man."

"And I want that, too. But you know I'm uneasy about the markets. Tate says they're on the way up, and maybe they are, but trading stock seems a lot like gambling to me, but maybe—"

"Yes, Will?"

"There are lots of booming businesses and others sure to follow. Automobiles, refineries, tires, electricity, radio. They're all growing fast. Maybe if we invested in something that's safer, a surer thing than a gold mine. Good businesses will probably do well over time and their stocks will go up. Maybe if we invest in a growing business, not just trade stock, we'll be okay. Let's be sensible. Let's not risk our daughters' futures."

Mary turned away. "You surely don't think that's what I want."

Will reached for her. "I'll tell you what. Give me a little time to think on it, to ask around and decide which companies have the best future. Then we'll invest, but not everything. I've made all the payments on our house and business, and we've saved four thousand dollars. Not many people can claim that much. I don't want to risk it all. We'll invest half of it and use the other half to pay down our mortgages. Let's play it safe. Okay?"

"We'll make money in the market. Everyone says so."

"Then we'll take out the profits and reduce our obligations. At least that way, the girls will have a debt free inheritance."

"Let's not discuss inheritance, Will, not yet anyhow."

That night, Will joined Mary in their bedroom, and on September 12, 1925, nine months later to the day, Catherine was born.

22

atherine was different from the beginning. Unlike Ruby, Catherine O'Shaughnessy came rapidly and quietly. Mrs. Alderson raced up the stairs to find Mary fully dilated and baby O'Shaughnessy's head beginning to show. By the time Dr. Ruggles arrived, Mrs. Alderson had cleaned mother and baby, and Mary cradled the infant in her arms.

"You came to check my work?" Mrs. Alderson said with a scowl on her face and a twist of the shoulder.

Will knew she was contemptuous of male attendees at her sacred rituals, even those with "M.D." behind their names.

Dr. Ruggles stepped around Mrs. Alderson, gently lifted the newborn from Mary's arms, and examined her. And the baby didn't utter a whimper until he gently slapped her on the bottom.

"That was hardly necessary," Mrs. Alderson said. "I cleared her throat and cleaned her mouth long ago." She snatched the crying child from him. "Now now, my dear, don't let that awful man scare you."

"And what should we call this wee lass?" Will said. "So calm and peaceful. She's no Boudica, that's for sure."

"Your mother suggested Malvina," Mary said. "A good Celtic name. You should like that. Besides it's a special name, a name that stands out. More distinguished than plain old Mary."

"Well sure, she's special. She's our daughter. But Mary suits me. The first two turned out quite splendid."

"Three would be a crowd. She'd be the only Malvina in Ashley Springs. You don't like Malvina?"

"Now I won't be knockin' a good Celtic name, mind you, but it's a bit highfalutin for my liking. Our neighbors' Marthas, Shirleys, and Agneses are special, too. It's not the name that makes the person. It's the person who makes the name. Look what that great Russian Empress did for the name Catherine."

"Catherine," Mary said softly, then louder, "Catherine."

"I like that," Will said. "A royal name for a fine little girl."

"Catherine," Mary said again. "A romantic name, a poetic name, a regal name."

And the name fit.

His business grew so fast that Will decided to employ another worker, but everyone thrived these days, so few were available for hire. He placed ads and asked around for a month, but until Saul Paxson came through the door, he had no takers.

"Mr. O'Shaughnessy," Saul said, "I hear you're looking for a worker."

"That I am, my boy. Interested? Have you ever repaired cars before?"

"Only farm machinery. But I plan to be a farmer someday, and soon, too."

Will perked up. Farmers made good workers. "That's how I started."

"No one wants to hire me. They know I may not stay long."

"How's that?"

"I've saved money to buy a farm. Almost have enough now."

Will liked his honesty. "So, you may not stay long?"

"That's the problem. But I'll work hard. I promise that."

"You really want to be a farmer? It's a hard life. I can tell you that. Maybe you'll like it here. Maybe you'll want to stay."

"Oh, I want to farm, always have."

Will smiled.

"I sure hope the economy stays strong," Saul said.

"All businesses benefit from a strong demand. But with farming, there's much more to worry about. You must know that."

"I've worked on a farm before."

"But it's different when you're the owner. Between weather, disease, and just plain bad luck, you're always putting Humpty Dumpty back together again. You've got to be tough."

"S'pose so."

Will smiled and slowly shook his head. He couldn't believe how much he sounded like Grandpa. "Come ready to work first thing Monday morning."

Will fawned over his newest daughter. "Why, she never cries," he said. "Our other children cried, but I seldom hear a whimper from this little one. Dad says he's never seen one like her."

"Didn't you say that about Michael?" Mary said.

Will winced. He'd tried to avoid thoughts of Michael since Sharon's birth. He didn't want to think about him, and was terrified that it would happen again.

"It's clear, Will. That little one has captured your heart."

"Fanny is about to foal," Will said. "Do you think the girls are too young to see the birth?"

"Sharon may be old enough, but no, she'd faint dead away. Better just show them the young'n after it's up and about."

Will didn't complain about having three girls who couldn't help at the shop. With three workers now, he would sometimes take Fridays off, but he couldn't stay away for long. Now that Catherine was almost a year old, Will bundled her into the stroller and took her into town to show her off. And he usually stopped at the shop first.

"Now, isn't she the spittin' image?" Ed said. "Why, she's got your dimples, Will."

Will turned Catherine to the light. "See, Ed, the lass has sunshine in her hair." He tipped her down to where the light accentuated her tresses. "Look close." He pointed. "See? There's a whisper of strawberry, too."

"Like your mother's."

Catherine beamed a broad smile at her father. He knew that she loved his attention. "Now isn't she the darlingest?" Will said.

But he knew that Mary wouldn't agree with his conclusion about their daughter's hair. He heard her say more than once that Catherine had hair just like hers, and Mary's was golden brown, like a field of ripe oats.

"How's the new fella doing? Do you think he'll be a repairman?"

"It'll take a while," Ed said, "but he works hard. I'm kinda excited about getting into sales. I've never been on commission before."

"You'll do well. You've got the personality. Gotta go."

Will lowered the hood on the stroller and turned toward the exit. Catherine cooed her approval.

"Sure's a good baby," Ed said. "Haven't heard a whimper from her."

"That's what I tell Mary."

"Let's see," he said as he pushed the stroller down the street. "I suppose mama would object if we stopped at Bennie's." But he waved when he saw Bennie and Mayor Burns exit the building.

"Hey, Will, is that the new baby?" Tommy Burns said as he stepped onto the sidewalk.

"Not so new. Almost a year old now." Will pulled back the cheese-cloth that sheltered her face. "I can't have her getting too much sun. Not yet anyhow."

"She's a beauty," Bennie said. "Looks like her mother. How do you deserve the two prettiest ladies in Ashley Springs?"

"'Tis the luck of the Irish"

"Lucky she doesn't have your looks," Burns said. "It'd be a terrible load for a lass to carry that visage around."

Will faked a body jab and Burns retreated.

"Have you invested in the market yet?" Burns said. "Make your hay while the sun shines, that's what I say. Why, you can buy a thousand dollars worth for only a hundred up front."

"I've bought a little, but I won't buy margin," Will said.

"I'll put my money in Scotch whiskey," Bennie said. "You can send your money overseas and buy it by the keg. And they'll hold it until it's aged, and by then our country's craziness will have ended. I should make some money there eventually."

"Do you really think prohibition will end?" Will said.

"Probably, but I shouldn't complain. I've never done better."

"Stocks are a surer bet," Burns said. "They're heading up. You better jump on the wagon while it's rolling downhill." He grasped Will's shoulder. "Easy money. Don't get left behind."

"I'm not so sure, Tommy. That hill may not be as long as you think."

"I'm sticking with Scotch whiskey," Bennie said. "If it doesn't boom, I can sell it to Tommy here, one drink at a time."

"You got that right," Will said as he carefully replaced the cheesecloth over Catherine. "Gotta show this lass the town. I'll see you, fellas."

Will strolled down the valley road. The spring sun was warm, but the emerging leaves in the overhead canopy protected Catherine from its heat. Before he reached the water, he turned back. Will hadn't visited that stream since he took Michael there, and he couldn't do it now. Instead, he walked around the block and back toward the small barn across the street from his shop, the barn where he kept Fanny and Mabel, a barn too small for three horses and their feed and bedding. He knew that when the foal came, he'd have to convert some of the storage space. "Let's visit our horsey."

But Catherine didn't hear a word he said. She was fast asleep.

Will pushed her stroller through the doorway and toward the stall. When he approached Fanny, she nickered loud enough to wake the sleeping child. Will wouldn't have known that she was awake if she hadn't babbled in response to Fanny's greeting, and Fanny talked back.

Will could see that Fanny was getting big. She must be close to delivery, he thought. He lifted Catherine from her carrier and held her up to his horse. When Fanny nuzzled her nose, Catherine laughed and reached out.

Will opened the stall's door and carried Catherine inside. Fanny leaned against his shoulder, but swung around when he tapped her on the flank. Then Will carefully placed Catherine on Fanny's back, but held tight.

Catherine squealed her approval.

"You're going to be the best little horsewoman in town," he said as he urged Fanny around her small stall.

Catherine grabbed Fanny's mane and shrieked her delight as they circled the enclosure. Fanny turned her head toward her new friend and nickered her consent; then, she nuzzled her old friend on the shoulder.

"I think you two are going to be pals," he said. "And I think you're already the best little horsewoman in Ashley Springs." He felt exhilarated by Catherine's fondness for his old friend, but he shivered at the thought of Michael, at the thought it could happen again. He wished that Mary hadn't resurrected his name.

23

Will paced the floor. He knew that deception had a way of fueling its own ambition. He felt ashamed that he hadn't told Mary right away. Heaven knew he tried, but when he'd told her he had talked to George Tyler, she misunderstood and said, "So you're going to join the progressive folk in town? I'm sure George will loan you the money. Have you seen the light? Have you decided to put money into mining stocks?"

"Well, no, Mary, I—"

"He won't loan you the money?"

"Yes, he'll loan the money, but it's—"

"Well?"

"It's not what you think. He offered me a chance—"

"Can I tell Miss Fontenot that we'll invest a thousand dollars?"

"Mary, I told you. I won't buy mine stocks."

"We've got four thousand in our savings, but if you don't want to use that … You just said that George will loan the money, didn't you?"

"We'll talk about it later."

Will was to meet George at two o'clock and they would go look at the place today. But he didn't have the courage to raise the issue again with Mary.

"Will, I know you want to return to farming," George Tyler said. "This is as fine a dairy farm as you'll find in all of Iowa County. I never expected to have the opportunity to sell it."

Will knew the farm, and he knew that Bill Yahnke had dropped dead unexpectedly. "Why can't Matilda keep her hired men and run it herself?"

"I suppose she could, but she doesn't want to run a farm. She says she doesn't think she can be a manager. Knows how hard Bill worked at it, for what good it did him."

Will thought about Grandpa's words and icicles trickled down his spine, but he felt a sense of triumph, too. "I suppose she wants to go to town."

"She wants to take the money and buy a house in town. She wants her daughter in town school."

"Maybe she'd be interested in our house."

"Maybe, but it's a bit large. There's only the two of them now."

"I suppose so."

"It's a big farm, Will. As far as I know, the most acreage in Iowa County. He milks forty cows."

Will thought about the time it would take to milk forty cows: 'bout ten minutes a cow by hand. Why, that'd be almost seven hours, twice a day. Twenty's the most Grandpa ever freshened, and that was only one summer. It took Grandpa, him, and Frank to do the milking and to get the harvest in.

"Is Mary up for it?"

"I haven't told Mary."

"Oh."

Will saw the big barn on the horizon. Everyone else had red barns, but this one was white, the only one like it in the county. It stood high on the hill and seemed to shout, "Look at me. I'm big and I'm mean, and I'll devour anyone who tries to manage me." This was the kind of barn Grandpa would have died for—Frank, too. "Are you sure the men will stay with a new owner?"

"They've been with Bill a good while, but he paid top wage."

What if milk prices drop? Will thought.

Will had to turn his head to see the whole complex: three full corn cribs, a machine shed longer than his father's barnyard, and a granary larger than his father's milk barn. When Will looked in the barn, he saw a wide cement slab runway with twenty-five stanchions down each side flanked by gutters all the way to the end.

"He's not even milking to capacity," George said.

The work it would take to keep this farm going! Will thought about Mary.

Back at George's office George pulled a contract from his desk drawer. "You'll never have another chance like this, Will." He snickered as he handed Will a pen and pointed to the signature line. "Buy this and you're going from a Ford to a Cadillac."

Will winced.

"Put your four thousand down, and I'll gladly loan the rest. It's a good deal for the both of us."

"I'm not sure I can make all the payments. Not until I sell the house and business."

"You'll have no problem selling your dealership. It should make a good profit, too. I'll charge interest-only until you've made the sale. You'll never get this chance again."

Will knew George was right. When he thought about returning to farming, he never expected anything like this, not in his wildest dreams. Wouldn't Grandpa be surprised? The best farm in Iowa County. He wasn't sure how to tell Frank: tell him outright, gloat a bit, or maybe take him for a ride and watch his jaw drop when Will ordered his men into the fields?

He put the pen on the paper and began to write, but then he hesitated. He thought about Grandpa's words, thought about Mary. He wrote, "William." He began the "O" in "O'Shaughnessy", but then he dropped the pen and stared at George, not saying a word at first. "I can't do it, not without talking to Mary."

This was the moment that Will dreaded. Supper was over, the girls were off to bed, and Mary darned socks in the parlor. He knew he couldn't hesitate. "Mary, we've got to talk."

"Yes, Will. You've had second thoughts about that mining stock?"

"No, I'll not buy mining stock, but I do want to buy the finest farm in Iowa County."

"A farm?" She dropped her darning needle. "Will, are you crazy? We're already doing better than most people in town."

"This is the first time I can afford a farm. But I never expected one like this, not in my wildest dreams. Bill Yahnke's farm. East of town."

"People say that's too ambitious for Iowa County. People say that farm killed Bill."

"He's got lots of workers."

"It didn't do Bill much good, now did it?"

Will cringed. That thought had passed through his mind as well. "You know I've always wanted to farm."

"But I'm not ready to quit teaching. Not yet anyhow."

"You can keep working. I'll have three hired men."

"Will, come to your senses. I've never farmed, but most of my students' parents do. I hear all the time how hard their mothers work." She stood and faced Will. "You say you'll have three men. Who'll cook their meals? Who'll wash their clothes? Who'll make their beds and mend their garments? Do you plan on staying in the house and doing that work while I'm off at school? And who'll help in the barn if a man leaves or gets sick?"

Will squirmed on his chair. He knew Mary was right. But he'd been so enchanted by this chance to surpass Grandpa and Frank. Hired men meant lots of work for the lady of the house. He hung his head, slumped in his chair, and exhaled. "I wasn't thinking clearly." He knew he shouldn't do it, couldn't do it.

"Will, I know how you've always wanted to farm, and I understand your feeling. But the Yahnke farm is a big undertaking, more than we're ready for, I think." She knelt in front of Will and took his hand. "I'll tell you what. Why don't you take some of that money and build a new stable for Mabel, Fanny, and the new foal." She took Will's head in her hands and kissed him tenderly. "It's not the Yahnke farm, but it's a step in that direction. And we won't have to sell the business or the house. And I won't have to quit teaching."

"S'pose so."

Mary was right. He should have talked to her first, but he was so close to having what he always wanted. He knew his passion for the Yahnke farm was driven by the wrong reasons. Still, he felt as if he'd lost his last opportunity. He'd never again have a chance like this to prove Grandpa wrong and to see Frank squirm with envy. Would he ever have his own farm, even a small one? He felt a tinge of regret, but a sense of relief, too. He'd been so distracted that he hadn't watched Fanny as closely as he should, but he knew it was getting close to the time for her foal's birth.

Will had scrubbed Fanny's stall and was lining it with dry, fresh straw when the first signs occurred. He wrapped her tail and had begun to pitch new hay into her manger when she circled her enclosure looking for a spot to lie down in preparation to break water. After finding a comfortable position, she pushed hard and groaned as the fluid gushed forth. Soon, Will saw another thin sac appear, and he could see the foal within as its front hooves pushed into the daylight, one slightly ahead of the other. When the legs were out to the knees, a nose and head began to appear. Will remembered the first time he had seen this miraculous sight, and he felt shivers run the length of his spine. He knew that he must help, so he grabbed the clean towel that he'd brought from home, wrapped it around the emerging feet, grasped tight, and gently pulled the front feet down toward the mare's hind hooves. This would help rotate the foal's head into position. He then pulled straight in line with the mare's spine until the head and shoulders were safely outside the mother.

He knew that Fanny needed some rest time before completing the process, so he waited fifteen minutes for her to calm and catch her breath. Then he extracted the foals feet, and when the mare stood, the umbilical cord broke with little bleeding. Will grabbed the iodine solution that he'd previously prepared and coated the newborn's umbilicus. This would help prevent infection. Then Will sat back and watched this new miracle of life as she searched for her mother's teat. Until now, he'd been so busy that he hadn't taken time to admire his new youngin'. To Will, a new baby, human or animal, was the most beautiful sight in his world. She looked just like her mother. As handsome as any creature that God had placed on this fine earth.

Sharon wanted to stay overnight with a friend, and said that she'd go see the foal later. So Will took his two youngest girls by their hands and said, "Okay, girls, cover your eyes until I say open." He led them into the stable and up to Fanny's stall. "You can open them now."

Ruby squealed, then climbed on the rail and leaned toward Fanny who nudged her outstretched hand. Catherine peered between the rails while Will stepped into the enclosure and urged the foal toward the girls. "Isn't she the cutest?" he said.

"Is that a Fanny, too?" Ruby said.

"Yes, she is. A fine young lady if ever there was one." He brought the girls into the pen, and they snuggled and petted the new baby. Fanny stood near and seemed quite satisfied to let her newborn get the attention.

When they got home, Ruby shouted, "Mommy, we just saw Fanny Too, our new horsey. She's beautiful, so soft and cuddly. Better than my teddy bear."

"I thought I'd call her Maud," Will said. "I used to have a Maud when I was young."

"Oh, no," Ruby said. "She's Fanny Too."

Ruby was so earnest and determined that Will didn't have the heart to disagree. "It looks like we've got a new horsey, and she's Fanny Too."

As Fanny Too grew, Will could see that Fanny's stall would soon be rather tight for the two of them, so he put money into a new horse barn to be built on the edge of town, closer to their home, and next door to Widow Schmidt's house.

Will rushed into the house. "Mary!" he shouted, but received no answer. When he looked out the kitchen window, he spotted her in the back flower garden, turned, and raced out the kitchen door. "Mary, let's go look at the new stable. The frame's up and they're finishing the roof today. It won't be long before it's ready." He took the trowel from her offering hand.

"I'm ready for a break." She arched her back. "I must be getting old. I don't remember being so sore last summer."

"There's twice as much garden this summer. And, Mary, I mailed the fire insurance premium."

"Most people say it's a waste of money."

"They never complain after their building burns down. Besides, the baker eats his own bread, now doesn't he?"

"But what are the chances?"

"I don't like taking chances. Come on, get your jacket. There's a cool breeze blowing from the west."

Will could see that the corners were square, the white pine studs straight, and the underlayment secure and tight. The roof, now completely shingled, looked as if it could withstand any wind that swept across the hills. "The Mangardi brothers do good work." He pointed as he led Mary into the structure. "Four stalls, and each one bigger than those in the Commerce Street barn."

Mary looked puzzled. "That many? We only have Fanny, Mabel, and Fanny Too."

"You never have too much space."

"People already think you're a bit daffy for selling cars and keeping horses. When they see this, they'll think you're completely off your rocker." Mary grabbed Will's arm. "You're not building your farm a barn at a time, now are you?"

"And I thought I could get away with it, yes I did. Should have known I couldn't fool a Corny woman."

Mary swiped at Will's backside, but Will intercepted her hand and led her around the wide aisle that circled the stalls, back to a six hundred square-foot space where double doors, each hung on three heavy cast iron hinges, opened to the outside.

"There's enough room to hold two or three weeks of hay and bedding. Dad won't have to deliver twice a week anymore."

"I wondered why you built out in the country. You sly, old Irishman. You are building your farm one barn at a time."

It's insane, Will thought. The stock market hit new highs at the end of Friday's trading, so he knew there would be a line at his door Monday morning. Henry couldn't produce cars fast enough, but he still lowered the Model T's price. Chevrolet dealers sold even more, but no one complained about competition. Will was glad for the added business, but he didn't think it could last. The market was on fire, too, he admitted, but there was no insurance to mop up that mess when it ended in cinders.

Will arrived at work a half hour early and found Mayor Burns pacing at the front door. "Will, I want to order a new Roadster. I'm giving my sedan to Bernie." Tommy took the sales book that Will handed across the desk. "He's got it most of the time anyhow."

"It'll be at least three months—probably more—before delivery. Henry can't keep up to the demand."

"Think I'll go to Hinton and order one of those Chevy's." He reached for the doorknob. "Folks say they're pretty snazzy."

"The last I heard, those Hinton folk don't vote in our elections."

Mayor Burns scowled at Will. "Get out your order book."

Will reached into his desk's top drawer. "You must be selling lots of dry goods these days."

"Sales are up, that's for sure, but it's not dry goods that'll make me rich. It's the market."

"I'm not getting rich, but I'm paying the bills."

"Every spare dime I've got goes into stocks, and they're booming. You can buy a lot of stock at ten cents on the dollar."

"Too rich for my blood. I think you're playing with fire, Tommy."

"The market hasn't been down in two years, not for long anyhow."

"Buyers'll run out of money someday. Stocks'll go sour. Then how will you make your payments?"

"Payments?" Burns whipped five one-hundred-dollar bills from his front pocket, peeled one off, and handed it to Will. "There's plenty more where this comes from."

"I'd not get too content, Tommy. Whenever I think I'm on solid ground, an earthquake comes along and shakes me up a bit."

Will took three more orders that morning, but he didn't think the boom times could last. Yet it seemed he was the only one with reservations. Could his friends be wrong? Should he reconsider? When he arrived home that night, he still had Tommy on his mind. "Mary, I think Tommy's in pretty deep. I sure hope—"

"Do you know what Ruby did today?"

Mary had problems of her own, it seemed. Will sat at the kitchen table, ready for the nightly report about his wayward daughter. "I have no idea, my dear. What did our little black lamb do today?"

"Why, she convinced Catherine that she was a puppy and had her nibble on the ham bone that I put aside for your father's dog."

"She's done worse. That girl sure has imagination." He didn't tell Mary that he saw Catherine snorting like a pig and eating cabbage leaves the night before—while Ruby urged her on.

"She has too much influence over Catherine," Mary said. "That's what worries me."

And Will worried, too, but he didn't let on; Mary was worked up enough already.

"I almost forgot. Your mother called today. She said your dad received letters that seemed strange to her. Someone who claims he can predict the stock market."

"Everyone thinks he knows the market these days. That's not so strange."

"But this guy has been right two times."

Will wondered why anyone would bother to send stock predictions to his dad. After all, he was just an old farmer. He would ask the next time his father came by the shop.

Thomas O'Shaughnessy drove into Ashley Springs with a wagon full of corn and oats on most Saturdays, and even though it wasn't the straightest route to the mill, he turned his team down Water Street, and then turned again onto Commerce to go past Will's shop. He told Will that he wanted to make sure he was attending to business, but Will knew he wanted to hear about the week's sales. And he knew that Thomas reported his progress to Gertrude after each trip.

Now with the girls demanding more time and Ed settled into management, Will was less likely to be there when Thomas drove past, but that morning he didn't want to miss his father, so he propped the front door open. Will heard the horses' hooves on the cobblestone before they turned onto Commerce Street, and he waited out front when his father approached.

Thomas reined his horses to the curb and jumped off the wagon. "I didn't think I'd find you here today. Beginning to think you're an absentee owner, like those tycoons I read about."

Will laughed. "No tycoon, just a proud father. I wouldn't trade the little darlin's for all their money. I hear you've been getting investment letters."

"Oh, those. Gertrude must been talking."

"Well?"

"Deep subject, son. Best keep out."

"Tell me about them."

"Just some guy who claims he can predict the market. Says he has inside information."

"And he wants you to send money?"

"He's been right two months running. Said the market would go up at the end of last month and down this month. Right both times. S'pose he's lucky."

"I suppose he wants something. He wouldn't send letters if he didn't want something. Better stick to sure things, Dad. Stick to your investments in Radio Corporation and Standard Oil, solid companies."

"You've made money these last years. Grandpa didn't know the favor he did when he took that farm away. Farmin' was good for a while, but since the war ended, we've got no overseas markets. I'm just scraping by now. My farm's too small, barely feeding us." He grabbed the seat-back, winced, and then pulled himself up on the wagon. "This lumbago raises heck every time I bend to a teat. If I can make some easy money, I may be able to retire one day soon."

Will liked that idea, too, but he wasn't ready. "Can I help?"

"I'm okay for now. I still have my savings. But like everyone else, I'd like to make some easy money."

25

Will couldn't dally any longer. Mary pressed his promise to invest half their savings in the market. Their account was twice what it was six months earlier, and it was growing by the week.

"All my friends flaunt their riches," Mary said.

"I've already bought stock: some Ford, General Electric, and Standard Oil."

"But you promised we'd spend half our savings."

"Yes, it's time, I suppose. But only if we pay down our debts, too."

"Maybe we should borrow more. Everyone's doing it. They say it's smart to make your fortune on borrowed money."

"You're right there. A national mania. But it's not good for the kids, spending other people's money."

"The kids?"

"A step away from stealing. It sets a bad example."

"We've got mortgage debt."

"That's different. The collateral's secure."

Mary shrugged, and Will knew she wasn't convinced.

"I'll leave it to your good judgment," Mary said, "but I think we should borrow, too. The market's been climbing for over two years."

"This surge may never end," David Tate said. "It doesn't have a peak. It just keeps rising."

"David, have you known anything that went on forever? One of these days, the bubble's bound to burst."

Will turned his attention to the continuous ticking of the tape machine as it spewed its winners and losers, and there weren't many losers these days.

David tore off a foot of paper and scanned the tape before throwing it down. "Well, it doesn't look like it's about to tank anytime soon. Will, I've got a tip for you."

Everyone had tips these days, it seemed. "Yes?"

"A customer told me his cousin works for Nash Motors, down in Kenosha, and they've added a new assembly line. He figures their production will double."

Will noted the glitter in David's eye and the devious smile on his face.

"Can't I sell you some Nash Motor stock? I hear they're a mighty good car. Some say better than a Ford."

"I'll hear none of those salacious rumors."

"They're made right here in Wisconsin."

Will turned toward the door. "I'll not listen to such talk."

"Hold on, Will. I've got other tips if you don't like that one."

"I'm ready to buy, but I don't need tips. I know the companies with a future."

"What do you have in mind?"

"I want Goodrich, Atlantic Refining, and Radio Corporation, and more of Ford and Standard Oil, too."

"Not much risk there. Maybe not enough upside either. Why don't you throw in a mining stock. If you hit it right, you can make lots of money."

"I'll stick with what I know, but don't tell Mary you recommended mining."

"If you're going with such stalwart companies, why don't you buy more then?"

"I can't afford it. For every dollar in the market, I'm increasing my mortgage pay-down the same."

"Go ahead and do that, but you don't need more money. I'll get you nine shares on credit for every one you buy. Why, you can get rich using other people's money."

"It's not for me."

"When your friends retire early, don't say I didn't offer."

"I know, most the town's in hock half way up the flagpole. A lot of that will go unpaid, I'm afraid. And unpaid debt's just theft out the back door. It's not the way I do business." Will wrote a check. "You could be right, David, but taking unsecured debt seems reckless to me."

Will walked to Ashley Springs Community Bank. This part he felt good about. He knew that George Tyler would be happy he was paying his loan down, even if it meant ravaging his savings account. But, at today's rates, George could do better.

"Hello, George. I want to pay down my mortgages. I'll take some savings to do it."

"Now that's a novel idea. I thought people only borrowed these days. You'd not believe how many of your friends have mortgaged to the hilt to fuel their gambling frenzy." He threw his pen onto the desk. "I'm losing business every day because I refuse loans and they just go elsewhere." He raised his hand to cover his eyes, as if he wanted to shut out the world. "Enough gloom. House, land, or business?"

"The business, George. The rate's higher. Makes sense to pay it first, doesn't it?"

"You'd be surprised at what I can get for that money now. A couple percent more than your mortgage. I could loan all the money I get my hands on, but there's not much coming in these days. But then, we don't pay the highest rate either." He dug a ledger out of his desk drawer. "Iowa County Bank's paying a full percent more than us. Beats all. Something's not right. They don't charge more on their loans."

"In a few months I'll have this paid off," Will said. "Business is booming."

"You may be the only guy in town who hasn't lost his senses. I'm glad you're doing well."

Will didn't mention the stock that he purchased earlier that day.

26

Will felt certain that Mary would be pleased. He'd been up since five o'clock, but now on the weekend, he was glad to let her sleep in. But he didn't want to go to the shop, not yet, not without telling her he bought stock yesterday. He stoked the cook stove and warmed oatmeal on one burner, but he didn't heat the fry pan. He wouldn't do that before he heard Mary stirring. He took out his pipe, but placed it back into the writing desk. Too darn early for a smoke, he thought. Besides, he noticed that Mary coughed a bit each morning until she cleared the stale night air from her lungs. He took the whisk broom, a dust rag, and dust pan from the closet and cleaned the hickory nuts from the dining table, those he'd husked the night before and which he'd told Mary he'd clean before heading to bed. But he began reading the *Farm Journal* and forgot all about his promise.

He was so intent on pushing each small piece into the dustpan that he didn't hear Mary until she harrumphed and loudly proclaimed, "Aw, ha, caught you in the dastardly act! Didn't you say you'd pick those up last night?"

"When the cats away, the mice … shirk their duties." He reached for her. "I thought I could get away with it." He raised her face and gently kissed her forehead. "I didn't expect to see you till noon. But you'll be glad to hear I bought more stock yesterday, another two thousand dollars' worth."

"Only two thousand?" She pulled away.

He couldn't win. "We're heavily invested."

"I suppose."

Best to change the subject, he thought. "I so wanted to get the horses into the new barn by the end of April. I didn't want to pay another month's rent. But with this rain, I'm not sure we'll get moved before May's over. These storms are trying my patience."

"The almanac predicts clear weather the rest of the week."

"Can't rely on it. It hasn't been right all spring. I hate to move horses with lightening around, but I'm ready to take the chance. I'm not going to pay again. That new stable's beckoning like a mare calling her newborn. I'll get Dad out in the morning."

Will smelled burned wood as soon he stepped out the door.

He didn't see any smoke though, probably because the night's rain had dampened it. He remembered waking up to thunder and lightening sometime while it was dark. Rain had pounded the roof but he'd soon fallen back to sleep.

As he walked toward his new building, the smell of burnt timber and hay frightened him. Having seen fires before, he knew that smell. He heard voices shouting in the distance before he saw Mrs. Schmidt's collapsed house. At first he felt a sense of relief, but as he raced toward the carnage, he saw smoke drifting from the west toward her seared timbers. Suppressed by the heavy air, the smoke hung low. And where his beautiful new stable had stood, nothing remained but a smoky hole in the ground.

Thomas and a few neighbors dug through Mrs. Schmidt's rubble while she sat on the grass, head in her hands, weeping like a disconsolate child.

"It's everything I've got!" she wailed. "It's all I ever owned. All gone now."

"We'll do what we can, Mrs. Schmidt," he said before he turned to Fred Kirkpatrick, a neighbor. "Get her away from here. Take her to her sister's."

But when Kirkpatrick took Mrs. Schmidt by the arm, she jerked free and threw herself onto the ground. "How could God do this? First my husband, now everything else. What could I have done to deserve this?" She lowered her head. "Tell me: what did I do?"

Will and Kirkpatrick gently lifted Mrs. Schmidt from the ground. "Find her pastor," Will said.

As Kirkpatrick led a resistant Widow Schmidt away, Thomas approached Will.

"I suppose it was lightening," Will said. "I should consider myself lucky my horses weren't here." He walked toward the remains of his ruined stable. "Poor Mrs. Schmidt."

"Will, did you notice how your stable is burnt to rubble?" Thomas said. "Nothing but ashes, while Schmidt's house is only partly burned? Lots of charred timbers still standing. Isn't that strange?"

"It rained mighty hard last night."

"Why didn't it put yours out, too? Her wood has dried for years. Should have burnt fast. Yours is green wood. It doesn't make sense."

"I'm glad I bought insurance."

"There's something else I want to tell you, Will. Jesse's back in town. Bennie saw him last week."

"You don't think he had anything to do with this, do you?"

"It must have been lightening."

But Will wasn't sure.

27

Will knew the price for having three children was to delay his return to the farm, but it wasn't a bad tradeoff. He loved time with his girls, loved to read stories at bedtime. One night it was *The Tale of Peter Rabbit*, and on another it was Hans Christian Andersen's *Fairy Tales*, but lately the girls begged him to read *Winnie-the-Pooh* and A.A. Milne's new book, *The House at Pooh Corner*, stories about Pooh bear and his adventures in the Hundred Acre Woods. Will reread the stories so often that the girls knew them by heart, but they pleaded for more.

"Daddy, take Pooh to his thinking spot," Catherine said.

But Ruby complained, "No, you did that last night. Read about the flood, about Owl losing his home."

"It's my turn to choose," Sharon said. "Read about Christopher Robin's birthday party."

"Now girls, if we can't agree on one, then we'll have none." Will closed the book and slid off the bed. Whenever the girls squabbled—and Sharon and Ruby squabbled often—Mary said that until they acted like proper young ladies they'd have to go without. And Will was happy to follow his wife's advice. She knew children.

"Don't go, Daddy," Sharon said. Then she turned to Ruby. "Okay, we can have the flood tonight, but tomorrow night I get the birthday party." She extended her hand. "Agreed?"

Ruby turned Catherine to her. "You'd like to hear the flood story, wouldn't you, Cathy?" Then she whispered in her sister's ear, but not so quiet that Will couldn't hear, "I'll tell you a new story about the thinking spot after Daddy turns out the light. Okay?"

Will smiled.

And Catherine agreed with Ruby. She always agreed with Ruby.

The girls tucked in and the light turned out, Will joined Mary in the parlor. "You sure have those girls figured out. When I closed the book and walked away, it didn't take long for them to reach an agreement."

"Compromise is easy when it's the only way to get what you want," Mary said.

"Just common sense," Will said.

"I would think so, but given the problems parents have with their children these days, common sense isn't all that common."

"But you're a teacher."

"I suppose teachers have the same proportions of common sense as everyone else." She dropped her last darned sock on top of five others in the clothes basket. "These should last you the rest of the year, then we should probably invest in new ones."

"Speaking of investments, ours have done well."

"Everyone says so. It seems we can't lose. It's probably time to buy more."

"I'm thinking about selling."

"Why'd you do that?"

"This can't go on forever, my dear." He took his corncob from the writing desk drawer. "Grandpa Duffy didn't give me his farm, but he gave lots of advice." Will touched a flaming match to the bowl. "That was part of our problem. Frank listened while I had my own ideas. But I do remember one thing he said." Will took two deep draws and blew smoke across the room. "Once, when I paid two dollars for a bike, polished it up, but turned down four dollars because I thought I could get five, he said, 'Son, don't get greedy. You'll never go broke selling at a profit.'"

"But, Will, everyone says there's lots more money to be made."

"That's what makes me uneasy. When everyone's in, who's left to buy? We've done well. We've almost made enough to retire our house and business loans. It's time to cash out."

"Oh, Will, I hate to sell the hen that lays the golden eggs."

"I'll tell you what, Mary. I think it's time for a second honeymoon. Lets take some of that profit and go back to Madison, but this time, let's do it right. Let's stay at the new hotel across from the Capitol Building."

"I hear it's exquisite. And the new Orpheum Theatre. It's just down the street." She threw her arms around him with so much fervor that she almost knocked the pipe from his hand. "Maybe a talkie will be playing. Why, there's no writing on the screen. Did you know the actors really talk, and you can hear them?"

What Will knew was that he'd hit the jackpot. Whatever displeasure Mary had about his intent to sell stocks was already forgotten, it seemed.

But he wasn't so fortunate when his father drove up the next morning. Will could tell by the way his wagon bounced off the cobblestone street that it wasn't loaded. "You're not so full today, Dad. How come?"

"I couldn't take the time. Wanted to catch Tate before he closes at noon."

"What business could you have with David? You're not buying into this market, are you?"

"No, Will, I'm taking your advice. I made a little profit. I'm selling. I wanta free up some money."

Will thought that David Tate would try to convince him otherwise, but he was resolute. "David, my mind's made up. I'm selling the whole kit and caboodle."

"All your stocks?"

"Yep, all of them, and you'll not talk me out of it. I'm going to pay off my loans."

"As you wish. But it'll take a couple days. My ticker tape's on the blink. I should have it back late tomorrow, at least by Wednesday morning."

"You're not going to talk me out of it?"

"Is that what you want, for me to talk you out of it?"

"Mary would."

"Too many have every dime they've got in the market. By the way, I shouldn't be telling you, but your Dad bought more."

"He said he was selling. He's not on margin, is he? It's not the stock he's buying that worries me: it's those letters that Mom said he's getting."

"I don't think he's done margin. Let's see." David sorted through the pile of orders that cluttered his desk.

"He probably didn't mention it, but someone's been sending letters predicting market moves."

"That's not new. Everyone thinks he can predict the market."

"But this guy's been right every time."

"Yeah?" David leaned toward Will.

"The man's written about a half-dozen letters, each predicting whether the market will rise or fall. And he's always right."

"That's weird. I don't believe in seers." David lifted a paper from the pile. "No, he didn't do margin. Does the man ask for money?"

"Dad says no, but maybe he wouldn't tell me."

"I know a fellow at the Branch Bank of Wisconsin in Madison. He knows what those scam artists are up to."

"Mary and I are going to Madison next week on a second honeymoon. I'll check then. What's his name?"

"Samuel Darch. Smart fella."

28

ill hoped his second honeymoon idea would pacify Mary, and it seemed to. So far she hadn't complained about his quitting the market. Once again Will hired Bernie Burns to chauffeur them to Madison. Mary had been so enamored with that pleasant young man, who had brought sunshine into that turbid day, that she insisted he accompany them again.

Will paid quadruple the amount this time, but he knew that Bernie could use the money now that he had a wife and a daughter who was almost Catherine's age. But Will couldn't remember her name.

"Opal," Bernie said. "She's the crown jewel in our lives."

Will looked across at Mary and wasn't surprised to see her smile back. How many times had she teased that Catherine was the crown jewel in his life, even though Ruby was named after a jewel?

"So you're an old, married man," Mary said. "Your father must be very proud."

"Oh, Opal and Grampa are two peas in a pod. He stops to see her every morning on his way to the court house. She knows if he's ten minutes late, and she won't leave the window until she sees him drive up the block. I shudder to think what she'd do if he didn't show up one day. She does love her grampa."

"Enjoy every moment now," Mary said. "They grow up so fast. Overnight my first-graders become eighth-graders, it seems." A frown crossed Mary's brow. "And they don't stay innocent for long either. Already Ruby wants to know about the birds and bees. Wants to see a calf born, and she's only five years old."

"I fix Opal's dolls," Bernie said. "I'll leave the birds and bees to Shirley."

"Coward," Mary said. "Just like all you men." She glared at Will.

"I don't think Ruby cares about birds and bees as much as she cares about physiology," Will said. "That girl's going to be a nurse."

"Why not a doctor?" Mary said. "The world's changing."

"Maybe we should send the girls to the farm to see a birth," Will said. "That first one changed my life."

"Sharon would faint away and Catherine's too young," Mary said. "I'm not sure Ruby's ready either."

Will wondered if Michael would have been braver about it than his girls, but he doubted that anyone could be braver than Ruby. "I was five," Will said. "I'll never forget. I didn't want to look, but once I saw those two little feet show, I couldn't turn away. It wasn't long before this beautiful little brown and white calf was on the ground tossing its head and kicking its heels." Will stared through the windshield. "'Twas a miracle. I wonder if Dad has any births coming up?"

"Being a town boy," Bernie said, "I've not had that experience."

"Everyone should," Will said.

"Dad took me lots of places but not to a farm."

"It's not his constituency," Will said. "But he's a good man, Tommy Burns, even if he is a politician. We're lucky to have him for mayor, and municipal judge, too. Two for the price of one."

At first, Bernie didn't respond.

"A good man," Will repeated.

"I'm worried about him, Will."

"Oh?"

"The market. He's in awfully deep. I'm afraid it could go sour."

"You're not in the market?"

"Not me. I have a family to raise. I'm not getting rich, but I'm doing okay."

"Well, son, if you ever decide to stop clerking at the grocery, stop and see me. I think you'd make a fine car salesman. I pay good, too." Will tapped Mary on the shoulder and pointed to a Ford dealership as they drove through Verona. Then he turned back to Bernie. "I worry about your father, too."

"That Tate fella has him bamboozled. Convinced him to borrow to the hilt to buy more stock. Not right to operate that way. Some people'll do anything for money."

"You're probably right about some people, but not David. He's as honest a man as you'll find in town."

"You know what big money does to a person. And all these profits are making Tate big money. He's bound to be corrupt."

"You're wrong, Bernie."

Mary pointed toward white board fences that flowed as far as the eyes could see. "Look at those beautiful horses."

Will counted a dozen elegant Morgans.

"I don't remember seeing that before," Mary said.

"It wasn't there before," Will said. "David said the head of his company built a horse farm just outside Madison. I bet that's it. Pull over, Bernie."

Bernie slowed the car and stopped on the gravel shoulder.

When Will got out to look closer, he heard Bernie say, "So that's where Dad's money is going. And you say Tate's not corrupt."

A half hour later Bernie opened the car doors in front of the Loraine. Mary held her breath as she looked up. "It's the tallest building I've ever seen. It must be a dozen stories high." She crushed the flowers on her hat as she held it tight to her head, tilted back, and looked into the sky. "One, two, three." Mary took a step back as she continued to count. "Nine, ten. I hope you didn't take a room at the top."

"No, my dear. I know your fear of heights, so I took a third floor room with an awning under our window. It's high enough to see the lake, but with the awning below our window, you'll think it's the ground floor."

"I won't look out the window."

"You'll have better things to do," Will whispered into her ear.

Bernie insisted on carrying both suitcases to their room. "I want this to be a special time for you, all pleasure and no work. I hope someday Shirley and I can take a second honeymoon like this. Our first one was in Ashley Springs at the Walker Hotel."

"Well, our first night together was at the Walker, too," Mary said. "Remember, you picked us up there." She blushed as she turned to Will.

Will's face warmed, but he didn't say a word because Bernie, a lascivious smirk on his face, caught his eye.

Mary raced ahead with Will at her heels, while Bernie struggled with the two heavy suitcases.

Two clerks talked behind the desk, and a bellhop stood straight as a plumb-bob in front of the counter, his arms folded across his chest.

The boy's eyes followed Bernie as he trudged forward with the heavy suitcases.

"Can I help you, sir?"

"Thanks, my man, but I gotta earn my pay."

Not a muscle twitched as the bellhop snidely warned, "The lift's being repaired. You'll earn it, all right."

Will scanned the local business directory while the clerk sorted through the reservation lists. "O'Shaughnessy?"

"Yes. Will."

He pulled a paper from the pile. "Room 348. The lift's down for an hour. If you leave your bags, I'll have the bellhop bring them up."

"I'll bring them, Will," Bernie called ahead to them.

The clerk pointed down a long hall. "Three flights up and to the right."

Mary ran ahead. "I can't wait to see our room!"

Will heard Bernie struggling on the stairs below and was about to turn back when Mary called. He hesitated, dug the key from his pocket, and then hurried in her direction.

Will fumbled with the key while Mary looked over his shoulder, but before he opened the door, he said, "Close your eyes and don't look until I say."

Mary placed her hands over her eyes as Will gently lifted her, nudged the door open with his foot, and stepped into the room. It was much larger than the one at the Baldwin, with furniture that stole Will's breath.

"Can I look now?" Mary said.

Will set her down, and they scanned the room together.

"It's not Queen Victoria's furniture," Mary said.

"Nor Queen Anne's either. Looks more like a bordello," Will said.

"Will! How would you know?"

Mary walked from one furniture piece to another, caressing the marble and hand-rubbed wood finish. Beside the three-door armoire with its adjustable shelves there was an amboyna burl bed, a bed larger than Will had ever seen; two night stands with beige, thick Italian marble tops; a matching amboyna writing desk; and a black, lacquered vanity with a beveled swivel mirror set in polished chrome.

On the far side of the room a rich brown leather sofa and two chairs looked inviting, so Will plopped down while Mary moved toward the bed, its blue chenille spread turned down to reveal mauve sheets and matching pillows.

Will heard the heavy breathing before Bernie turned the corner and dropped the suitcases inside the doorway. "I thought I'd never get up those steps. Should've paid the bellboy." He pulled a hanky from his hip pocket and wiped perspiration from his brow, and then flopped into a wingback chair in the corner. "I suppose you'd like me outa here." His smirk dissolved into gasps for air. "Do you need anything else?"

"Just place the suitcases by the bed." But when Bernie struggled to get off the chair, Will took pity. "I'll get them." He grabbed the two suitcases and, with little effort, hoisted them onto the racks. "That's what clerking does to you, son. You could use some exercise."

"I shoulda waited for the lift to git fixed." Bernie eased off the chair and stumbled toward the door. "I'll be here Thursday early. I'll need to get back for work at one o'clock."

Before Bernie turned down the hallway, Will called, "Bernie, I think you're wrong about David Tate. I think your father's blinded by the color green."

Will closed the door, walked across the room, and sat by Mary on the bed. "Bernie thinks David's hornswoggled Tommy, but he's wrong. He's right to be worried though. Tommy's leveraged to the hilt."

"Will, you worry too much."

"I don't want to think about Tommy or the markets. I just want to enjoy our time alone."

"Just you and me, all alone tonight."

Will pulled Mary close. He inhaled. The scent of almond, her favorite cologne, filled his head and weakened his knees. He clung to his wife and felt tipsy, like that day he'd stayed too long at Bennie's. He was so ready for this evening together. No stocks, cars, or children—just the two of them. But he couldn't help but think ahead a bit. It was the next night that worried him.

Mary opened her suitcase while Will looked out the window. "I can see Lake Mendota. It's as calm as the water in my horse tank. Let's take a walk before the sun sets."

Mary sorted through her clothing.

"Glad you're unpacking now," Will said. "We may be busy later."

Will led Mary, hand in hand, to the business directory. "Let's see if there's a place we want to visit."

But Mary's attention was elsewhere. She scanned a giant poster with the title "Now Playing at the Orpheum." "Look, that talking movie's in town, *The Jazz Singer* with Al Jolson. There're no subscripts."

"I hear the Orpheum's a beautiful building. It's just a couple blocks down State." Will thumbed through the fliers. "What else would you like? There's Brown's Book Shop, Kessenich's Gift Shop, the Rosemary Beauty Shop, Ward Brodt Music, Lawrence Restaurant. I've heard their food's good. They're all within six blocks."

"I'm not up for a long walk tonight. Maybe tomorrow when we're fresh."

"I wouldn't want to tire you out. Not tonight." He sidled over to Mary and put his arm around her waist.

She pecked his cheek. "No, we wouldn't want to tire out now. Let's stroll down to the Orpheum. I'd like to peek inside."

"The Lawrence restaurant is just a few blocks farther. We can go there for supper."

"It's been a long day." She grinned as she hugged his waist tightly. "Let's eat in our room tonight."

The Orpheum Theatre, which opened in 1927, wasn't quite two years old. They had just turned the corner onto State Street when Mary spotted the sign two blocks ahead. "It's lots higher than our third floor room."

Will thought it's probably not that high, but its flickering lights danced with the stars.

Mary tilted her head back as she followed the lettering upward. "It illuminates the whole block!"

The marquee did have more lights than Will had ever seen in one place before. From a block away, the words "*The Jazz Singer* with Al Jolson, America's First Feature-Length Talking Film" dominated their horizon, and although the movie didn't begin for another hour, the line of people trailed a block away from the box office.

"Popular as a hog trough at feeding time," Will said.

"They've never heard actors talk before." Mary was jostled by people who rushed to get in line. "Do you think they'd let us look into the foyer?"

When she stepped toward the entrance, the doorman said, "The ticket line ends down the block, ma'am."

"Can't we just look in?"

He opened the twin glass doors and beckoned her forward. "You don't want to miss this one. It's the movie of the century. Never been one like it."

Will almost stumbled over Mary when, just inside the foyer, she stopped short. "Will," Mary raised her hands to her face and scrutinized the interior, "have you ever seen anything so grand?"

A giant glass chandelier, matched by four-tiered sidelights, illuminated the room like sunshine at midday. Matching staircases commanded the room's sidelines, each covered with rich, royal blue carpet imprinted with golden eagles, a reflection of the décor which looked down from the ceiling. A long brass railing separated two wide aisles that ended with doormen guarding two sets of closed mahogany double doors. Will imagined the bedlam when the doors opened and the crowd rushed down those aisles to the more than a thousand seats which waited inside the mahogany doors. He supposed the doormen earned their paychecks.

Mary wandered to the right stairway and caressed the shiny wood rail as she looked up the twenty stairs that led to the balcony. She looked around and inhaled.

Will, too, savored the freshness of new carpet, the smell of popcorn and sweet candy; then he closed his eyes and breathed deeply to fully appreciate the wonderful aromas.

"Oh, Will, it's so grand. Can we come back for the movie?"

Will saw that the building's splendor mesmerized his wife. "You'd like to see the inside, I suppose."

"It's the most beautiful place I've ever seen."

Will had plans for the next night as well. But he wasn't certain that Mary would like those. The theatre might be the ticket to get her in a receptive mood, but he didn't think that would be a problem tonight.

"Do you remember our first night together?" Will said.

Mary blushed as she nodded and slid across the sheet toward him. They caressed and exchanged love words that fueled Will's passion and warmed his soul.

"I don't know how you ever fell for an old hayseed like me, but I'm sure glad you did. It was the luckiest day of my life. I've never been happier, and I'll love you forever," he said as he slid his fingers across her soft skin and stroked her upper back and neck.

Mary arched her back and wiggled her shoulders.

"It feels wonderful," she said.

"You're incredible," Will said as he pulled Mary close. He shivered with excitement, and, as the evening progressed, he found, once again, just how amazing his beloved wife could be.

Will wasn't sure how Mary would respond to his plan, so he was uneasy. She was a dyed-in-the-wool Methodist.

Mary pulled her new dress from the armoire and held it before her.

It was stunning, Will thought. A black silk crepe dress with georgette ruffles, the torso covered with large gray stars filled with iridescent, cobalt beads. He stepped back and admired his lovely wife. "My dear, it's a gorgeous dress. Perfect for the most beautiful lady I know. Only a prince could deserve one so lovely. I pinch myself every morning to make sure I'm not dreaming, that I've not turned into a frog."

"Git on wit you, my bold prince. You and your Irish blarney." She slapped Will's arm as he reached in her direction.

"Now is that any way to be treating royalty?" Will undid his checkered necktie and realigned the ends. "We're a long way from home, my dear. When in Rome." He wrapped the long end twice and fished it through the loop. He held it out. "Why can't I ever get this right?"

"Here, let me help." She nudged him toward the mirror. "Stand where I can see."

Mary stood behind, undid Will's mistake, wrapped twice, threaded the long end through the loop, and pulled it snug under his chin. "That's not so hard, is it?"

Will looked down at the perfectly aligned ends. "You don't teach that in school, now do you?"

"You'd be surprised how many I've tied before school events." She finished dressing and snatched her new cloth hat and a jacket from the armoire's top shelf. "We better get going. I don't want to stand outside too long."

Will knew that this first part would be easy. He hoped it would electrify Mary so that she'd be receptive for the main event.

They hurried the two blocks to the Orpheum, but the line wasn't as long as the night before. "Probably not so many come to the early show," Will said.

"It's been here two weeks," Mary said. "Maybe everyone's seen it already."

Will noticed a restaurant scene on the outside billboard and stepped between Mary and the picture. He wasn't ready to discuss their night's meal, but he was too slow.

"I'm getting hungry. We should have eaten first. We usually do."

"The place isn't open."

"I thought we were going to the Lawrence Restaurant."

"Not tonight. This place is special. Rocco Galli, the chef at Walker House, told me it serves the best steak in Madison."

"I don't like steak. You know that."

"He says their chicken cacciatore is scrumptious, too."

Will was thankful when the man behind pointed ahead and said, "Step up lady. Don't lose your spot."

And the ticket agent said, "How many, please?"

At first Will and Mary couldn't get to the aisle. The crowd stood at their seats and clapped, whistled, and cheered. "Jolson, Jolson," rang through the theatre. After they pushed their way out, they were continually jostled as they made their way up the walkway. "I wouldn't have believed," Will said.

"What?" Mary leaned toward him.

"Movies will never be the same."

Mary slammed into Will when she was pushed from behind.

Will spun around to face her assailant, but Mary grabbed his arm. "Let's get outside."

"That was bedlam," he said. "They acted like animals."

"They lost their heads in the excitement," Mary said.

"I thought they were going to attack the screen when Jolson said, 'Wait a minute, you ain't heard nothing yet.' Did you like it?"

"I kinda liked Jolson. His voice brings tears. But it's not my favorite music."

Will knew that Mary's favorite music came straight from the Methodist Hymnal.

Mary clutched Will's arm as they walked down the street. "I couldn't understand all the words. Could you?"

"It's like any new technology, I suppose. It'll get better."

"Where's this restaurant you say is so good?"

"Just down the street. In the next block."

"What's its name?"

"Rocco called it Al's Place."

"Al's Place?" Mary slowed, grabbed Will's arm, and spun him toward her. "It's because of the movie. It's named after Al Jolson."

"I don't think so."

"I've read he has businesses all over."

"Not this one."

"Then what is it? Tell me."

"It's a … you know, one of those places you read about." He dug his fists into his topcoat pockets. "A speakeasy."

"She spun to face him. "One of those illegal places? You know I'm against liquor. How could you, Will?"

"Now, Mary, it's not that bad."

"Don't you placate me."

Will took her hands in his. "Rocco says it's a high class establishment. Only the best people are allowed in. And you don't have to imbibe."

"What would the ladies at the Church say if they knew?"

"I doubt we'll see those ladies, my dear. And I've always wanted to see inside a city speakeasy. I've read so much about them. You'd rather I took you with than go alone, wouldn't you?"

Mary turned back, but slowly. "I suppose." She frowned "But don't you tell everyone at Bennie's. I'll skin you alive."

At the end of the block, Will reached for the handle of a door that looked like it might lead to an apartment above. "Rocco said it's over Kessenich's dry goods store. The door at the end," he said. "This must be it."

They ascended a narrow stairway, opened another nondescript door, and stepped into a short hallway which ended with split wall-to-ceiling mirrors separated by a plain oak panel. "Rocco said to go to the mirrors and knock three times on the wood panel, but no more."

Will knocked and waited.

"This is weird," Mary said.

After a minute, a mirror slid back and a portly, pockmarked man stared down on them. "Yes?" he said.

Will knew the password. "Valentine's Day surprise," he said.

The big man stepped aside, but before Will and Mary entered, he demanded, "That'll be twenty dollars."

Will dug for his billfold.

"Twenty dollars for two meals?" Mary glared at the man. "That's outrageous. Why, it's more than I spend in a month."

The man shrugged and turned to Will. "Twenty dollars, sir," he said. Will pushed two sawbucks forward.

A dance floor occupied the room's interior, and at the far end was a stage where a piano, a bass, and a row of music stands promised entertainment. Linen tablecloths set with fine Richard Ginori china and spotless sterling silver adorned each table. Gaudy murals decorated the walls.

A woman took the table next to them. Her hair was bobbed, and her bright red lips matched the color of her heavily rouged cheeks. She wore a feather in a beaded headband. When she sat, her straight, loose dress slipped above her knees. Layers of beads hung from her neck over a silk blouse and flattened breasts. Smoke curled from a cigarette that dipped off a long silver holder. And while Mary stared, her mouth agape, the woman hiked her skirt and lifted a flask from under the garter, which anchored her silk stocking.

Mary turned to Will, her jaw still unhinged. She looked back toward the young woman who didn't bat an eye in her direction, blinked, shook her head as if to void the horrible image, and then, speechless, she turned to Will once more.

He couldn't help but smile. "You're not surprised, are you?"

"The floozy. She probably rides a bicycle."

"You supported suffrage."

"Not this, for heavens sake. You wanted women to vote, too, Will."

"You've gotta be careful, you know. Might get what you ask for."

He forced a wicked smile. "See what happens when you open the floodgates."

Mary harrumphed and nodded toward the seedy girl. "Seems the equality she got is the tawdry kind."

Smoke wafted across their table, and Mary fanned the air with her silk napkin. "This is a different beast than the suffrage I supported." She coughed. "Do you think we could move to another table?"

"How havoc rains down when the oppressed are unchained."

Will motioned to the maitre d' who, upon seeing him, rushed to their table. "May I get you a setup, sir?"

"What?" Mary said.

"No liquor served here, ma'am, but the setup's included in your fee."

"No," Will said. "But can we get away from this smoke?"

"Certainly, sir." He pointed across the room. "There's lots of empty tables, but I'm afraid none will be smoke free before the evening's over."

He led them away from the haze, and only then did their neighbor acknowledge their presence: As they rose from the table, she sneered and flicked ashes at their feet.

"If she were a student of mine," Mary said, "I'd rap her knuckles."

Will savored his porterhouse while Mary nibbled at her chicken. The room filled with people before they were half finished, and Mary continued to be bothered by the smoke that floated around them. "I never realized how oppressive cigarette smoke could be."

"You've not spent much time in barrooms."

"Well!" Mary snorted. "I don't need smoke for an excuse to shun those places. But it can't be good for you. At least your pipe smells good."

"It tastes better, too. You know what Tate says about a cigarette, don't you?"

"I can think of lots of things to say, but none of it ladylike, I'm afraid. What does he say about cigarettes?"

"Another nail in your coffin. That's one more reason I never took to the smoke sticks."

The room filled with applause as a black man dressed in a tux, white shirt, and bowtie entered from behind the curtain and ran toward the piano. He stopped, doffed his straw fedora, and bowed repeatedly as he edged toward the instrument. He paused over the bench, lifted his coattails, and plopped onto the seat, then held his fingers over the keyboard as if he were uncertain what to play, turned to the diners who to a person had tabled their utensils and stared, anticipation on their faces. And when the cry "play Tootsie" echoed across the room, he launched a stirring rendition of "Toot, Toot, Tootsie."

"It's right from the movie!" Mary said. "This is Jolson's place after all."

29

Mary pressed the wrinkles from her skirt while Will shaved. "If my friends hear about last night, I'll leave town."

"The food was good. You'll have to admit that."

"That hussy was disgraceful."

"Tell them about Jolson."

"We should have come back here after the movie."

"It wasn't that bad."

"Do you think I should get one of those new pageboy cuts?"

"Like that young lady wore last night?"

Mary frowned.

"And a flask and some cigarettes, too, my dear. You'll make a lovely flapper girl." Will rolled his room receipt, hung it from his lips, and puffed away while he shuffled his version of the Charleston, all the way across the room.

Mary collapsed on the bed with laughter. "You'd look marvelous, my dear, in a knee-length skirt and a string of beads."

Will cringed in terror at the suggestion, but soon joined her on the bed. "You'll always be the most beautiful woman in Wisconsin no matter what you wear." He pulled her close and kissed her tenderly.

After leaving Mary at the beauty parlor, Will stepped into The Branch Bank of Wisconsin. He picked the March 27, 1929, The *Wall Street Journal* off the table, scanned the front page, and read, "Charles Mitchell says his bank will keep lending. Market recovers." Will didn't know the market was down, but he wasn't surprised.

A voice startled him. "Mr. O'Shaughnessy, you're here to see me?"

A tall, bald, and corpulent man approached.

Will held the paper up. "I didn't know the markets were off. I've avoided news the last few days."

"Quite a scare, but I doubt it's over. Are you in deep?"

"I took my money out last fall."

"A smart man. I feel sorry for those buggers on margin. What can I do for you, Mr. O'Shaughnessy?"

Will dropped the *Journal* on the table and held out his hand. "Mr. Darch, David Tate said you could help me." Will felt strength in the man's grip.

"David sent you? A good man. We worked together for a while. I started as a broker." He beckoned to Will as he turned away.

The small, sparse office smelled like cigar smoke. Darch walked to his large overstuffed roll out, pulled a smaller wheeled chair away from the desk, and motioned for Will to sit. "What is it that David thought I could do for you?"

"He says you're an expert on scams."

"I've seen them all, I suppose. And, yes, I advise worry."

"It's not me. It's my dad. He's been getting letters."

"I bet I can tell you. They say the market will rise one week, fall the next."

"You've gotten these mailings?"

"It's an old con game." Darch flicked the lid off his humidor, pulled out two cigars, and offered one to Will. "But it still attracts the naive."

"No thanks. Only smoke a pipe."

Darch dropped one big cigar into his container and fingered the other.

"I haven't seen the letters, but Dad keeps getting them, and he says they're right every time."

"He's one of the winners." Darch paused. "It's more accurate, I suppose, to say he's a loser."

"How's that?"

"Well, it goes like this. The scam artist sends out, oh, say, twenty thousand letters. Half of them predict the market will rise in a given week, the other half that it will fall. Now he's got ten thousand interested people."

"And my dad was one of them."

"But it doesn't end there. He now sends letters to those ten thousand who already believe he may have special powers, and once again, he tells his story. Half the letters say the market will rise, the other half that it will fall."

"Now he's really got believers."

"Yes, and by the time he's repeated the process a half dozen times, he only has a few hundred left, but he's got them by the short hairs. They're ready to be fleeced."

"I suppose he asks for money."

"Oh, sure. He may ask them to pay for his advice, or worse yet, he'll tell them to send money, probably lots of it, money he'll invest for them."

"How does he know the investors?"

"May be random. It seems everyone is eager for a hot tip these days. But sometimes he has a contact inside the stock exchange or a large brokerage office who gives him the names and addresses of the players."

"Thank God that Dad doesn't have the money to do much harm, but I better tell him."

"The promise of sure, easy money has a terrible draw. He wouldn't be the first one suckered into the morass."

Will knew that he must tell his father about the scam. Thomas said that he wouldn't send money. Nevertheless, Will worried. Maybe he could convince him to get out.

Will smelled the familiar barnyard aroma as Fanny approached his dad's farm. The cow manure, corn silage, and hay dust blended into a pungent odor, one that would offend city folk, but it smelled like home to Will. He hitched Fanny to the post in front of the house, but he didn't see his father. Now, late in October, Will knew the corn was in, the year's harvest done, but it was too early for milking. He wasn't likely to be in the barn or fields. Maybe the house. Even though he knew his boots were clean, out of habit Will slid them across the scraper at the door's entrance. Seemed like his feet had a mind of their own. Strange how the body repeated old behaviors.

His mother pushed the door open before Will touched the handle. "Well, Will, this is a surprise. I thought you'd forgotten we live here. Seems you're too busy to visit nowadays."

Will ignored his mother's complaint. "Best to pay no heed to what you don't want to hear," Mary had cautioned him. Of course, she didn't countenance that when she had something to say.

"Is Dad in the house?"

"So you didn't come to see your old mother?"

"Yes, Mother, I came to see you, too." He knew Mary would object, but old habits die hard. "But first I must talk to Dad."

Gertrude shrugged and pointed towards the pasture. "He's out repairin' fences."

Will knew his mother wasn't adequately appeased, but he'd already humored her more than Mary would have liked.

Will unhooked Fanny from the post and turned toward the lane. Fanny raised her head, whinnied, and picked up her pace. "So you know we're home. It does feel good, now doesn't it?" Will tugged on the reins. "Slow down, old girl."

At the far fence line Will's father stood on his wagon, maul in hand. Will marveled at his father's strength. At sixty-nine, he still could swing a fourteen-pound hammer from his heels, and swing it harder than his sons. When Will got closer, he hollered, "Hey, Dad, got a minute?"

Thomas reached the maul toward Will. "Came to help, did you now? Here, son, show me how it's done."

"Don't think I could lift it anymore. I do all my work from the bottom up, and not much of that since I hired help."

"Gittin' soft, are you?"

"I've got more pressing matters. Come on down." Will took a flask from his jacket pocket and reached it towards his dad, who dropped the maul, sat on the wagon's edge, and reached for the liquor.

"I thought that would get your attention."

A ring-neck pheasant, wary of the pounding but spooked by the silence, flew from the tall weeds under the fence. Will couldn't understand how people could shoot so beautiful a bird.

Thomas smacked his lips as he handed the flask back to Will. "One swig's good for a dozen more posts."

Will returned the container to his jacket without taking a drink.

"You haven't gone dry on me now, have you, son?"

"Mary doesn't like it."

"Domestication'll do that every time." He took a tin of Red Man from the pocket of his OshKosh B'gosh bib overalls. "Have to beg for your

treats, just like an old dog. Your mother doesn't like my tobacco either."
He pasted a pinch inside his cheek.

"Dad, about those letters—"

Thomas turned from Will and spat into the tall grass along the fence line.

"The ones that predict the market."

"Oh, those."

"Have you gotten more?"

"Don't you worry about those letters, son. The market's back up."

"Did he ask for money?"

"He's been right every time. Not missed once."

"But did he ask for money?"

"Well, yes, but he's always right. Never seen anything like it. Guy's a genius."

"Do you know how he does it?"

"S'pose he's got powers."

"Trickery, that's what he's got."

"You say?"

Will explained how the correct predictions dwindled until the man had a small group convinced he couldn't be wrong. "You certainly didn't send him money, did you?"

"Where would I get money? Put mine in those stocks you recommended."

"It's time to sell those, too, I think. The market's topside heavy."

"Soon, Will. Farm income's about to pick up. The House of Representatives passed a tariff resolution last May, and I read that Congress plans to put restrictions on imported goods any time now. Farm income's bound to improve when we stop that foreign competition."

"Don't be so sure those tariffs will help. When your adversary's barefoot but you're stark naked, it's not a good idea to stomp his toes. You didn't send that man money, did you?"

"But the man's Irish, you know."

"What makes you think so?"

"He said he is." Thomas dug a crumpled envelope from his coverall pocket, extracted a letter, and pointed to the last line. "See?" He handed it to Will.

Will read aloud, "'Take it from another Irishman, there's gold at the end of this rainbow.'" He threw the letter down. "He didn't even sign it. Anyone can say he's Irish."

"Not many claiming to be Irish these days, not since the war. Why'd the man say so if he weren't?"

"It's addressed to O'Shaughnessy. You don't suppose your name had anything to do with it, do you?"

Thomas picked the letter off the wagon and stuffed it into his pocket before he hoisted the maul.

"You promise you'll see David and sell those stocks."

"I'll get to town next week. Won't be comin' through this Saturday."

"The sooner the better."

"The market's been up the last four years. No need to drop everything now, is there?"

30

Will stewed over the slowness of the fire investigation. "Mary, I want to get that stable rebuilt before the snow flies. The Mangardis say they'll start when I give them the word. I want Fanny in her new stall before winter."

"What's the holdup?"

"The sheriff suspects foul play, and the insurance company won't pay until the cause is known."

"Your dad said it looked a bit fishy."

"He questions why green wood burned to ashes when dry wood didn't. I suppose the sheriff wonders the same."

"Didn't he say?"

"He's bringing someone in from Madison to investigate a bit. I want to get that building going."

Two days passed, then another week, and still there was no word. So Will stopped in Stover's office on the way home from the shop. "Sheriff, have you heard anything from the investigator?"

"I haven't got to yesterday's mail yet. Bunch of young shenanigan's raising havoc at the farms. Hazing the cattle. This younger generation." He thumbed through the mail on his desk. He held up an envelope, grabbed a scissors, and snipped off the end. "It's from the state fire warden's office. Probably what you're looking for. Let's see." He read for a couple minutes. "Yep, just as I thought."

"What is it?"

"It's not clear from the evidence but it might be arson. They found a kerosene can in the lot behind. Of course, it could have been thrown there by anyone."

"What about Schmidt's house?"

"They don't think it was lightening. The fire's updraft probably carried embers downwind to the widow's house, and they set her roof on fire. They believe hers started from sparks thrown off yours. Your stable may have burned a while before the storm hit. Hers, not so long."

"Poor lady." Will felt responsible. "A kerosene can, you say?"

"It could be tied to the fire."

Will remembered his father saying that Jesse had been seen in town about that time.

Business had languished throughout the summer, but now in September and early October, sales were dismal. While Will worried about the plight of his income, an unexpected obstacle threatened his economic well being. For the first time, he would have competition in town. A stranger to the area, Brock McDougal, opened an Oldsmobile dealership up the street. When he heard, Will rushed to the bank to see George Tyler. The bank was empty and George sat alone in his office. Apparently his business suffered, too.

"George, what do you know about this new Olds agency, about this McDougal fella?"

"Not much. He doesn't bank here, but rumor has it that he's got a good business head. He came up from Chicago. They say he wanted to get away from the city with all its problems. I'm told that he sold a prosperous dealership there. Said to have made big money."

"It doesn't seem like the time to be opening a new dealership."

"Probably got the Larsen building cheap. It's been sitting vacant a long time. I hear that he plans to redo it throughout."

"I wouldn't put new money into my business, not now. But maybe he knows something that I don't."

On Thursday, October 24, 1929, Will sat staring at his ledger. Car sales were down again, the eighth month in a row with sales fewer than the month before. Repair receipts lagged, too. How long would this continue? Will couldn't understand it: the stock market still boomed, probably still propped up by bankers' dollars. But he was thankful he no longer had mortgage payments and had a tidy sum in the Iowa County Savings Bank. He could get by for a while, but he didn't know how long he could keep his employees.

Will heard shouting in the streets, but being deep in thought, he ignored it. Then his door flew open and Silas Murrish burst through. "The market's in freefall. People are panicked."

Will bolted from his chair.

"The radio says it's the worst crash ever."

"Oh, my God." Will hollered into the garage, "Watch the shop, Ed. I'll be out for a while." He rushed toward David Tate's office in the Ashley Springs Community Bank building.

But when he arrived, he couldn't get through the door. The office was full and people pressed to get David's attention. David stood on his desk and tried to quiet the throng. "I can't sell your stocks, not now. The New York ticker is running way behind, but don't panic fellas, remember last spring. Mitchell stemmed the tide. Mark my word, the bankers will step in again."

And David was right. By that afternoon, a group of bankers pooled their money and invested in the market, calming the fears. If those insiders invested their own money, many said, then there's no reason to panic.

Will met Tommy Burns on the street that afternoon, and Tommy was cheerful. "It had me worried for a while," Tommy said. "Not so that I wanted to sell, but, I'll admit, I was a bit nervous."

"I'm glad I'm outa the market," Will said.

"Now's the time to jump back in. Bargain prices. I'm heading to David's now. Gonna double up on Bethlehem Steel and Postum."

Will watched Tommy race to double his risk, and he shuddered. He wasn't so sure it was fixed, but the market thought otherwise. People bought again.

31

The market vacillated, but it didn't crash over night. It took two days. On October 28th, the Dow Jones Industrials was off 38 percent. On October 29th, it fell another 30 percent.

The country panicked. Margin calls went out. The New York Times reported people jumping from windows. Gun and ammunition sales increased to the highest level since the Great War ended. Lines formed at banks, and people gathered in the streets.

That night, Will's dinner grace continued beyond his usual, "Bless us, O Lord, and these thy gifts which we are about to receive through Christ our Lord. Amen." This time, Will fervently thanked his Lord for their good fortune. "And thank you Lord for opening my eyes to the risks of the market. Thank you that my family, my father, and brothers are not overwhelmed by this terrible plague that threatens our nation." And Will was truly thankful even though he knew that his father may have lost his savings in this market collapse.

But it could have been worse. He didn't worry about Frank. Frank didn't trust banks, let alone the markets. Frank would have money. And poor Jess: he doubted that any of this would touch Jess, wherever he was. But Will worried about his neighbors. "Please, O Lord, give them strength."

Six-year-old Ruby said, "Daddy, won't we have food?"

Catherine, who had turned four a month earlier, began to cry.

"Why do you ask, my dear?"

"You said the market. I can tell you're worried. You've never prayed so long."

Catherine cried harder.

"Shush, Catherine," Mary said.

"We'll be fine. There's plenty of food. You can help Mother in the garden."

But Will knew that a lot of children would go hungry soon enough if this market didn't recover.

And it got worse. Many lost everything when they couldn't meet their margin calls. Others watched their profits collapse and their principal erode until it was lost forever. Short market upswings gave hope, but hope vanished when the market crashed downward each month. Gloom hung over Ashley Springs like a fog.

Will hated facing Ed and Ray. He thanked the Lord that Paxson had found another job. If his business didn't pick up soon, he would have to let one go, maybe both, and it wasn't likely they could find other employment, not now. Thankfully, neither one had families.

Will wasn't sure whether everyone in town was broke or if they just stopped spending, but he hoped it would change. He hadn't sold a new car in months and he wasn't getting many repairs. But that didn't surprise him. He wasn't buying many things, either. And it wasn't because he held back available money.

Will puttered around the office while the boys worked under his last repair job. When he had arrived that morning, Lou Carey's Model A sat in front of the shop with a note attached to the steering wheel: "Thought I better get this transmission fixed while I still have a dollar left in the bank. Slips out of third gear now and then."

That afternoon, Will had another visitor: Sheriff Stover.

"Haven't got much news," Stover said. "Not much to go on."

"You have no ideas?"

"Could be Jesse, but there's little enough evidence. The last we heard, he hopped a westbound freight."

"What makes you think it's Jesse?"

"He was seen at the hardware store a few days before the fire. And he was cussing you out."

Will winced at the thought. He turned to the sheriff. "Do you believe he did it?"

"No way to know. Everything's circumstantial."

Hadn't Jesse had enough trouble? Hadn't he been punished a hundred times over all ready?

"Will, I wish we knew more. Mrs. Schmidt's in a terrible way."

And that troubled Will the most.

That night before bedtime, Will told Mary the news. "And it might be Jesse. How did we ever get so estranged? But Mrs. Schmidt lost everything. I wish we could help her."

"Will, you bought the insurance, even when I belittled you. You're a smart man, and I love you with every fiber in my body. I couldn't have a kinder, more caring husband." She paused, smiled up at him, and took his hand. "I think we should give the insurance money to widow Schmidt. We may be hurting but she's destitute."

Will had been thinking about that, too, and he felt a bit ashamed that he hadn't mentioned it. He should have known that Mary would agree.

Will hadn't read the advertisements in the Ashley Spring's Weekly at first. But when he did, he crumpled the page and ran toward his shop. He rushed toward Ed, who sat at the desk, and pushed the advertisement into his hands. "That damn McDougal is trying to drive me out of business."

"Whoa, Will. I haven't seen you this worked up since you emptied that oil pan over your face."

Ed smoothed the crumpled paper.

"Look at that." Will jabbed his finger at McDougal's advertisement. "I can't compete with those prices—and he offers free oil changes, too."

"Don't they call it free enterprise?" Ed said.

"Carnivorous business practice, that's what it's called."

But Will couldn't think of a thing that he could do. And he knew he couldn't match McDougal's prices.

The October rains came in torrents, leaving the streets as quagmires. November began the same. It reminded Will of those Asia monsoons he read about. Everyone was gloomy, but rain was the least of their problems. It seemed as if all the gods were against America and nothing could go right. Will wondered what the next calamity would be.

Today he was glad to be inside, even if more rain wasn't expected that day. For a while he doodled on his spiral ledger but didn't open the cover. The morning light flooded the room and illuminated cobwebs that Will knew were there but had neglected to clean when more pressing jobs demanded his attention. He bent over his desk and searched the top drawer for the dust rag but couldn't find it. The closed ledger loomed large in front of him, but he tried to ignore it. He knew what was there. He checked the second drawer but found no rag. No matter. He couldn't reach the cobwebs anyway, not unless he stood on a ladder, and his ladder was out back.

The broom? He remembered using it on the mud that Dennis Newberry tracked through his office earlier that morning. Dennis didn't have business—just wanted to pass the day—but that was no surprise. Will wished they'd notice the new mat he placed outside the entrance. Just because it said "Welcome" didn't mean they should rush by with nary a nod. After all, it'd cost five dollars. It sure wasn't earning its keep. Where had he put that broom? The broom closet? Now that would be a first. He opened the closet door, but it wasn't there either.

He might as well go home and play with the girls. He knew that after a few minutes with his daughters, his spirits would ascend from the depths of anxiety. It never failed. "Hey fellas, I'm leaving for the day," he called out back.

To avoid the standing water along the tracks, Will walked the longer upper road home. Besides, the train was about due, and it'd probably delay him at the lower crossing.

Will had walked two blocks when he saw Tommy Burns' new Model A coming toward him. Tommy usually whipped down the street, but today he drove slow—mighty slow for Tommy. But then, it was that kind of day. He probably wanted to avoid getting his pretty car all muddied. When Tommy came alongside, Will waved and shouted, "Hey, Tommy, some weather we've been havin'. Looks like I may have to swim home." He supposed Tommy wouldn't take time to shoot the gab—he was usually in a rush this time of day—but Will expected at least a hardy good morning.

But Burns drove past. He acted as if he hadn't seen Will. No wave, no hello, no recognition at all. Not like Tommy, but the world weighed heavy, Will knew. He was probably trying to sort his way through his problems. Tommy had been gloomy all month.

Will trekked through the wetness, but he had to watch the path or he'd be in the market for his second pair of shoes this fall. Mary tried to get him to wear galoshes, but he hated the darn things, hated pulling them on and off. Most of the time his shoes came off with them. He might as well go barefoot.

Will heard the train whistle and knew it would only be moments before the Milwaukee Road passenger train sped through town on the tracks below. It didn't take long, not at thirty-five miles an hour. Will didn't know why the village allowed it. He knew that Tommy was trying to set speed limits, but they had to keep their schedule. If he glanced through the trees, maybe he'd see the train pass through the crossing. It was a beautiful machine, sleeker and faster than the freights. Will recalled his father telling about when it came to town almost seventy years earlier. It put Ashley Springs on the map, but back then it was called the Milwaukee and Mississippi.

Even from a quarter mile away, Will heard the tracks sing. Sound swooped down the valley and carried up the hill. Then he saw Tommy's car slowly approach the rails.

That's strange, he should have passed the crossing long ago. Tommy stopped, not before the tracks, but on them.

His engine must have died, but Will didn't remember Tommy saying his car was giving trouble.

Will saw the train racing, a hundred yards away now.

Get out Tommy.

The words surged through Will's head, screamed through his consciousness.

Without thinking, Will began running in that direction.

But Tommy didn't get out.

The last thing Will remembered before the car exploded was the exhaust.

The engine ran, but Tommy didn't drive off the track.

And Will never saw Tommy, not before the collision, not at impact, and not when pieces of his Model A littered the roadway for a quarter mile down the track.

When Will walked into his shop the next day, Ed Spencer waited at the door. "Someone shot David Tate last night as he left his office," he said. "They say he's in bad shape."

Will knew that David had lots of enemies these days.

David lived, although he couldn't name his killer. He remained in a coma for a week, then slipped away. Will was despondent, the town was despondent. After Tommy Burns's death, Bernie was nowhere to be found. Will and Mary visited Tate's family that day. Their minister was there, along with three other friends, but most of the community went about their business.

Sheriff Stover searched for two men, Bernie Burns and Tate's killer, and when he found one, he found the other as well. Bernie didn't try to hide the thirty-eight revolver, one shell expended. And he didn't deny his guilt. "The bastard had it coming," he said.

Mary spent the afternoon with Maud Burns and the evening with Bernie's wife, Shirley. Will visited Bernie inside his cell in jailhouse ally. He didn't know what to say. He was exhausted by the dual tragedies. Will was glad that Tommy couldn't see his son caged like an animal. And Bernie paced the ten-by-twelve enclosure like an animal, too. At first, Bernie looked wild-eyed at Will, not acknowledging his presence. Will scanned the sparsely furnished room and wondered if Tommy would have paid more attention to the comfort of his cells if he knew his son would soon be confined in one. Will sat at the end of the sleeping cot, the room's only furniture; its blanket lay crumpled on the floor and its sheet was disheveled.

"Can I do something to make you more comfortable?"

"I'm glad I killed the vermin." Bernie continued to pace. "He sold death to the innocent like a snake-oil man sells his poison."

"Tommy—" It was no time for accusations and too late for preaching.

Bernie paused in front of Will. "I think about Opal waiting at the window for her grampa every day."

And now she'd wait for two men that she'd never see again. But Will didn't voice his thought. "What can I do for Shirley? For Opal?" Will shuddered as he thought about his own daughters waiting for him to come home.

"I'm done for. That's for sure. Be nice to her, Will. She's got no one now." Bernie fell to his knees and sobbed.

Will knelt beside him and took his hand. "I will, Bernie, for you and for Tommy."

Will felt dazed as he stumbled from the jailhouse. The past week had been a nightmare for his little village, and the deaths were so unnecessary.

That night Will and Mary sat side-by-side on the settee. "I promised Bernie I'd help Opal," Will said.

"And I promised Maud and Shirley I'd help them. I said they could feed from our root cellar this winter and from our garden next summer."

"There's misfortune all around and we've barely been touched. How lucky we are, my dear. It's the least we can do."

Will didn't mention his rapidly decreasing sales.

32

"What can I do for you today?" George asked Will.

"It's Dad. Mother called this morning and said you're calling in his loan. Can't I help?"

"He doesn't have a loan here. He paid it off last spring." George dropped his head and sighed. "Try the Iowa County Bank, but I hear they're in trouble. He's always banked here. I'd be surprised if he went elsewhere."

Will cringed. "Mother sounded desperate."

"The Iowa County Bank took a lot of my business. I hear they're calling loans, but he wouldn't go there, would he?"

Will didn't remember his mother mentioning the Iowa County Bank. Although he wasn't surprised to hear the market had touched them, he was shocked to hear her say they were losing everything, that the bank was taking their farm. "How can that be?" he'd asked. "I inquired about his sending money to that man the other day and he denied it. I'll be right out, Mother."

Will had dropped the receiver and buried his head in his hands.

"Will, what's wrong?" Mary said.

"It's Dad. Mom says he's losing the farm."

"How's that possible? It's paid for. He told me himself."

Will had driven Fanny to his childhood home. She sped up when they turned onto Tredinnick's Road, the township road that ran past his place. Will supposed she remembered the grain his father scooped into her manger at day's end. It wasn't long after they weaned her that Fanny discovered life's other pleasures. At dusk each summer day, she would race up the lane towards the barn, so intent on her treat that she didn't pause to greet the cows as they streamed past toward their night pasture. Will could tell the time by her arrival home. Fanny did like her oats.

"Those were the good days, weren't they, old girl?" And Mother said they were going to lose it, but maybe she's wrong. She never paid much attention to finances.

Will rushed to the house. He wanted to talk with his mother first. "Mom, are you in here?"

"Out on the sun porch."

Gertrude looked through the screen at her bright flowered mums. When she turned toward him, Will saw that her eyes were red and puffy. He had never seen his mother cry. "I just weeded those flowers last weekend." She pointed toward her mums, the earth around them loose and black. "If I'd only known, I'd have saved the effort." She grimaced as she stretched her back. "Oh, Will. We're going to lose it."

"Are you sure?"

"You know I don't pay much attention to bills, but this time … " Tears ran down her face.

Will wanted to hug her worries away, but he held back. He hadn't hugged his mother since he was a boy. But she worked so hard. "Mother, sit down." He took her hand, led her to the wicker chair, and pulled another to the front so he could face her. "Tell me what's happened."

"You know about those letters."

"Dad said he wouldn't send money."

"But he did."

"How? He spent his savings on a few stocks."

"He borrowed."

"Where?" But Will knew.

"I saw the letter from the Iowa County Bank. They're calling the loan, and we don't have it. They'll take the farm." Tears rolled down her cheeks, but she didn't utter a sound. She just waved her son away.

"Where's Dad?"

"Maybe the barn. He didn't say a word but just threw the letter down and went out."

Will walked across the barnyard. This was where he grew up. It wasn't much of a farm, but it was home. It had possibilities if farmed right. He glanced upward toward the top of the yellow, glazed tile silo that didn't look near so tall now. How he'd hated pitching silage when it piled toward the dome and he'd have to climb down the creaky outside ladder. The barn needed paint and boards were missing. His dad hadn't replaced them after winter winds sent them sailing over the southwest Wisconsin hills. Will shielded his eyes so he could see into the lower barn. "Dad, are you in here?"

His pupils not fully adjusted, Will couldn't see much, but he smelled the pungent odor of the full gutters. Dad hadn't shoveled the manure after milking that morning. He stepped inside and waited for his eyes to adjust to the darkness, but his father wasn't there. He began to worry. Will stepped outside the dark interior and rushed around the building, toward the ramp that led upward. The wagon sat unhitched beside the barn, so he knew his father hadn't gone to the field. He ran up toward the hay mow.

"Dad, are you in here?" But there was no answer.

Sunlight streamed through the sixteen-by-ten opening, illuminating dust that floated above the dry hay. Will began to feel weak-kneed and nauseous.

He was about to go back to the house when he thought he heard a moan behind the loosely piled timothy and broom. He eased around the hay, and there, half buried in the stack, Thomas lay still. Will rushed to him but immediately knew what happened. He didn't need to read the label on the empty quart bottle that lay by his dad's side; the smell of liquor permeated the air. Will lifted his father's head and fanned his face.

Thomas groaned.

"For the love of St. Patrick, you smell like a vat of beer."

Thomas groaned again, but when Will tried to lift him, he slumped back to the floor. Will knew how to speed this up. He gently lowered his father's head, jumped up, grabbed a pail that sat by the door, and ran down the ramp. A minute later, he was back with the bucket full of water. At first he sloshed a little water over his dad's face, but when that didn't rouse him, he dumped half the pail.

Thomas gasped, flailed his arms, shook water from his face, but didn't open his eyes. "Don't drown me, you son of Cromwell." He licked his lips and frowned. "It's bloody water. I don't need another baptism." He groped the floor with his hand. "Where's my bottle?"

"You don't need more liquor, either." Will grabbed Thomas's arm and pulled him upright, but when he tried to slide under his shoulder to give support, Thomas waved him away. He took a few steps, staggered but made it to a grain sack in the corner. Will clutched the empty bottle. Most men would be out all day. Thomas O'Shaughnessy could hold more liquor than any man he knew. "What's this all about?"

"Now don't get excited. The man said he'd pay."

"What man?"

"You know who."

"Where'd you get the money?"

Thomas tottered but Will grabbed his coverall strap and snapped him upright.

"I thought you invested your savings in the market."

"Now, son, don't go gettin' all worked up."

"Mother showed me the bank's letter. They're taking our farm. And you don't want me to get excited?"

"He said he'd send the money. He's always been right, now hasn't the man?"

"You talked to him?"

"No, but he sent a thank you. An Irishman, you know. Said he'd send dividends each month."

"How much has he sent so far?"

"He will."

Will grabbed the half full pail and dumped the remaining water over his father's head, then ran down the ramp.

Will drove toward Frank's, a road he had traveled many times, first with his father, then behind Fanny, who now trotted smartly along. She probably expected her oats this time.

He tied the reins to Grandpa's cast-iron hitching post and hurried toward the barn. He supposed that Frank would be doing the evening chores. He found his brother forking hay down the manger. "Frank, it's Dad."

"He didn't go have a heart attack, now did he?"

"Naw, he's fit as a fiddle, but snapped a string or two, I'm afraid."

"How's it concern me? Don't see him much anymore."

"Do you see anyone?"

"I keep my nose to the grindstone."

"Dad's going to lose the farm."

"No surprise there. Grandpa said Dad played loose with his money. Grandpa said if you don't take care of the little things, the big things'll eat you up."

"But he was scammed." Will explained. "He still thinks he'll reap a reward, but the bank won't wait."

"How's that concern me?" Frank spat a stream of tobacco juice to the side. "Do you think he'll get some money?"

"Not a cent. These people are crooks."

"So?"

"So we gotta help."

"Dad's always stumbled through life, him and all the other drunkards in town. I heard the market's crashed. Hope you didn't buy in, Will. Might as well have bet on rainbows."

"Will you help?"

"Grandpa would say, 'He got into the shit, let him dig his way out.' What you got in mind?"

"I've got a couple thousand in savings, but that's not enough to unravel him without your help. We'll have to act fast."

"See what you can do." He turned to a pile of loose hay and buried his fork. "I gotta get the milking done."

Early the next morning, Will hurried toward the Iowa County Bank. Maybe this could turn to his advantage. Perhaps he could pay off the loan, buy ownership in Dad's farm. A down payment on his future, so to speak.

Before Will entered High Street, he was told four times, "Heard the news, Will? The bank's shut down."

Will ran the five blocks to the bank, but from a block away, he could read the big handwritten sign: "Closed for Business." There had been no warning. Little likelihood he would get his money now. One thing was for sure: there'd be no down payment on his father's farm.

The news spread rapidly. The Iowa County Bank put its money in stocks, gambled its customer's deposits. And like everyone else, they'd lost. There were no reserves for customers, and rumor had it that the Board of Directors lost their money as well. Although people screamed for their arrest, the directors proclaimed their innocence. They said they wanted the highest possible profits for everyone. But their grand vision crashed along with the market.

He'd avoided an overheated market by placing his money in a safe bank account, but that didn't look so prudent now. An additional one percent was a poor return indeed.

"He's our father, Frank," Will pleaded. "I don't have much left, but maybe we can pool enough to save him."

"Whoa, not so fast, my big-hearted brother. You're sure free and easy with other people's money. I worked hard, kept my cash at home, didn't blow it in the market or risky banks." He spat tobacco juice toward Will's feet. "Dad acted stupid and greedy. You, too, it seems. You're barking up the wrong tree if you expect me to fund his foolishness." He spat again. "I'll tell you what I'll do, though. I need the help. There's plenty room in the house. They can live here, do the cookin' and cleanin', and I'll pay twenty dollars a month. That's more than Dad paid me."

"But, Frank, they'll lose our farm."

"They can take it or leave it."

With no better option, Thomas and Gertrude moved in with Frank at the end of the month.

Mary laughed when Will told her. "Gertrude with Frank? He may be getting more than he bargained for."

But Will knew he'd not be going to the home farm again.

33

Sharon was angry with Ruby and they both fumed at Catherine. They squabbled over a puppet man, but Will steered clear of their quarrel. He knew it had something to do with the circus they attended while at their Grandma Tregonning's the previous weekend. And it was apparent that Catherine was disturbed over it. Will had never seen his gentle little girl so belligerent.

"I won't do it," she said.

The Ashley Springs Talent show was to be the next Saturday. "Annual Talent Show at the Village Center. All Ages Welcome. 7 P.M., October 19, 1932" plastered walls all over town. Will supposed his little girl was out of sorts because she was anxious, this being her first time. Sharon and Ruby participated the prior year, and Sharon said she was nervous this year, too, but not Ruby. "I'll dazzle 'em with 'Playmates.' I wish you'd sing a duet with me, Cathy."

"I want to be Shirley Temple."

"But we don't have her music," Mary said.

Mary turned to Will. "Ever since we took them to *War Babies*, all I hear is Shirley Temple."

"I've been practicing her dance." Catherine swayed, whirled, and twirled. Then she stopped and mimicked Miss Temple, hands on her hips and a smile as wide as the dining room table. "This is when the ice cream drops down my back." She squealed, wiggled, and shook like a dog escaping an unwanted bath. "Can I wear a red rose in my hair?"

"How do you know it's red?" Ruby said. "It looked black to me."

"It was red," Catherine said. "Look in our garden. Our roses are red."

"Not all roses are red," Ruby persisted. "Some are yellow."

"And lots of other colors, too," Will said.

"Where can I get a big sucker?" Catherine said. "I don't think Shopley's has any that big."

"No Shirley Temple," Mary said. "I think you can find something other than *War Babies*."

"Oh, Mom." Catherine stomped her foot. "I want to be Shirley Temple."

"My, my, you're even snappish like that young lady, but no, not this time."

"Let's do 'Playmates,'" Ruby said. "I'll let you have the best parts."

"That's a good idea," Mary said. "I'll make you matching outfits. Just like the song says."

"But I don't want to sing with Ruby. I want to do Shirley Temple."

"If you forget your words, Ruby'll be there to help you," Will said.

"I know all the words," Ruby said. "I've been practicing since school started. If you forget, I'll sing your part, too. They'll never know."

"I'll still be scared," Catherine said.

"Just look at the ceiling and pretend you're singing to Mama and Papa," Ruby said.

"That's easy for you. You sing all the time. But Daddy says I sing better, don't you Daddy?"

"Now, Catherine, my dear, don't be getting me in trouble, but you needn't worry. You sing like a nightingale."

Ruby glared at her dad. "Dad thinks you do everything better." Ruby curtsied and stuck her tongue out. "Daddy's pet. Even Sharon says so. Don't you, Sharon?"

Sharon nodded but said nothing.

Will knew that after a few years of mending Ruby and Catherine's squabbles, his oldest daughter had learned to be the diplomat.

"I'm not cheeky like you," Catherine said. "Mama says you should watch your tongue."

"Well fiddle-dee-dee. You're just a little 'fraidy cat."

"I guess you're right." Catherine emitted a strained giggle. "I'm afraid to go on stage."

The morning of October 19, Catherine wouldn't eat breakfast, saying she had a pain in her stomach. But her sisters said it was nerves, so they ignored her complaint. Mary felt Catherine's forehead and proclaimed her a bit warm, but the thermometer registered ninety-nine, not enough for concern. Catherine moped around the house all day, but didn't resist when Mary called them into the dining room to try on the dresses she sewed. Two little maids dressed in blue gingham pinafores, matching sunbonnets, red stockings, and the glittery red shoes that her teacher, Miss Bridge, had promised.

And because Catherine sang the spiteful refrain, her mother painted large brown freckles on her cheeks, and her father taught her how to grimace like an angry leprechaun. Sharon said that Catherine looked absolutely wicked when she called out, "I don't like you anymore." And before they left home, Mary wound matching braids, which hung to the middle of their backs.

Children over ten went first, so Ruby and Catherine wouldn't contend with Sharon who sang "I'll Take You Home Again Kathleen." Catherine knew Kathleen was spelled different than her name, but still, whenever her dad sang it, she said the song was written just for her.

The nine young contestants drew numbers to determine their order of performance. Ruby and Catherine drew fifth. As her time approached, Catherine said she felt dizzy and her stomach hurt, but after calming her fears, Will and Mary left for their seats. And when their names were called, Catherine skipped on stage just like she practiced all week, but she stumbled and almost fell when the footlights blinded her. The audience gasped, but laughed and applauded when she regained her balance and waved at her mother and dad who sat in the front row.

The piano music began, and dressed alike, Ruby followed Catherine onstage. At the front, they joined arm in arm and sang about their love for each other. Then, one day, they quarreled. Catherine spun away but stopped and turned to face Ruby, her eyes full of venom. She wagged her finger in Ruby's face while she sang that she no longer wanted to be her playmate. The girls circled, glared at each other, and then abruptly turned and separated. When they reached opposite ends of the stage, they stooped and cried alone in sorrow. The footlights dimmed for a moment, then turned their brightness on the sisters who ran to each other, hugged, and sang about the good times once more.

The sisters kissed each other's cheeks and walked hand-in-hand off the stage. As they approached the back, the crowd applauded the next contestant when she rushed onto the stage, but Will noticed Catherine stagger and fall. Ruby lifted Catherine and helped her off the stage.

He turned to Mary. "Something's wrong." He jumped from his seat and reached for his wife. "Let's get back stage."

Miss Bridge pulled Mary aside as Will rushed over to Catherine. He grasped her hand and felt her forehead but jerked his hand away.

Catherine whispered, "My side hurts bad."

"We'll get you home, my dear. Get you into your own bed." He turned to Miss Bridge and frowned.

"She's a sick child," Miss Bridge said.

Catherine affirmed Miss Bridge's declaration by vomiting alongside the cot.

Miss Bridge turned to Debbie Price, one of the older contestants. "Get Dr. Ruggles. I saw him sitting in the back row."

Mary felt Catherine's warm brow, but before she responded, Dr. Ruggles ran across the back stage toward them. "So we've got a sick little girl, but a brave one." He bent over Catherine, felt her head, pulled aside the light blanket that Miss Bridge had thrown over her, and examined her stomach.

Catherine winced when he touched her right side.

"Pretty sore, is it?"

"It hurts when I move."

Dr. Ruggles pressed firmly, then he quickly let go.

Catherine tensed and scowled. "Ouch, that really hurt. Will I be okay, Doctor?"

"We'll take good care of you, my dear." He turned to Will. "Her abdomen's tight as a drum. I think it's the appendix. We need to get her to the hospital." He reached down and closed his bag. "Get Charles Roehl to bring his panel truck to the back door."

Will dashed away as Dr. Ruggles called to Miss Bridge. "Do you have more blankets? We need to keep her warm when we get her outside. We'll leave her on the cot, load it into the truck. I don't want her to move until we get to the hospital."

Piano music and singing, punctuated by applause, accompanied the drama back stage, but Catherine might as well have been a township away. The audience didn't know little Catherine had fallen, and Catherine's family was too preoccupied to appreciate the talent that Ashley Springs presented that night.

The doctors operated before midnight. "We couldn't chance it," Dr. Ruggles told Will. "And it's a good thing we did. Her appendix had already burst. Pray to God that peritonitis doesn't set in."

Catherine went delirious later that night. The nurses took turns watching over her.

"It'll be touch and go, but I'll stay until the crisis is over," Dr. Ruggles said. He shouted toward his head nurse, "Get cold water over here fast! And bring some ice. We've got to get that fever down!"

Nurse Fitzsimmons brought towels which had been soaking in a tub of ice cold water, and Dr. Ruggles laid them over Catherine's overheated little body. "Will, you can help." He handed a pile of warm, wet towels to Will. "Take these to the sink and ring the water out."

Will felt weak as, with shaking hands, he rapidly exchanged towels. He couldn't believe how fast the cold cloths turned warm. They worked through the early morning and Will fought back tears each time Catherine tossed or groaned. He thought about Michael, how Michael suffered before he died. His stomach knotted and he wiped the sweat from his brow. He couldn't bear to see a repeat of that terrible day. He prayed silently, "Please let my little dear live. You know how I love her." And he remembered his prayers for Michael, prayers that went unanswered. "If it be your will, O Lord, please let her live."

Dr. Ruggles and Nurse Fitzsimmons worked over Catherine's tortured body throughout the early morning hours. About sunrise, Dr. Ruggles said, "She's cooling down some. I don't think it's over, but the worst may be behind. Keep her cool, Miss Fitzsimmons."

Will urged Mary to go home where his mother waited with the girls. "Sharon and Ruby will be frantic. I'll call if there's a turn for the worse."

Mary looked toward the doctor.

"She's comfortable now, so go get some rest. I'll be leaving, too." He turned to Miss Fitzsimmons. "Send for me if she worsens. This may not be over yet."

Dr. Ruggles checked back early evening. "So far she's holding her own, but watch her closely," he said to the nurse. "She's still a very sick girl."

Will watched while Catherine rested throughout that night. He was glad that she seemed calm, but jumped up whenever she moved. And he continued his prayers.

Early the next morning, Mary returned. Catherine lay quiet in her bed. "How is she?"

"The doctor hasn't been in yet, but she doesn't seem any worse."

"Will, you look plumb tuckered out. You won't do any of us any good if you get sick, too, so go home and rest for a little while. I'll call if you're needed."

Will hesitated, but Mary pushed him toward the door.

Will turned toward home, his thoughts were with his little girl back in the hospital room as he shuffled down High Street. He was glad the street was quiet this Sunday morning. He wasn't in the mood to answer questions about his daughter. He wanted to rest a little and get back to the hospital. When he passed Samuel's Department Store window, he saw the big wooden rocking horse with a long silver mane that Catherine wanted for her birthday. But they told her she would have to wait. With income tight and savings depleted, he and Mary decided to buy something less expensive. "Don't be crying over a wooden horse," he had said to her. "You've still got Fanny Too." But when that hadn't stilled Catherine's tears, he'd reminded her that Christmas fast approached.

Will stumbled through the front door and found Sharon and Ruby still in their nightclothes, slumped bleary-eyed and pale at the kitchen table. He should have called home earlier. They couldn't have gotten a stitch of sleep. The sisters were at his side before he hung his coat on the hook.

"Is Catherine okay?" Sharon asked.

"Her fever's dropped, but Dr. Ruggles says it'll be a while before we know for sure."

"Mom went to early church," Sharon said. "She said this is no time to be offending God."

She hadn't told him, but Will wasn't surprised that she consulted God before visiting her daughter at the hospital. "You didn't go with her?"

"She didn't think God would be too put out if we stayed here," Ruby said. "Told us she'd send you home and someone had to get your breakfast."

"Girls, I'm too tired to eat. A couple hours rest and then I'll go back to the hospital. Make sure I'm up by ten."

Later that day, Dr. Ruggles met Will at Catherine's door. "She's still a pretty sick little girl, but I'm hopeful. Her fever's stayed down, but it may go up again this afternoon. "I'm going now, but I'll be back a little later. Nurse Fitzsimmons will call if there's a need."

Will took the door handle, but hesitated.

"You can go in. I think she's awake. But don't stay long. She needs rest."

He slipped into the room. Catherine reached down the sheet and caressed her tummy. "Oh, Daddy, it hurts."

"Be brave, my dear. It'll get better soon. And—," He was about to tell Catherine that she won the blue ribbon, but remembered that Ruby wanted to bring the news. "And when you get home, I'll have a big surprise for you." He decided he'd buy that wooden rocking horse.

"Daddy, will I be okay?"

"You'll be on your horse before you know it."

"Can you bring Fanny Too here?"

Will laughed. "Not here, my dear, but we'll go see her as soon as you're able."

"Please stay with me, Daddy." Catherine twisted toward him, but groaned when she moved.

"I'll stay for a while. But Dr. Ruggles says you need rest. Try to sleep."

Will thought about how he'd sung her to sleep when she was a baby. "Rest, my dear." He began to sing, "Too-ra-loo-ra-loo-ral," his favorite Irish lullaby. And by the time he was halfway through the refrain the second time, Catherine lay still on the pillow.

Will sat and watched. He was glad to be alone, alone with his thoughts and prayers. He knew he didn't worship as fervently as Mary, but he hoped that God wouldn't visit the sins of her father on his dear child. He prayed aloud, "The Lord is my Shepherd; I shall not want. He maketh me to lie down in green pastures—"

Catherine improved each day. Dr. Ruggles said if she could get through Wednesday she should be okay. His spirits soared at the news of Catherine's recovery. How unimportant his financial plight seemed now. Mary stayed with Catherine while Will went to his office on Monday and Tuesday morning to catch up on paper work. But he didn't get much done, so he returned to the hospital each afternoon. Lost in thought, he wandered down the valley road, drawn to the stream he hadn't visited since he took Michael there. He began to turn away, but he heard the water's song and the birds' harmonious response, and he felt compelled to go on. He approached slowly, hesitant to go forward, but he couldn't go back. The cowbird was there and so were the thrushes, but no matter how hard he looked, he couldn't see the indigo bunting. He remembered telling Michael how rare they were.

He paused for a moment, his thoughts on Michael, and then on Catherine. The longer he listened to the woodland stillness, broken only by the babbling water and birds singing their songs, the more at peace he felt. How silly he had been to never bring Catherine to this lovely spot. They'd come as soon as she was able.

After Dr. Ruggles proclaimed Wednesday a crisis point, Will planned to stay at the hospital all that day, but Bert Whitford brought his Model A in that morning, and Ed needed help separating the drive train from the engine.

Will called home each hour, but there was never any word. By noon he began to relax, but then the phone rang while he was under the car. In his haste he tore his arm on a protruding bolt as he scrambled from underneath, but he didn't notice until he saw blood running down the telephone receiver. When he heard the news, Will grabbed a chair to steady himself, but as soon as he knew it wasn't about Catherine, he felt a sense of relief, too.

Upon his reentering the garage, Ed asked if it was about Catherine.

"It was George Tyler. He said they just sentenced Bernie Burns to life in prison."

"Justice was served," Ed said.

"It's a sad day."

It was a terrible day when news of someone else's tragedy brought him relief, but it did. "God forgive me," he whispered to himself.

The afternoon passed slowly, but with no more phone calls, Will felt better. They'd dropped the drive train, and Will, at the sink, scrubbed grease from his hands when the phone rang again. Will dropped the grimy rag on the floor and raced to the office. He listened for a moment, and then, without a word, he threw the phone down and ran to the front door. But he stopped and hollered back, "Ed, I'm leaving. Catherine's taken a turn for the worse." He rushed outside.

Will and Mary waited while Dr. Ruggles and Nurse Fitzsimmons worked over his daughter. Will glanced out the window at Ashley Springs' largest sugar maple tree, which had inhabited these grounds for as long as anyone could remember; it probably was there before his grandmother came from Ireland. He prayed that Catherine would have long life, too.

When Dr. Ruggles turned toward him, Will feared the worst.

"Will, we need to get Catherine back into surgery. The wound's abscessed. She's a mighty sick little girl. I'm not sure she'll make it, but we've got to get it drained. We've gotta get that poison out of there."

While Dr. Ruggles talked, two nurses wheeled Catherine out the door and the resident surgeon, Dr. McReynolds, followed them down the hall toward the operating room. He didn't stop to explain but hurried after the gurney. When Catherine was wheeled past Will, she looked right at him, but didn't smile, didn't whimper, and, worst of all, didn't move. Will took Mary in his arms and helped her to the settee.

Will paced the floor. He took out his pipe. He put it back in his pocket, unlit. In between, he consoled Mary, told her that Dr. Ruggles and Dr. McReynolds were excellent doctors. They'd bring her through. He had told Catherine to be strong, and reminded himself that he must be, too. An hour passed. Another half hour. Then Dr. Ruggles walked toward them. Will thought he looked grim. He took Mary and Will's hands. "We've done all we can. We drained the infection, cleaned the wound, and placed a tube to remove the seepage. We can't do more. It's in God's hands now."

"Can we see her?" Mary said.

"Not yet. She's not recovered from the ether. We'll call as soon as she's conscious, as soon as the effects have worn off."

Will and Mary waited in silence, alone with their worries. He wanted to tell Mary that Catherine would be all right, but he didn't dare promise anything, especially anything the doctors couldn't deliver. He didn't blame them; they were only human. Dr. Ruggles had said that Michael would recover, he was sure of it, and Will believed, but he was wrong. He couldn't be wrong again. He couldn't try to know God's will. Not this time.

They wheeled Catherine into her room. She looked so frail and weak that Will wanted to take her in his arms and hold her, keep harm away, make her healthy again. Mary took Catherine's hand and Will thought he saw a glimmer of a smile on Catherine's face, but he wasn't sure. She lay so still.

"We'll keep her here under close watch," Nurse Fitzsimmons said. "You can sit in these chairs," she pointed to two straight-backed, wooden chairs, "or you can sit in the waiting room. The chairs are softer there. We'll call you if there's any change."

Will looked at Mary, and without a word spoken, he turned to Miss Fitzsimmons and said, "We'll wait here."

Nurse Fitzsimmons checked every half hour, and Will stood close behind, waited for each report. "Is she okay?" he asked after each examination. And between the nurse's visits, when his little girl's wellbeing fell on his shoulders, Will reacted to Catherine's every move. When her breathing seemed labored and irregular, he panicked and started toward the nurse's station. But Mary held him back. Then he fussed because Catherine seemed so quiet. And then when she cried out, Will rushed to her side, but Catherine lay still. He lowered his ear to her chest. Her breathing seemed normal. It must have been a dream. It would be a long night.

"She's resting well now," Nurse Fitzsimmons said, "but tonight is critical. If she makes it through tonight, she should be okay."

Mary dozed in her chair, but Will stayed awake through periods of panic and calm. Why couldn't he be like Mary? Why couldn't he leave it in God's hands? He paced the floor. He bent over Catherine and listened intently, listened for each breath, listened to catch any whimper or word. He watched and waited. The darkness wouldn't go away, and the night wouldn't end. His body wanted to quit, to drop on the floor beside Catherine, but Will wouldn't give in. He couldn't go to sleep. He drank cup after cup of coffee, and then he saw light on the far horizon and felt a sense of relief. Catherine had made it through the night.

The next three days, Will and Mary took turns staying with her, and she improved rapidly. Early on the fourth day, Nurse Fitzsimmons proclaimed Catherine well enough for visitors, so Will raced home to catch Sharon and Ruby before they left for school. And he was just in time. He found them at the hall closet discussing whether it was cold enough for winter coats. "Grab your jackets, girls," he said. "No school today. Today we celebrate. We're going to see Catherine."

"She's okay?" Sharon said.

"Just a minute," Ruby said and rushed up the stairs. She was back in a minute with a big blue ribbon in her hand. "I've waited all week to take this to her." She glared at her father. "You didn't tell her, did you?"

"Not a word."

When Catherine saw it, she cried out, "We won? My first ribbon ever. We really won it?"

"Don't get too excited, young lady," Will said. "Don't tear your stitches."

"And Miss Bridge said that you did so good and were so brave that she's going to give you those red slippers," Ruby said.

"And red slippers aren't all," Sharon said. "Just you wait until you get home."

"Now, Sharon," Will said. "Don't you go telling secrets. Besides, I think Catherine's had enough excitement for one day."

One week after her second operation, Catherine slept in her own bed. But she didn't sleep alone. Sharon and Ruby had placed the big wooden horse alongside Catherine's bed where she could reach out and hug it.

When they brought her into the room and she saw it, Catherine squealed with delight. "That's for me? I've got my own horsey?" And when she was assured that it was hers, she responded, "I'll take good care of him, I promise."

And Catherine didn't complain, not once, that she couldn't ride. Although she looked uncomfortable to Will, Catherine slept through the night, her fingers grasping the horse's silver mane. And Will felt sure that she dreamed about adventures they'd have together.

But Will had another surprise in mind. As Catherine regained her strength slowly, they walked around the yard and down the block for exercise. Each day, they went further until he was sure she was ready. Then one day they walked down the valley road, the road that Will had never taken Catherine along before.

They listened to the current sing its song and watched the birds flit from branch to branch at the water's edge. "That's a brown-headed cowbird," he said. "A lazy bird. Must think she's well-to-do. Leaves her young with a nanny."

Will described a red-winged blackbird, a brown thrush, and a meadow lark.

Catherine squealed her delight when a German brown trout surfaced to grab a bug.

Then Will saw it. "Look over there. It's an indigo bunting. See the blue speck?" Will pointed across the stream to where the iridescent bird darted among the hawthorn branches. This was the first one he had seen since that day he sat with Michael at this very spot, and he was sure it was a sign that all was well with his little family. Even while the world fell apart around them.

35

By July 1932 the Dow Jones Industrial Average dropped 89 percent below its 1929 peak, and by early 1933, twelve million workers, 25 percent of the workforce, were unemployed. Many Americans took to the rails, searched for a living they couldn't find at home. Others lived in the streets. With each passing year, food lines grew longer. And with despair came violence. In Los Angeles County Mexican immigrants were deported, and demonstrators were killed at Ford's production plant in Dearborn, Michigan. Farmers slaughtered cattle, dumped milk, and demanded better prices.

When Will O'Shaughnessy saw the plight of others, he knew he had reasons to be thankful. But he was affected, too. The O'Shaughnessies scrimped on the ever decreasing income that flowed from the dealership. Will sold few cars and his customers jerry-rigged their repairs. To boost his income, he installed lightning rods on Iowa County's high barns.

As a practical lot, farmers found it less expensive to avoid a loss rather than pay insurance premiums, so while Will's insurance business plunged, his lightning rod business grew, but ever so slowly. It was dangerous work—a job that most shunned, even in these hard times—but work that Will embraced. He felt at home on the farms, loved the road time with Fanny, and after many years climbing silos and repairing rails high in his father's hayloft, he knew no fear when hanging off a barn roof.

Besides, it let him keep Ed Spencer a little longer. He hated the thought of letting Ed go, but knew it was just a matter of time.

And Mary mentioned Ed, too. "Has Ed said anything about marriage? I heard he proposed to Nancy Sherman last week, and that they're getting married this fall."

Will had noticed that Ed had been somewhat distracted lately. "He hasn't said anything."

"It's not a good time to start a family."

"Love is blind."

"Have you told him you'll have to let him go?"

"I'm trying to avoid it. Maybe I'll get more barn jobs."

"And maybe this awful depression will be over, but not anytime soon, I'm afraid. You must warn him, Will."

"I'll talk to him."

Catherine shuffled into the kitchen, and at a good time, Will thought.

"Daddy, I had a bad dream in the hospital."

"But it was just a dream."

"I was scared."

"Yes, a hospital can be scary, but you're better now."

Sharon and Ruby drifted into the kitchen, but not without words. "Ruby, you did so take my gold necklace."

"You said I could wear it. Don't be a spoil sport."

"Mamma, I said she could try it on, not keep it."

"Whoa, don't bring your problems to me. You work them out."

Will eyed his older daughters and waited for the resolution. He knew that Mary showed good sense when it came to their girls. And he knew what was coming.

"Why, it's not even gold," Ruby said. "It's only yellow paint."

Sharon grabbed for the necklace, but Ruby was quicker. "Spoil sport," she called.

Mary turned back to her stove. "In five minutes I'll be done with these pancakes. If you're still arguing, I'll have myself a new necklace, and I don't care whether it's gold or paint."

"But, Mother," Sharon said.

Mary ignored Sharon's plea and turned the cakes.

Sharon glared at her mother's back, but Will knew that wouldn't bring her relief. Mary was resolute when it came to managing her girl's petulance.

For a few moments Sharon continued to frown, but when Mary paid no attention, Sharon's anger dissipated and she proposed a practical solution. "Okay," she said, "you wear it until after breakfast, but then I get it back."

"I'll wear it all day," Ruby said, but when Mary scowled in her direction, she relented. "Okay, after breakfast."

Will wasn't surprised that Ruby, without much enthusiasm for the bargain, agreed. The girls lost more than one pretty trinket when they wouldn't solve their own problems. His Mary was a smart woman. She sure knew how to stop the bickering, and with so little effort.

But Catherine hardly noticed. It seemed that her mind was on other things. "Daddy, I still dream about the puppet man."

"Puppet man?" Will supposed she referred to the Punch and Judy stories he read at night. "They're not scary. They're just dolls, my dear."

"They can be scary, Will." Mary dropped a buckwheat cake onto his plate. "For a little girl. They do pound on each other. Maybe it's best that you not read those stories to Catherine, not just yet anyhow."

"I don't think Punch and Judy stories scare her," Sharon said.

"Oh?" Mary said.

"I think it's the real puppet man," Ruby said.

"What's that?" Mary said.

"Ruby," Sharon hissed. But it was too late.

"What's this real puppet man?" Will said.

"The one at the circus," Ruby said. "He looked awful." She grimaced. "His face was all wood and tin."

"He was sad," Catherine said.

"We weren't going to tell," Sharon said. "Grandma told us not to go to the sideshows, but we disobeyed."

"But we thought you wouldn't mind," Ruby said. "We talked about it. It was just a puppet show."

"And was it?" Mary said.

Ruby fidgeted. "Well, not quite. Not like Punch and Judy."

"Tell me all about it," Mary said as she turned to her oldest and most reluctant daughter.

Sharon broke down in tears, but she confessed all. She told how Grandma had warned them not to go to sideshows, and then she pointed her finger at Ruby. "She bought the first ticket."

Ruby remained silent, but Will saw her eyes spit daggers at her older sister.

Sharon told how the puppet man was big, how he danced and laughed and even sang if you gave him money. And she said that Catherine gave him a penny, told how Catherine wandered away when they were on the Ferris wheel. "I knew we shouldn't have left her alone," Sharon said. And she broke into a dismal crying spell.

"Go on," Mary said.

Sharon caught her breath and told how Mr. Heinzelman found Catherine with the puppet man. How Heinzelman was mad and sent the puppet man away. "I know we shouldn't have done it," Sharon said. "It was my fault. I'm the oldest and should have stopped them." She glared at Ruby. "We should have obeyed Grandma."

"Tell me about the puppet man," Will said. "What did he look like?"

Mary turned to Catherine. "Did he scare you?"

"When he yanked me. But I was mostly scared when Mr. Heinzelman hollered."

"When he yanked you?" Mary said.

"When he pulled me away from that naughty man."

"Did he hurt you?" Mary said.

"No. Puppet man was nice," Catherine said.

"Mr. Heinzelman didn't think so," Ruby said. "He was mad as he chased him away."

Will persisted. "Tell me about him. Everything you can remember."

That night in bed, Will said, "Do you think it could have been Jesse?"

"Not likely. There are lots of wounded veterans out there these days, them and other poor vagrants. It could have been anyone."

"But it could have been him. The description fits."

"I guess we'll never know."

Will wasn't about to give up. The next morning he called Mary's mother. She told him, "I don't know who brought Heinzelman's Circus to town, but I'll ask around. Someone must know."

"Do that, Mary, then get back to me."

36

Will knew that Frank was desperate and would do anything to get Gertrude out of his house. Will wasn't sure how they'd do it, but he promised his brother he'd help move their father's new two-story, eight-room house a quarter mile up the hill to a lot that Frank purchased at the north end of Ashley Springs. Now that the price of everything had plummeted, Frank looked like a genius for hoarding money over the years. He was one of the few people that Will knew who had available funds. And cash was king these days.

The house, owned by St. Mary's Catholic Church and on the Church grounds, had been converted into a school, but with enrollment plummeting and repairs needed, St. Mary's was eager to be rid of it. So they sold it to Frank for a dollar. And Thomas intended to convert it back into a home. With time on his hands, he planned to do the needed repairs.

"I didn't think Gertrude's living with Frank would work." Mary laughed. "Gertrude means well. She's like her father. She thinks she knows what's best for everyone."

"Frank just shakes his head when I mention Mom, but he sure complains about Dad's swigs on the bottle."

"I'm with him on that." She glared at Will. "Frank may be the only sensible man in the family."

"Did you hear that Dad had to wet Father McCrery's tonsils to get permission to move the house to Thomas's vacant lot? It took a quart of good whiskey to convince him." Will pulled a blanket up to his chin. "It's getting nippy out. I hope there's no frost on the hill tomorrow."

"Surely he didn't think your father would live on the parish grounds."

"Father McCrery wanted them to hire a mover, but Frank balked at that."

"I suppose Father McCrery thinks you'll drop it on parish property, and they'll have a mess on their hands."

"Kinda nervous 'bout it myself."

The next morning began cool and cloudy. Will hoped they wouldn't get caught with a muddy slope. When Will arrived at seven o'clock, Frank, Thomas, and five of Frank's neighbors busied themselves around the house, but it was the horses that caught Will's attention. A stunning sight. Three teams of Belgians and two of Percherons. Will didn't think there could be a more beautiful sight than a matched pair of Belgians. Magnificent beasts, almost twenty hands high with long golden manes, the same color as the hair tufts over their hocks. Stately animals. And they knew it. They moved with the egotistical gait of royalty. He was told that Clydesdales were more impressive, but he hadn't seen a Clydesdale, so he wasn't about to demote Belgians to second place.

"Frank, how can I help?" He saw they already removed the front porch and jacked the house a sliver above the foundation. Knowing Frank, Will supposed they had been there since daylight.

"Jump down in the hole and give Les a hand," Frank said. He pointed to a trench they had started to dig toward the east side of the house. They dug for an hour while the five others worked in their holes. All except Thomas. He supervised. "You gotta make those holes longer, boys." Thomas removed a flask from his coverall pocket and took a long swig, but he didn't offer it around. "We'll never get those big logs underneath if we can't shove them across level. We're not digging post holes, now are we?"

Les groaned, but Will nodded in agreement. The old man knew his digging, but Will wondered if he'd show his flask at the far side, where Frank was.

By noon, the six holes were dug. Then they placed four inch flagstones at the bottom of each hole, against the openings in the foundation. "Lay them firm, boys, and be sure they're level," Thomas called down. "It's not patio work we be doin' today, now is it?"

Thomas ran from one side to the other, suggesting and cajoling while the men sweated under the rising sun. Whenever he was away from Frank, he pulled his flask. "Gotta wet the tonsils, keep the voice strong," he called down to Will while brandishing the flask in his direction. "Can't be misunderstood, now can I?" Sweat trickled off his brow. "Could lose the whole house if you boys don't do it right. It's an awful responsibility." He took another swig.

After a morning of preparation, Thomas shouted the horsemen forward, but when the ten horses pulled, the logs creaked and groaned as if in agony, but nothing moved.

"Will, go get a couple pails of pea gravel," Thomas said. "Works like ball bearings. My wagon's full of the stuff. And Les, get the fellas to help you bring those saplings that I piled alongside the house." He bit a chaw from his tobacco plug. "We'll move this old house uphill on ball and roller bearings."

Thomas took another swig from his flask but didn't bother to hide it from Frank. The old man was feeling his oats. Will marveled at his father's wisdom. He may drink a bit much, but he knew his stuff, and everyone there believed it. Thomas was king of the hill today.

They inched upward, and whenever the skids slowed, Thomas dumped pea gravel along the path or urged the men to lay another sapling. Slow but steady, and when the house listed to one side, Thomas and his sons shoveled dirt and laid pebbles in front of the lower skid to bring it level.

By early evening they had dragged the house onto the vacant lot. Thomas looked to the skies. "If the Lord keeps that rain up there, we'll get her done in the morning." He spat a stream of tobacco juice in front of a skid. "Gertrude might be fretful 'bout a swimming hole in the basement. Wouldn't trouble me none, but she can't swim." Thomas removed the flask from his coverall's pocket and took another swig, once again paying no attention to Frank.

That night Will told Mary about the day's work. "Frank may be paying for it, but it's Dad who knows what he's doing. I think he works best lubricated with a little whiskey."

"How would you know? He's always a bit lubricated. No wonder Jesse took to liquor. At least Frank has some sense, but I'll never know how he escaped your father's influence."

"Have you heard from your mother? About the circus."

"Why, yes, I almost forgot. Mother said that Mr. Liddiecoat—he's the storekeeper—brought the circus to town. Said he'd call the booking agent to get their schedule. Mother'll get back to us."

The next morning, Will arrived at the worksite early. He knew they would need the whole crew to get the house on its new foundation. It was bound to be a touchy operation.

But apparently his father had no concerns. As chipper as a robin snatching worms after a rainfall, Thomas directed the crew through the job. Will noticed the flask peeking from his father's coverall pocket, but didn't see him take a drink, not yet anyhow.

"Now, fellas, our problem is getting this old girl centered." He spat a wad of tobacco. "If we don't get her lined up square, we're in for trouble, now that's for sure."

When Will saw his father take out his flask, he knew that Thomas had a plan. He always launched his ship with a swig of whiskey. "Okay, boys, unload those butt end logs and stone flats I hauled from the old foundation this morning, and run those logs through the rock we took out."

Will watched his father work and noticed that no one, not even Frank, argued with his commands. And Frank didn't complain about his drinking either, although Will saw him wince each time his father took a mouthful.

Later Thomas watched the horses slowly pull the house onto the new foundation. "Gotta keep her perfectly straight," he yelled. He took another swig from his flask, wiped the back of his hand across a trickle that flowed down his chin, but never took his eyes off the timbers.

Will had never seen his dad waste a drop of good whiskey before.

"Keep her movin', boys, but go slow."

The big, two-story house inched across the void.

At first Will wasn't sure they would make it that day, but at the noon whistle, they lowered the house onto its new foundation.

Will was glad to see Gertrude and Mary trudging up the hill with picnic baskets and pitchers. "Have you heard more about Heinzelman's Circus?" he said.

"Mother called back," Mary said. Heinzelman changed booking agents. His old agent has no idea."

While they ate their ham sandwiches and drank lemonade, Will told Frank about Catherine's puppet man, how he thought he might be Jesse. "He's probably some place out West. I'd sure like to find him."

"No matter," Frank said. "Got no time to chase after another drunk."

Will hoped that Jesse fared better than most of the other vagrants in this land of despair.

37

ill slammed the front door behind him as he rushed into the house. "Mary. Mary, do you know what the village board has gone and done?" But when he couldn't find his wife in the downstairs, he barged through the kitchen door into the back yard. When he saw Mary on her knees weeding her lily-bed, he shouted as he ran in her direction. "Mary, they've cancelled the Fourth of July parade."

"Why'd they do that?" she said.

"I saw Mayor Zimmerman coming from Shopley's. He said the village board voted last night four to three to cancel. Those who voted no said we couldn't afford the extravagance. Said they needed the money to repair village streets."

"They do need that," Mary said. "I've never seen so many ruts."

"But I ordered a new sedan to transport the village dignitaries. I don't think Henry will let me return it. I've never cancelled an order before—not after production has started."

And that was Will's frustration. Ever since he bought the dealership, he had transported the county's dairy princess, the mayor, the board president, and the parade's Grand Marshall in the Fourth of July parade. And he planned to do it this Fourth of July, 1932, too. His leading the parade in a new, polished, black Ford sedan had come to be expected by Ashley Springs' townsfolk, and since the '29 crash, it was the only vehicle he ordered from Dearborn each year without a buyer at his end. The car's visibility to people from all across the county and their patriotic fervor for this event had always led to a quick sale. But this year he had hesitated. Then after vacillating for a week, he placed the order, hoping that, once again, his position of prominence in the parade would result in a quick sale.

When Will tried to convince Zimmerman to press the Board members to reconsider, the mayor responded, "I campaigned on fiscal restraint, Will, but even so, I spoke for it at our meeting. My hands are tied. There's not much more I can do."

"But it's our country's birthday," Will said. "We've always had a parade." He wanted to plead the financial hardship this decision posed for him, but he knew that almost everyone in town had financial hardships these days.

At first, it was just a rumor. Rich Turner stopped in his shop and said that he'd heard the village board was reconsidering their decision to cancel the parade. On the way home from work that night, Will poked his head into Mayor Zimmerman's office. "Frank, is it true? Are we going to have a parade, after all?"

"I don't know, Will. I've heard the board members are talking about it. I'm not sure what they are doing. But I wouldn't get my hopes up if I were you."

Will thought it was strange that Zimmerman was so evasive. He knew the mayor would have been in the middle of the discussions. If Tommy were still here, he'd be more forthcoming.

Will planned to ask Mary if she had heard anything, but that night, she'd left for a choir practice before he got home, and later, when she stepped through the door and before he got his question out, she proclaimed, "Good news, Will. Evelyn Krause said we're going to have a Fourth of July parade, after all."

Will knew that Evelyn's husband was a Village Board member. "That's wonderful," he said. "What made them change their mind?" Now he hoped the new sedan would arrive in time. "I talked to the mayor on the way home. He didn't seem to know much about the decision."

"That's strange. Evelyn said they decided at a last minute meeting yesterday morning. It seems they've received some private money to help fund it."

Will couldn't think of anyone in town who was generous enough to finance a parade. But he was glad that someone was so publicly spirited.

His new Sedan arrived on July 1st, enough time for him to wax and polish the outside and scrub the inside. With so little other work, he spent more time than usual spiffing up his new baby. He wanted it to be a proper carriage for this year's dignitaries, and he knew the parade route would be lined with people. Free events brought crowds like food brought ants because freebies were the only kind of entertainment that most people could afford these days. He knew that many people along the route would admire his new Ford sedan, but only a few would have the money to purchase it. This car would shine like no other he'd offered to the public. If there were no buyers, it wouldn't be because he hadn't prepared it properly. He was never sure why, but being the leader in such a prestigious event attracted far more attention to his vehicles than anything else that he did. It was the best advertising he could get. And at so little cost: a day's worth of elbow grease. With renewed vigor, he continued his waxing into the afternoon.

When on July 4th he drove his car from the building, it sparkled in the sunlight. Will thought that it was the best prepared vehicle that he'd ever taken into the parade. If this Ford didn't attract a buyer … He didn't want to think about that. He'd spent the business's last dollar bringing it to town.

An hour before the parade's start, Will drove to the Methodist and Episcopal churches at the top of High Street to establish his usual place at the head of the line. When he backed to the curb at the parade's starting place, Mayor Zimmerman rushed toward his car and beckoned him out.

"Will, there's been a change in plans." He pointed toward the edge of town. "You're to wait up by the water tower."

Will felt confused. He looked up High Street, then back to Zimmerman. "We've never started the parade that far up the street before. It's too close to the highway. It could lead to all kinds of confusion."

"We're not starting the parade up there, Will. But that'll be your position this year."

"My position?" He twisted the cloth that he'd brought to remove any dust he'd accumulated on his trip up the street. "I've always led the parade. I've always driven the dignitaries. I spent all my cash for this sedan. Why didn't someone tell me?"

"Sorry, Will, but it was a last minute decision."

"Why?"

"Because it's the only way we can have a parade this year. Brock McDougal funded it, but only on the condition that he'd drive the dignitaries, that he'll take your position up front."

"But, Frank—"

Will knew it was no use. Money talked these days, and McDougal had the money. He heaved the dust cloth through the open window. It wouldn't have been like this with Tommy.

38

Will's daughter looked up, tears in her eyes. "But, Daddy, you promised!"

Sharon turned to her mother. "Dad said I could have a new dress for my class's spring ball." She ran from the living room.

Will hung his head. He felt dejected, but thought he'd done the right thing. How many promises would he break before this awful depression was over?

May 1935, almost six years after the crash, and there was no end in sight.

The O'Shaughnessy sisters were now as different as three sisters could be. Sharon, almost fourteen, looked like her father: short and, as he liked to say, pleasingly plump. But her disposition wasn't his at all. Like her Cornish ancestors, she was serious, and like her Cornish mother, practical.

Ruby was Cornish, too, and she looked it from head to toe. At eleven years old, she was almost as tall as Sharon, and she was strong and rawboned like her Grandmother Tregonning. But unlike her sisters, she was confident and strong-minded.

Catherine, two years younger than Ruby, was all O'Shaughnessy, but you wouldn't know it by looking at her. She was built like her grand-mother O'Shaughnessy, who was short and willowy like all her ances-tors before her. But like her father, Catherine was a scholar and a roman-tic. Unlike her sisters, she saw the world as she wished it to be. And she was already attractive; Will knew that when she matured, she'd be the belle of the ball.

Mary started to follow Sharon toward the stairs but instead turned back to her husband. "I know we can't afford much, but Mrs. Spaight makes beautiful feed sack dresses to sell at Samuel's. Didn't Earnest O'Doul come in to pay his bill today?"

Will had expected the payment, the money for the promised dress. "He came in, and he offered the money, but he needed medicine. His little Shaunty has the croup. They're afraid of pneumonia." Will winced at the thought. "He said he'll pay in two weeks." But Sharon's dance was this weekend. Will slumped into his big horsehair chair. "I didn't have the heart to take Shaunty's medicine. He promised he'll bring it."

"You've got a pocketful of promises, but those promises won't buy a dime's worth of groceries."

"Should I have taken it, Mary?"

"No, you couldn't take Shaunty's medicine money." Mary settled her hands into her lap. "But I feel so bad for Sharon."

Will sold few cars anymore. Now most of his work came from repairs, and they provided more promises than income. Fortunately Southwest Wisconsin farmers were becoming interested in protecting their investments, so his lightning rod sideline provided a little money.

"Did I tell you what happened up on Bill Young's barn? I'd tacked the tripod on the roof and was dropping wire down the side when a gust of wind came up. There must have been a nest under that peak, and when the wind gusted, a pair of pigeons flew at my face. I ducked to the right just as the tripod toppled over my left shoulder. If it wasn't for those birds, I'd have gone tail over teakettle off that roof."

"How odd. Might those be the same pigeons that saved you on Wes Schmidt's barn?"

"They must be my guardian angels."

Will sighed. All the stories in his imaginative reservoir wouldn't solve his financial problems. He longed for those days before the crash, for the days he sold so many cars that he couldn't keep up. Will hadn't believed his grandfather, hadn't believed that being heartless was necessary to succeed. But he was beginning to wonder.

Will continued to fret about his inability to buy Sharon a new dress, so when Mary's cousin approached him, he was receptive to Joe's idea, but he wasn't sure that Mary would agree to the girls' missing school.

"Joe wants Ruby and Catherine to plant his potatoes this year," he said to Mary.

"I thought Ira's boys planted for him."

"Not this year. Ira needs them at home. It should only take a couple days."

"Missing one school day shouldn't hurt, but that's all," Mary said. "They can finish after school."

"My prayers have been answered," Catherine said. "I so want to help Sharon."

"We'll have to work fast, though," Ruby chimed in. "Sharon's ball is Saturday night."

Will saw them coming down the street. They were so intent in their argument that they failed to see him.

"Cheating is bad," Catherine said.

"Cousin Joe would want to help Sharon," Ruby said.

"Then why didn't we tell him we dumped—?"

"Whoa, girls," Will said. "What's this about cheating?"

Ruby stopped short.

Catherine turned red.

"Miss Angel caught that nasty Wright boy cheating in math today," Ruby said, "and she lectured us all."

Will wondered what cheating had to do with Cousin Joe, but he let it go.

Ruby reached the five dollar bill forward. "We want you to give this to Sharon," Ruby said.

"I can't give it to her. You earned it."

"It's the broken promise that's upset her. We want you to give it." Ruby turned to Catherine. "Don't we, sis?"

Catherine nodded.

"Girls," Will said, "I can't take your bill. I've already broken the promise, but I couldn't help that. I can't lie to Sharon, too. You earned it, you give her the money. We can't tarnish your generosity with a lie, now can we?"

39

Will had thought that summer driving would bring increased business, because the cars stored through the winter might need repairs, but it appeared he was wrong. He studied the books. Five pages full of debtors and not one from whom he could demand payment. Profit was meager as cash trickled in. Why hadn't he taken an agency that catered to the money in town, like the Olds' dealership down the street? He could have bought that dealership, but he was so sure that Henry was right, pricing cars for the little guy, that he never considered taking a more prestigious brand.

Since the crash, only the guys with money could afford new cars, and they weren't buying Fords. He knew now that he'd made a mistake, but it was a bit late to whine about it. Will knew that opportunity always looked bigger from the back side. His customers needed repairs but had little money to pay for them. He supposed that's why they were called the little guys.

Will was wary when Ernie Peavey ambled through the front door. Ernie had never been in serious trouble, but he was known for cutting corners when it benefited him, even if it came at another's expense. Will remembered the time that Ernie sold a genuine Civil War rifle that he said was fired at the battle of Shiloh. It turned out to be a parade piece that had never seen a battlefield. Apparently Ernie had never made an effort to authenticate the rifle—or so he said when threatened with a lawsuit. But he gave the money back.

Ernie swatted the gumball machine.

"Hey, go easy on that, Ernie. I can't afford repairs."

"I thought there might be a loose one waitin' to pop out."

"Do you need a penny?"

"Only if it's on the house."

Ernie strolled through the shop fingering a few items as he worked his way toward the tire display. "Kinda lean pickin's, I'd say." He looked close and squinted as he rotated a tire. "Seventeen-inch, I'm in luck. I'm desperate for a set of tires. Back and forth to Madison each week has worn mine to a frazzle. I don't think I'll make it another week. I gotta feed the wife and kids, you know."

"Can you pay for them?" Ernie made good money as an office manager in Madison, better than he could in Ashley Springs, but being gone all week must be hard on Amber and the kids. Ten, if Will remembered right.

"I've been home all week, but I'm driving back this afternoon. Got lots of catchin' up to do, but I get paid tomorrow. I'll bring the money Saturday and pay the whole bill."

"I'm sorry, Ernie. I can't give credit anymore. I don't have anything left to replace those tires. It's been rough."

"It's only two days."

"Sorry, Ernie."

"Say, Will, did you see that old man Kelsey died last week? Do you remember that time when he was about to call the sheriff on you? I saved your butt that day. Remember?"

"I found out later that you stole those melons. I was unlucky enough to be hunting near by."

"It would have been your sweet ass if I hadn't told him I saw those Hinton boys with a car full of melons."

"Maybe so."

Ernie approached Will and looked him in the eye. "Do you remember the time I told Principal Perkins you were at my house helping Dad fix his hay rack, when you'd really skipped school to go fishing? Do you remember, Will?"

Will nodded.

"You owe me."

"I haven't any money to replace my inventory. I have three kids."

"Three? Try ten on for size. I've got to get to Madison. You'll have your money Saturday. I'll be here by noon."

Will didn't know what to tell Mary. He hoped there would be repair money, but he doubted it. He didn't even have lightning rods to sell.

Will felt down all day, but he took pleasure in Sharon and her sisters' excitement over the new dress. They'd place it on layaway at Samuel's, and Mrs. Spaight would fit it Saturday afternoon, just in time for the ball that night.

Two days seemed endless. With little repair work, Will tinkered with old parts, cleaned empty shelves, and scrubbed clean the greasy floors. Walt Frederickson wanted a set of seventeen-inch tires, but he went to Brock McDougal's when Will told him that he wouldn't have any until next week. How long could he hold out? His grandfather was right. He had to get nasty.

For the rest of Thursday Will practiced saying "no" while he imagined friends asking for credit. He seemed to be gaining ground on nastiness when he heard Ruby tell Catherine, "Daddy's sure out of sorts." His new-found temperament shouldn't affect his family, he thought, so on Friday he tried being nice.

On Saturday Will left home early. He didn't want to miss Ernie. Today he decided to squeegee out the oil pit—a dirty job—but he felt the need right now. He would work until Ernie got there; then he would go home for the day. He'd hitch Fanny to the buggy and take Mary for a ride, maybe to her mother's in Hinton. She'd like that.

Will scrubbed the grease pit until his knuckles bled. He knew he couldn't get the pit any cleaner, but he still scraped. It was almost noon, but no Ernie. He said he'd be here before noon. Will scrubbed another hour, and then he went to his office. What could have happened?

How many rings? Was it three shorts and a long? Where was that phone listing? He looked through his desk drawers, in the magazine rack, and behind the gum dispenser, but found no list. Then he remembered: Bridget O'Shea borrowed it the week before. She must not have returned it. He rang one long, the operators signal, and waited. Probably on another line. He paced the floor for a while before trying again. This time, he heard, "Operator."

"This is Will O'Shaughnessy. Can you ring me through to Ernie Peavey? I can't find my listing."

"Sure, Will, but you're not going to find him home. I overheard his wife talking to her mother this morning. Ernie didn't come back from Madison today. When she called his office, they said he'd not been at work all week. Neither had his secretary. His boss suspects they've run off together. Amber was in tears. Poor woman."

Will dropped the phone. Poor woman indeed, but what would he tell Mary? His nastiness had come too late.

Will strolled toward home. Grandfather was right.

At first Will thought Mary was going to cry. Then she lifted her head and lightly caressed his cheek. "Will, these are bad times, but we'll see them through somehow."

"I should have known better. Ernie didn't become a scoundrel overnight. I was bound to get muddied, wallowing with a pig. But—"

"Let's take a ride in the country, Will."

When they returned, the three girls waited in the parlor. "Daddy," Sharon said. "Ruby heard that Ernie Peavey ran off and didn't pay his bill, that you can't afford more tires. We went to Samuels' while you were gone, and he agreed to take the dress off layaway and not charge a thing. I want you to have the money for a new set of tires. We all want that."

Will sat down. "I can't take your money," he said. "It's because of me that you needed it."

"We all agree," Sharon said. "Our family is more important than any ol' dress. We want it this way. We're family, good times or bad."

Will watched Mary attach a blue sash to the old mauve dress and add a panel and pleat to enhance the bodice. It was as close to store bought as any old dress could be.

"It sure looks like new," Will said.

And the three girls agreed.

Will surged through his door, a newsprint advertisement in his hand. "Did you see this?" he shouted toward Mary who sat mending a dress. Will thrust the advertisement under her nose. "That McDougal has cut his prices. He's offering an oil change and full vehicle inspection for half my cost. He can't even cover his expenses at that amount."

"It doesn't sound like good business to me." Mary said.

"Not unless you want to drive out the competition. It's the Chicago way. I'll bet his inspections will produce more money than an oil change price."

And it didn't end there. A stream of advertisements followed offering cut-rate prices on every repair that Will did, prices below Will's cost of materials and labor.

Then by chance, Will met Brock McDougal coming from Samuels' Department store. At first he thought he'd ignore him, but when McDougal had the audacity to ask if his business was thriving these days, Will couldn't hold back. "What are you trying to do McDougal, drive us both out of business?"

"I don't know what you mean, O'Shaughnessy." He flashed an easy, confident smile. "My business is doing just fine."

And to look at him, you'd have believed every word of it. He wore a custom-tailored brown suit with a tight-fitting, narrow-shouldered jacket and a pinstriped trousers. A gold watch fob hung from his vest pocket and his brown shoes reflected the sunlight. He looked more like a banker than a car repairman. But Will knew that McDougal never saw the underside of his customer's automobiles.

"You can't afford those prices you're advertising," Will said. Are you trying to do drive me out? Are these bloodthirsty practices your Chicago style?"

"I sell Oldsmobiles, or I should say, they sell themselves. I don't worry about competition. They aren't writing songs about Fords." He turned and walked down the street, but not before he smiled in Will's direction and loudly hummed the chorus of "In Your Merry Oldsmobile."

Will couldn't believe the man's nerve.

41

Will resolved to get tough but he knew that making resolutions was easy. His new Goodyears filled his window display space, and today he busily installed brake linings on the Ford sedan that Tony Filardo dropped off that morning. His business from Italians increased monthly, and he was thankful for that. When treated fairly, these first generation Americans became loyal customers.

Mr. Parker, a teller at the Ashley Springs Community Bank, inquired about a new Ford roadster and even spent time looking through the pretty promotional pictures. A bright red, five-window coupe caught his eye.

"You'll look mighty sporty in that when you drive about town," Will said.

Parker said he'd get back to him.

Will's spirits lifted. Maybe he could get a little farther ahead of the red line.

The bell which Will recently installed interrupted his pleasant rumination. He'd decided to install the doorbell when he found it difficult to hear customers while he worked in the rear. Will shielded his eyes from the morning sunlight that surged through the bay window. "That you, Charlie? How can I help?" Charlie Nesbitt was one of Will's favorite customers. When he lived at home on the farm, Charlie and his wife, Esther, were his parents' neighbors and best friends.

"I need to take Esther to St. Louis to see her sister. We got a call saying she's pretty sick, may not last much longer. I don't know if I can make it though. Tires are bad. I need a set of seventeen inchers. I'll make the payments."

What was it with seventeen-inch tires? Will felt that he was the one with family at risk. He sighed, sat down, and pulled the spiral ledger from his desk drawer. "You know I'd like to help, but I can't do it anymore." He held the notebook out and flicked through the pages. Tough, gotta stay tough, he thought. "All these entries are customers who owe me."

"I'm sorry, Will. I suppose I'm in there, too. Still owe on that engine work."

"I'm not meanin' to push you for that money, but I can't do more credit. You probably heard that Ernie Peavey ran off with his secretary. Well, he ran off with my seventeen-inch tires, too." Will walked to the window display and placed his hand on a tire. "The kids gave me the cash to buy this set. I can't do it, Charlie. I don't have the money to replace these."

"I'm not sure what I'll tell Esther." Charlie Nesbitt hung his head. "She's in a bad way. They're close, her sister and her. I'll just have to chance it, I guess."

Will slammed the ledger down and stepped toward the door. "Let's look at those tires."

Charlie followed him into the street.

Will walked around the Model A, a frown on his face. "Not good, Charlie. Don't think you'll get far. Can't you delay the trip until you can afford the tires, or … I'll tell you what." He turned to Charlie. "Wait until I get a little money ahead. Mr. Parker was in this morning. You know, the bank teller. He's interested in a new car. If I get that money, I'll give you credit. I'll do that, Charlie."

"I don't think we can wait much longer. The doctor told Esther that Susan may not have a month left."

"Try to delay a bit." He grasped Charlie's arm lightly. "I should get that money soon. Not likely you can survive a trip and not have a blowout. That front left one doesn't have many miles left in it."

"It wouldn't be the first tire I've changed, except I don't have a spare."

"No spare? I've got an old tire out back. It's not much, but it's no worse than that front one." Will pointed to the bald tire. "You can have it for free. Try to hold out a bit longer. I'll call when Parker buys that car."

A week passed, then two. Will didn't hear from Parker, but when he dialed home to tell Mary he would be late for supper, Mrs. Clark told him that Parker purchased a new Oldsmobile that very morning. She also said that Charlie and Esther Nesbitt left for St. Louis. Will slammed the receiver onto the hook. Charlie had no business risking their lives.

That night at supper Will and Mary sat alone. The girls were away practicing for the village's annual summer concert. Will told Mary the Nesbitts had left town. "I should have given him the tires. He always pays his bills. Mother'll never forgive me if something happens to Esther." Will shook his head and grimaced. "You know how much Mother likes her."

"Will, stop your worrying. Most of what we worry about won't happen anyhow. You can't be responsible for everyone. Your name's not Carnegie, you know. Besides, where would you get money to replace those tires?"

Will forked through his beans. "I know. I had little choice, but I just have a bad feeling."

"Eat your supper, dear. I promised Ruby and Catherine that we'd go to their performance tonight. They've been practicing all week. Ruby's voice is stronger, but Catherine's is so sweet it brings tears to my eyes when she sings 'Londonderry Air.'"

"That and 'Galway Bay' are my favorites." He cleared his throat. "Oh, Danny boy—"

Mary gave him a push. "Git outa here, you big lug."

Will spent most of the next two weeks on barns, working on two lightning rod jobs which came his way. He always felt better when he led his horses from their stalls and drove his wagon into the country. Even the rigging felt good in his hands. And it felt like home every time he drove past the fields and into a farmer's yard. He'd slow Fanny or Mabel and survey the crops. He always felt excited when he saw new growth emerge after the rains, and he'd look the cattle over carefully whenever he approached a barn where the cows milled around the yard. He tried to identify the high producers, those that he'd want for his herd. And he inhaled deeply whenever he smelled the pungent odor of corn silage. Why, even the manure smelled good to him.

Lately, the urge to return to the land edged into Will's consciousness more than ever before. He had always planned to do it, but the time was never right. Now, what did he have to lose? He wasn't sure how much longer he could take the strain of a failing business. But it was his family that worried him the most. How could he ask Mary to leave their lovely home? But that wasn't the pressing problem. How was he going to get out from under his sinking ship?

Until Saturday afternoon, when their son-in-law stepped into his shop, the Nesbitts were lost in the shadows of Will's mind. "I didn't expect you here today. Your sign says you close at noon."

"Usually, Hank, but I've got some paper work. Have you heard from Charlie and Esther?"

"Jane talked to them yesterday. They're leaving tomorrow. If all goes well, they should be home Tuesday."

Will thought about the tires and his stomach churned, but he didn't mention them to Hank.

"Esther believes her sister's a bit stronger. The doctor said her visit has perked Susan up, and he thinks there may be some remission, but the prognosis is bleak. Esther's happy they took the trip now, though."

Will nodded, but he couldn't keep his mind off the tires.

Then on Tuesday morning the shop telephone rang. It was Mrs. Clark. "Will, Jane just got a call from some burg in Iowa. Esther was killed in an accident this morning, and Charlie's in the hospital, hurt bad."

"Dear God, no!"

"I don't know the details. Hank and Jane are leaving immediately."

Will closed the shop and shuffled the ten blocks home.

"You don't know it was the tires," Mary said. "And even if it was a tire, you had to say no."

The funeral was Saturday. Thomas, Gertrude, and all their friends attended. Frank was there, two aisles over, but Jesse was nowhere to be seen. Will supposed he didn't even know, wherever he was. Charlie, still confined to a hospital bed, couldn't be there. The church was filled with Esther's family and friends, but Will sat in back.

After the burial, Will waited in the parking lot by Hank's car. "Have they found out more about the accident, Hank?"

"I talked with the local police but didn't learn much. They said Charlie's car veered across the highway into a truck. I didn't ask Charlie, not yet."

When they were ready to return home, Fanny eased forward when Will flicked the reins over her back.

"Esther looked real nice," Mary said. "You'd never know she was in an accident. It's too bad Charlie couldn't have seen her. She looked so peaceful."

Will didn't answer. Her death was so unnecessary. They should never have taken the trip. Not on those tires.

Mary grasped her husband's arm. "Snap out of it, Will. You told him not to go."

"Do you know that their car veered across the road into a truck? It must have been a blowout. That's the only possible explanation."

Will continued to think about Charlie. He even considered driving to Iowa, but Mary soon dissuaded him of that idea.

"First, Will, the doctors won't let him come home, so they probably don't want him to have visitors either. And what's to be gained?"

Will thought that peace of mind was worth something. He'd feel better if he knew that it wasn't a tire that caused the accident.

"Talking to Charlie about it won't bring Esther back, and so soon afterwards, it might make Charlie worse. You'd not want that, would you?"

Will knew that Mary was right, but he fussed all day until his attention was yanked in another direction when he picked up the Ashley Springs' *Weekly* that afternoon. When he slipped the newspaper from its wrapper another of Brock McDougal's advertisements fell to the floor. And when Will reached for it, gigantic headlines grabbed his attention: "THEY DON'T WRITE SONGS ABOUT FORDS". Then McDougal wrote a ditty in which he asked Lucille and every other lady in Ashley Springs to come ride in his merry Oldsmobile. And he had the audacity to promise anyone who currently owned a Ford that if they'd switch to an Oldsmobile, he'd give them a ten percent reduction in their price and free oil changes for a year.

Will stormed to his desk, crumpled the advertisement, and threw it against the wall. McDougal had badmouthed Fords ever since he opened his Olds dealership two months before the market crashed. Will had thought it was bad timing, but he hadn't accounted for some people profiting while everyone else went broke. With prices plummeting, cash was king, and those who had cash were Oldsmobile customers. Will didn't have the money to compete against McDougal's predatory attacks. Will wanted more than ever to get away from this madness, to get back to a sane life. The farmers he knew might strive to outdo their neighbor, but they always helped when things turned bad.

Two weeks later, Hank brought Charlie home. Although Dr. Ruggles recommended only family, Will couldn't stay away. He found Charlie awake in bed, propped up by two pillows. Clean bandages covered the left side of his head, and his left leg, a large cast on it, protruded from under the light blanket. He flashed a wan smile when Will entered the room.

"Charlie, I'm so sorry. Was it a tire?"

"I've thought about the accident every day since. I don't remember much. I must have blacked out. Iowa has those curbs along the road, you know."

Will nodded.

"We got started early that morning, and the sun was in my eyes. The last I remember is bouncing off that curb."

Will watched Charlie twist on the bed, could see he was uncomfortable.

"The sheriff told me that the left front tire was flat after the accident, probably from the collision. The other tires were still good. If a blowout pulled me into that curb, it would have been a right tire, don't you think?" Charlie winced, adjusted his pillow, and pushed himself higher. "Rest easy, Will. I don't think the tires had anything to do with the accident."

42

Will couldn't get farming off his mind. Somehow, he had to find a way to get back, but that was impossible unless he could sell his business. And nobody was buying businesses these days, certainly not a failing one. He knew that McDougal was trying to undercut him, trying to push him out. And he hated the man for it, but maybe he could turn McDougal's zeal to his own favor. Will gathered all of McDougal's attack ads that he had saved, packaged them, attached a letter, and dropped them off at the post office. If he wanted to get back to farming, it was time to make a bold move.

Will walked through his competitor's front door. He could see that McDougal wasn't hurting for inventory. Two new Oldsmobiles set on his large showroom floor, and floor-to-ceiling shelves loaded with parts hid all the outside walls. Tires of every imaginable size filled racks spaced across the room. McDougal wasn't short of money. But the thing that made Will cringe was what he saw through the big doors that opened to the back showroom, the room where McDougal displayed his used cars: three Model A Fords with large for sale signs stuck to their wind screens. McDougal's advertising was paying its way.

As Will approached, McDougal got off his chair and stepped toward him. With a wide smile plastered across his face, he reached for Will's hand. Doesn't this man have any shame? He'd rather be anyplace else, but it was his only chance to get back to the farm.

"What can I do for you today, Will?"

Will cringed. McDougal acted as if they were old friends. "McDougal, you've been pushing hard to get me out of the way. Why don't you make a good offer for my business?"

"You want to sell you're dealership? I don't think I'd want it."

"Looks from here like you might have an interest. You've been doing your best to pry it loose these last few months. There are lots of Ford owners in the area." Will decided to stick the knife in a bit. "Most wouldn't be seen dead in an Oldsmobile."

"Most couldn't afford an Oldsmobile," McDougal countered.

Will knew that McDougal was right, and he also knew that was his advantage. "Someone will want to service their needs if I leave. And there will always be customers for reasonably priced cars. This depression can't last forever."

"I can probably have both dealerships if I wait long enough."

"Don't be so sure about that. Come over to see me in a week or two. I may have information that'll burst your pipe dream. Good day." Will tipped his fedora and turned toward the door.

A week later, to the day, Brock McDougal walked through the door.

"Good morning, McDougal. Did you decide to make an offer?"

McDougal smiled, but without a word, he walked through the office and into the garage. He engaged the lift, raised it a foot, and then lowered it back to the floor. He walked to the sink, pumped water, and watched it drain; then he turned his attention to the two used oil barrels. After shaking each, he reentered the shop, turned the tires, and inspected their labeling. McDougal ambled over to Will's desk, but remained silent. He took the promotion book from Will's desk and thumbed through the pages, scanned each picture.

"I can see you're having a tough time making a go of it. You've got little inventory. You're selling cars outa the book. And your oil barrels are empty, but Smith hasn't been around to collect used oil for almost a month. You must be cash poor." He set the promotion book back on the desk. "There's no profit in your dealership now, but this depression can't last forever. I have the resources to see it through, and someday people will buy Fords again. I plan to be here when they line up at the door."

"So you'll make an offer?"

"Why'd I do that? It looks to me that if I wait awhile, it'll fall into my hands."

"McDougal, I think you've outsmarted yourself this time." Will pulled an envelope from the desk's top drawer. "If you want this dealership, you're going to pay for it."

"I don't give out gifts, O'Shaughnessy."

"And you'll pay a fair price."

Will pulled a letter from the envelope. "Listen to this, then rethink your position."

Will read:

Dear Mr. O'Shaughnessy:

You've represented the Ford Company well these last twenty years. We've never had a complaint from your customers, and you've honored your contracts with us. I'm sorry to hear that you are considering the sale of your dealership, but I know how difficult it's been for our business these last six years. I don't think this economy can continue in the doldrums forever, but I admit, I can see no end to it soon.

If you decide to sell your dealership, we will transfer your contract to the next owner as long as he is financially solvent and, in our opinion, able to conduct a successful business. But if you terminate your contract because of an adverse competitive situation, we will be hesitant to continue doing business in Ashley Springs.

I have personally inspected all of the advertising materials that you have mailed to me, and I assure you, if you are forced to close your business because of these predatory practices, we will not negotiate a contract with Mr. Brock McDougal.

Sincerely,

Howard H. Smithson
Dealership Relations
Ford Motor Company

Brock McDougal pulled a chair and sat down.

Will slowly reinserted the letter into its envelope, then he walked to McDougal and looked down on him. "It looks like you may have some thinking to do. You just said that you want this dealership. Make me an offer."

McDougal didn't respond, but he got off his chair and walked slowly toward the door. Before he stepped through it, he turned back to Will.

"O'Shaughnessy, I underestimated you, it seems. Give me some time to think about it. I'll get back to you."

Will wasn't sure just how badly McDougal wanted the business. What if he didn't make an offer? And what if he did? How would he tell Mary? Will closed the shop and strolled to the stable. Fanny Too looked up but didn't move. Mabel stood in the back of her stall and chewed a mouthful of hay, but Fanny stopped eating, plodded forward, and nuzzled his face. Good old Fanny. Will scratched her neck. She seemed to feel his distress. "What do you think, old girl? Can we make a living if I sell the business?"

Fanny nickered softly.

"You think we can, do you? I'd like more time together, old friend. But I think you want to be rid of those awful machines, now don't you?"

She tossed her head and whinnied again. Will suspected that she knew exactly what he said.

When Will told Mary about his interaction with McDougal, she wasn't as enthusiastic as Fanny. "How can we pay the bills? Can you expand the lightening rod business? Can it provide more than food money? We don't have to sell, you know."

Will paced the kitchen floor. "The more I think on it, the more I think this may be opportunity calling. Grandpa Duffy would say, 'When you're at the bottom of a deep hole, it might be time to stop digging.' I don't know if I can make a living selling lightening rods. Maybe that's not the answer, but I know it's hard to sell a business at a fair price anymore. Few people have the money. But Brock McDougal sure does."

McDougal caught Will in the garage changing oil on Dennis Newberry's Model A. "I'm starting to fill that oil barrel, McDougal. Business is picking up."

"Not fast enough to save you, O'Shaughnessy."

"You're still playing hardball?"

"I want your dealership. I'll pay you a thousand dollars for it. That's a fair offer. Better than you'll get elsewhere."

"I'll think about it, but you think, too, McDougal. I'm not so desperate that I have to sell now." Will felt far more desperate than he let on. He wanted to get out. "Give me fifteen hundred and I'll think real seriously about it. But I'm printing ads to send to Milwaukee and Chicago." Will hoped there would be businessmen who wanted to escape the city as badly as he wanted to get back to farming. But he knew it was a long shot. "I'll accept the first good offer."

Mary wasn't convinced. "You paid two thousand for that business, and that was twenty years ago."

"Times have changed, Mary. Fifteen hundred's a mighty good price these days. It'll give us the money to get started farming."

"Oh, Will, don't you think our business will get better soon? It was good for so many years."

"Don't worry too much over it." Will hated that Mary wasn't as enthused as he was. "He hasn't offered my price yet."

At midmorning the next day Will took a break from the garage and walked uptown to the Ashley Springs Community Bank. George Tyler knew the area. Maybe he could help. "George, do you know any farms hereabouts that are selling for a reasonable price?"

"Five years ago I had half a dozen the bank would give away, but they're long gone. I can't think of one."

Will winced.

"I know you've always wanted to farm, but what about your dealership?"

"Brock McDougal's interested in buying. I'm waiting for his reply."

"He's got the money. How much?"

"I told him fifteen hundred."

George tilted his head and arched an eyebrow. "It's more than I'd expect you to get these days, but if he sees a future in it, he'll probably pay." Tyler stood and walked around his desk toward Will, reached out a business card. "You could look for a farm away from here. I've got a brother who manages the Willow bank. Maybe there's something down there."

"Down on the Wisconsin River? That's pretty far."

"It's still in Iowa County. Looks like you'll have to leave Ashley Springs if you want to farm again."

Two days later, McDougal returned to Will's shop. "O'Shaughnessy, you've got me over a barrel. I want your business but fifteen hundred's robbery. You've got no heart, man."

Will couldn't help but laugh. "Seems to me the worms turned on this one. Not so long ago I was convinced you had icebergs in that chest. Fifteen hundred's my bottom line."

"Fifteen hundred you've got. I hope you ask forgiveness when you say your prayers tonight."

Will was already saying a prayer, but the word forgive hadn't entered his mind.

That afternoon, before Will told Mary about McDougal's offer, Tyler called and asked him to come to the bank at three on Friday. His brother would be there. This was moving too fast. He had to talk with Mary.

"Mary," Will said, "McDougal agreed to the fifteen hundred that I asked. And, I talked with George Tyler yesterday. He wants me to meet his brother from Willow."

"From down on the river? Why'd he want to see you?"

"I mentioned farms to George. His brother's a banker at Willow. Maybe he wants to push a farm on me. Maybe he wants to clear his books."

"Oh, Will." Mary slumped onto the settee. "You're intent on leaving our beautiful home?"

Will sat beside his wife. "I hadn't expected to hear back so soon. I'd have told you. You know I would have." Will saw fear in Mary's eyes. "Will you come to the meeting, too?" He took her hand. "Three o'clock, Friday."

Mary lifted her hand, stood, and straightened her dress. She looked down and frowned. "I can't. I promised Evelyn Krause that I'd help mend the choir robes. But, Will … " She paused a moment, then turned and rushed from the room.

On Friday evening Sharon carefully set a knife, fork, and spoon by Will's plate at the head of the table.

"Where's Mary and the girls?" Will said. "We need to talk."

"Mother said she might be late, that we should go ahead. Ruby and Catherine are doing a sleepover at Francine Hoskings'. What's wrong, Dad?"

"It's important, my dear, but I don't want to say anything until Mother gets here."

Will hadn't finished eating his meatloaf when Mary rushed into the house. "I don't know where we'll get the money. Those robes are threadbare. They won't last the winter. Evelyn says we'll buy new ones, but our coffers are as bare as the robes."

"Calm down," Will said. "I've got news. After we finish eating, I'll tell you about my meeting with Tyler."

Will handed his empty dish to Mary, turned toward the parlor, and took his pipe from the secretary. Then he beckoned Mary and Sharon to the living room. "I met with Tyler's brother Ron today." He lit the pipe and nodded toward Sharon. "Mother knew. I told her about the meeting yesterday. He seemed like a reasonable man."

Will glanced at Sharon who slouched in her chair and looked as if she were contemplating a visit to the dentist.

"Get on with it," Mary said.

"Well, he's got a farm on the Wisconsin River that he wants off the books. He'll let it go cheap. He—"

Sharon shrieked. "You're not thinking about leaving Ashley Springs. Leave my friends? Daddy, how could you?"

"Calm down, Sharon," Will said. "We'll decide as a family."

Without a word, Mary walked back to the kitchen.

Will wasn't surprised about Ruby and Catherine's response to leaving Ashley Springs. Mary heard them talking and later she told him, "Ruby's all for it. First she worried that she'd miss her friends, then she stomped her foot and proclaimed, 'Oh, fiddle-faddle, I'll get new ones soon enough.' But Catherine had to explore the idea before accepting it. She told Ruby, 'We'll have animals to care for: cows, sheep, and maybe a gaggle of geese.' Ruby laughed over that. But it was clear that Catherine liked that word. She kept repeating, 'Gaggle. Gaaaggle. I'll have a gaggle of new friends.' She told Ruby the word circled her throat before it flipped off her tongue."

Fanny leaned forward when Will opened the stable door. "You think I'm going to find you a scoop of oats, do you, old girl?" Will ladled a dipper from the feed bag and held it out to his horse. "And it's not just oats I be bringing this fine day. It's good news, too." Fanny crunched away on her treat. It seemed that nothing could rival a mouthful of that tasty grain. She reached toward the half full scoop. "You'd better listen. This is important. We're going farming again."

Fanny lifted her head and nuzzled Will's shoulder.

"I promised years ago, but I almost let it slip away. It's time. Yes, it is, old girl. It is time."

Fanny reached her head over the stall and whinnied her approval, but Will knew it wouldn't be so easy to persuade Mary and Sharon.

43

They gathered in the front parlor. This would be difficult, but he had to get it right. The more he thought about it, the more certain he was. He was meant to be a farmer. If he could just convince his family.

Sharon's face was tear-stained. Mary looked glum. He had't yet begun, and he was already two votes down. Ruby bounced into the room. "Daddy is it true? Are we going farming?"

"That's what we're here to discuss," Mary said. "Just sit down, Ruby. As soon as Catherine gets here, Dad will tell us all about it."

Sharon flopped into the straight-backed Quaker chair and rocked as if the frenzied movement could whisk this nightmare away. "Well, where is she? She's usually the first one here."

"Don't be cross," Mary said. "I asked her to find something. She'll be here soon."

Will was glad to delay the confrontation. He hated making life harder for Mary. It seemed their marriage had known nothing but hardship lately. He knew that she loved Ashley Springs. Like in Hinton, her birthplace down the road, the rock houses that protruded from the hills were all that remained of her Cornish heritage. Taken from the escarpments which anchored them, those houses would stand long after their wood-framed neighbors had rotted and collapsed, long after their own beautiful home was gone. And Will knew she didn't want to leave.

Catherine rushed into the room clutching a paper bag. Whatever could Mary have asked her to find? Will paused for a moment but knew he must get on with it. No use delaying the inevitable, but … "Did you hear about the old man who woke one morning and said, 'I'm dead.' His wife said, 'Don't be silly, Chester, what makes you think you're dead?' He said, 'I woke up this morning and nothing hurts. I must be dead.'"

"Daddy!" Sharon shrieked. "Are we leaving Ashley Springs?"

Will looked away.

Ruby leaned toward him. "We're going farming, aren't we, Dad? We'll have cows, chickens, and pigs. Must we get a tractor? I don't like those loud, smelly things."

"No tractors and no pigs," Will said. "But let's not get ahead of ourselves. I have a chance to buy a farm at Willow, down on the Wisconsin River."

"On the Wisconsin River? That far?" Sharon screamed. "Leave my friends? I won't do it. I won't go." She sobbed.

"Sharon," Will said, "I want your support. That's why we're here now. I want to go, and it's time. I've always been a farmer at heart. I hope you understand that." He set his jaw and straightened in his chair. "I've put it off too long. This is an opportunity I don't want to miss."

"I'll go," Ruby said. "I can't wait to ride the horses. I'll ride every day."

Will thought that it might not be so much fun when she had to do it every day.

"Let Dad tell us," Mary said. "Can we make a living at it, Will?"

"It can't be much worse than the car business right now. And we'll not go hungry, that's for sure."

Catherine raised her hand.

"Yes, Catherine?" Mary said.

"Can we take the Fannies and Mabel?"

"Everyone else is buying tractors," Mary said.

"We can't afford a tractor," Will said.' Besides, I've seen enough engines for a while."

"How can we afford any of it?" Sharon said. "If we don't have the money to live in town, how can we afford a farm and cattle? It doesn't make any sense, none at all." She broke into tears once more. "I don't want to go." She stopped rocking and stomped her foot on the floor. "I won't go!"

Will turned toward Sharon, but Mary, ignoring her irate daughter, looked toward Will and said, "Go on, Will."

"I've got an offer for the business that will give us the thousand down payment and five hundred more for working capital. The bank is eager to loan money. They're selling for the balance on the loan, and their terms are generous, too. They'll even give the money to buy the cattle we need, but I hate to take that much debt. You never know—"

"They must want it off their books," Mary said.

"I'm sure they do, but I can't get in too deep. If we can sell the house, I'll use that money to buy cattle, equipment, and seed."

"What if it doesn't sell right away?" Mary said.

Will saw the fear in Mary's eyes, but she sat straight and tall, like a teacher facing her first classroom.

"We'll rent until it sells. I'll have to borrow more, but the rent will make the payments." He eased off his chair and slowly circled the parlor, hands folded behind his back. "I've been thinking. I've got lots of ideas for farming. Better than what they're doing now." He stopped in front of his wife and reached to her. "We can make it, Mary. I know we can."

"I won't go!" Sharon screamed. "I'll ask Aunt Kate if I can stay with her. I won't leave Ashley Springs!"

Will kneeled before his daughter and took her hand. "I don't want the family to break up over this." He turned back to the others. "Do you feel the same as Sharon?"

Ruby stood, hands on her hips. "I want to—"

But Mary waved her down. "Hush, Ruby. Not yet."

Ruby scowled at her mother. "Well fiddle-dee-dee, at least I don't throw a conniption like her." She pointed at her older sister, but she sat down.

"I asked Catherine to find something for me, and I think she's got it," Mary said. "Bring it here, dear." Mary took a picture from the sack. "I found this picture in the bottom of Grandma's trunk."

"What is it?" Ruby said.

Will smiled when he saw the picture. "That's my Grandma O'Shaughnessy, my dad, and his brothers and sisters. That's their farm in the background."

"It is," Mary said. "It's their homestead, and there's a message written on the back. Read it, Catherine."

Mary returned the picture to Catherine who read, "'This is for you, Father. The farm you always wanted but never saw.'"

"Grandma O'Shaughnessy wrote that on there," Will said.

Sharon took the picture and looked closely.

"Tell them again, Will," Mary said.

"My grandfather saved every penny he earned back in Ireland so that he could start anew here in America. He didn't want to spend his life working to pay someone else's debts. He wanted his own land. His brother had come here before him, so Grandpa sent him money to buy land outside of Ashley Springs. Why, he bought the land from Governor Dodge himself. But Grandpa never saw that land. He died of pneumonia twelve miles from his new home."

Mary stood and faced Sharon. "I think that Great-Grandpa should be the last O'Shaughnessy to not realize his dream. Let's sleep on it and gather after breakfast."

Late that night, Sharon stepped into the parlor where her father sat alone, his head in his hands. "Daddy, I want what's best for us all. I want to stay part of this family, even if it means leaving Ashley Springs."

Will reached for Sharon and pulled her close. He may have an uncertain future, but he still had his family, and he knew that was far more important.

Early the next morning, while dressing for the day, Will told Mary about Sharon's decision. "I know that she's not happy, but she doesn't want to break up our family either. It's an awful bind I've put you into, isn't it my dear?"

"Will, I don't need to tell you how I hate to leave Ashley Springs, hate to leave my nice home. But when we married, I said for better or for worse. I may not be convinced that this is for the better, but I know that it's not the worst. During these last few years I've seen so much worse every day. I do know how lucky I am."

And Will knew how lucky he was to have a family that cared for each other. He knew he was assuming a heavy load, that he had to make this new venture successful so his family could live happily ever after. But he also knew that it wouldn't be easy. Happy endings were only certain in fairy tales.

"But, Daddy, why do we have to wait until spring?" Ruby said. "Can't we go now?"

"Most farmers freshen their cows for spring, so it's hard to find a cow that gives milk in winter. We'll need to get settled and be ready to milk at the beginning of March." Will was certain that Grade A milking was the road to profitable farming, although most everyone else in Iowa County milked Grade B. But he couldn't go Grade A without good cows. He worried that he couldn't find the high producers he wanted.

"And Mother needs to pack a house full of memories, yes she does. You'll just have to be patient, Ruby. If I can find the right cows, we'll move to Willow at the end of February."

"I don't like being patient."

Will sighed. He knew that Ruby expected the world to bow to her wishes immediately, and not a moment later. "Ruby, my dear, you'll learn that a stew needs to simmer all day before it reaches full flavor. Not everything should be done right now."

Will heard footsteps in the hall. "Ruby wants to go farming now," he called to Mary. "She doesn't want to wait until February."

Catherine shouted from outside, and Ruby ran from the room.

"It does seem inefficient to milk only three quarters of a year," Mary said. "But I'm no farmer, so I probably don't understand."

"There are better ways. And I plan to make lots of changes, but it'll take time."

Will had thought about farming ever since he'd come to town. But he shouldn't regret too much; the car business served them well for a long time.

Mary took a hot iron off the cook stove and began to press the girl's blouses. "Don't you think it's time we find a renter? It doesn't look as if the house will sell anytime soon."

"Paul Swartz was—"

"It's disappointing. I hoped the house money could go for a tractor."

"I'll not be needing a tractor. Four or five horses will suit us fine. Besides, I think tractors are too expensive for these small plots. And I've always been fond of my horses, you know that."

Mary set the cool iron back on the hot stove and shoved the handle into the newly heated one. "Horses aren't the modern way. I thought you wanted to be modern."

"I do. Oh, about Paul Swartz. He was in today. He still wants to rent the house come spring. He says with a new youngster coming they'll need more rooms."

"I feel sorry for his wife," Mary said. "She has all those kids and now had another on the way. But I'm not sure we want him. I've heard he spends too much time in the taverns."

"He's held a job at the feed mill ever since the war, and he earns a steady paycheck. That's better than most these days." Will edged toward his wife, wrapped his arms around her waist, and nuzzled his cheek against her neck.

"Will." She pulled away. "This iron's hot."

He lifted his head but didn't let go. "You can't hold a few drinks against him. Besides, he goes to Church every Sunday."

Mary set the iron onto an asbestos tray and twisted to face him. "Will, sitting in a pew doesn't make him a saint anymore than sitting in a stall makes you a horse."

Through the fall and winter months, Will visited the auction houses. He bought farm machinery and cows whenever the price was right. With farmers moving to tractor-pulled machinery, horse-drawn equipment was plentiful and cheap. Milk cows were another matter; there was plenty competition for young, quality livestock.

With no repair work and no customers, Will left the shop early again. Bennie's was almost empty. One customer sat at the bar and a fella with a bright green coat slumped over a shot glass at a back table. "Hey, Bennie," Will said as he stepped in out of the sunlight, "Pour me a Mineral Springs, will you?"

"Not drinking whiskey?"

"You'd be surprised at how good a five-cent beer tastes when you've only got change in your pocket."

"Can hardly keep it in stock. You'd think our town was full of Krauts. Good for our brewery though."

Will held the brew to the light, admired the amber color of the last few drops, and then he emptied his glass.

"I better get on home. The wife doesn't like me spending time here. You're not her favorite citizen, you know."

"She'd prefer I go broke."

"That she would, but she's a bit quiet after our recent attempts to outlaw it. Not clambering to ban it anymore. One night at a speakeasy numbed her enthusiasm for prohibition."

"Business was better then."

"Say, Bennie, who's that colorful fella in the back? I haven't seen him before."

"He's new to town. A cattle dealer."

"I'm looking for cattle. Calls himself?"

"Finian McCarthy. That's what he goes by."

Will approached the back table, but at first McCarthy didn't seem to notice. "Mr. McCarthy," he said.

McCarthy sprung off his seat and waddled toward Will. "Sir, what can I do for you?"

Will almost laughed aloud. McCarthy wasn't exactly ugly, but he was far from handsome. He was a short fella who looked overfed. His ruddy cheeks blended into a bulbous nose. Thin lips stretched upward toward his eyes and anchored his cherubic face. His smile lines twitched when he spoke, and it was that broad smile that drew Will forward.

But it wasn't his physical appearance that rendered Will speechless. It was the man's attire. He wore a brown checkered derby hat with matching knee-length corduroy breeches. His swallowtail jacket was emerald green, his shirt field-corn yellow, and his buckle shoes a bright red. Will hadn't seen such sparkle since last Christmas.

McCarthy grasped his arm. "Don't be smitten, my man. A little color grabs the attention. Pays to advertise, you know?" He released Will's arm, bent forward, and gawked into Will's eyes. "So, sir, can I be of assistance?"

Will shook the astonishment from his brain and tried not to smile, but he just couldn't help it. "Mr. McCarthy, you do command attention. Only an Irishman, I think."

"Your name, sir?"

"Will O'Shaughnessy." He shook his head again, tried to bring the glitter into focus. "I never thought I'd see such a sight, not this far from the wee folk in the Wicklow Mountains."

"A Wicklow man, now are you? I was raised in Avoca, yes I was. Spent many a pleasant hour at Fitzgerald's."

"I've never been there," Will said, "but I know Thomas Moore's poem, 'The Meeting of the Waters.' Can't be a more beautiful place." Will looked away as he recited the words of the poem.

"Drank many a Guinness there at The Meetings," McCarthy said. "The thought brings a tear to my eye." McCarthy swiped the back of his hand across his cheek. "Now we've established kinship, how can I help you, my man?"

"I hear you're a cattle dealer."

"Two of the man's drink, if you will," Finian called to Bennie. He dragged a chair away from the table and urged Will on to it.

When Will pulled change from his pocket, Finian grabbed his arm. "Put your money away," he said. "This ones on me."

McCarthy gulped his beer and called for a second round.

Will waved Bennie away.

"Drink up, my man," McCarthy said as he pushed a full glass toward Will. "How can I help you?"

"I'm going farming. I need cows. Good high producing cows. Know of any?"

"Hard to come by but I'll keep my eyes open. Like to help a Wicklow man."

McCarthy snatched Will's untouched glass and emptied it before Will reached the door.

But he was true to his word. By the end of December, McCarthy found all the high producing cows that Will could afford.

The new year was upon them before Will was ready. With the first month of 1936 at its end, and the house not sold, Will rented to Paul Swartz who moved in with his family on February 25th, the day after the O'Shaughnessys left for Willow.

But Mary wasn't happy. "I have a bad feeling about this. I think it's going to cost us. I don't like renting our lovely home to a drunk."

"He just takes a nip now and then."

Will thought that Mary's temperance obsession colored her opinion of Paul. But they didn't have a choice. Mary knew that.

When Paul handed him a fresh twenty-dollar bill, Will felt vindicated. He was glad to have new money in his pocket when they loaded the sleds for the trip north, and now, he'd have that income every month, a supplement to his unknown farm income. But he felt a bit uneasy, too. Will didn't like going against Mary. She was a good judge of people.

They removed the whatnots from the shelves, loaded the furniture, and swept the bare floors. Tears streamed down Sharon's face as she wandered through the empty rooms, but Ruby never glanced back.

Will, Bert Whitford, Dennis Newberry, Charlie Nesbitt, and Rich Turner brought five sleds, one for the family and four full of furniture and belongings. The breath of eight giant Belgians wafted through the frosty air, reminding Will of winter mornings when the steam locomotive chugged into the Ashley Springs depot. Two new family members, Ted and Ned, mixed breeds, pulled their sled. Although not as beautiful as the Belgians, they were big and strong, and Will thought they handled right smartly. Fanny, Mabel, and Fanny Too seemed content to trot along behind.

Will had heated soap stones through the night to warm his daughters' toes. Each girl was bundled in a hat, earmuff, scarf, mittens, and a greatcoat over a felt jacket and a wool sweater. Will piled straw under their feet, behind their backs, and along their sides, and covered them with blankets. Little Catherine looked like a bug in a rug, and a well warmed rug at that. But the trip hadn't yet begun, and Will knew it would be a long, cold day.

Catherine sat in back between Ruby and Sharon. They had just tucked the blankets tight across their legs and stuffed them around their sides when Ruby threw the covers aside and jumped up. "Ruby, sit down, please," Sharon said. "Don't make this harder than it has to be."

Ruby jumped off the sled and ran into the house but soon emerged with their cat. "I almost forgot Emily," she said. "Dad would never forgive me if I made him turn back for her."

"And you would, too," Sharon said with a frown.

"How could I ever have forgotten Emily?" Catherine said. "That's worse than forgetting Ruby."

Ruby scowled in her direction.

They sledded all day. At first they rode the ridge for two hours. Then they left the rolling hills and gentle depressions behind and descended through peaked hilltops and sharp valleys toward the river. Some trees pushed out from their rock and earth foundations before turning upward toward the sunlight, while others fought their way through brush and undergrowth until they stood as sentries overlooking their brethren below.

And when the sun rose high in the sky, Catherine pushed the blankets off her legs. "It's beginning to feel like spring," she said.

Mary reached for Will's hand. "Do you think we'll have room for the furniture?"

"Nine rooms. They should hold it all."

"I hope the girls do well in school. I want them to have careers, Will."

She squeezed his wrist so hard that Will's fingers began to numb.

"Ashley Springs' schools were very good," Mary said. "I knew all those teachers."

"Our girls have an advantage. They have the best teacher in Iowa County at home. They'll be fine, my dear."

"You say so."

"I'm sure of it." He dropped the reins into his lap, pried her fingers from his wrist, and cradled her soft hand between his two burly ones.

They rode through shadowed valleys with rock outcroppings which glared down from above. Then they rose from the darkness into sunlight which reflected off the spotless snow, their tracks the only blot on its pristine surface.

"My cheeks tingle but my heart's warm," Catherine said. "It's so beautiful. What a wonderful adventure!"

After ascending each hill, they stopped on the ridge and rested the horses before attacking another valley. The descent was harder than the climb and the sleds slid side-to-side, fighting the giant horses for dominance on the steep slopes. The horses' hooves probed the rock and frozen ground for secure footholds on their downward passage.

Six hours into the trip, Will hollered back during one of their rest stops. "It won't be long now. After the next hill, we'll see the river. Then it's another ten miles, all on the level."

"Can we drive on the ice?" Ruby said.

"Not on Wisconsin River ice," Will said. "The currents are far too treacherous to chance that." He reined his team and turned to his daughters. "Girls, if you don't remember anything else I tell you, remember to treat the river as your lethal enemy. She's a temptress who promises an early grave if you listen to her call."

At the top of the last hill, when the sleds exited the trees, an unexpected sight greeted Will below. He'd expected to see river ice, but instead a gray-white mass of fluff snaked its way through the valley for as far west as he could see. A vast feathery world lay before him.

"The river must be open," Will said. "The ice-cold water is teasing moisture from the warmer air."

When they descended into the whiteness, their senses were fooled by a mist that obscured all landmarks. It was an eerie world where potential dangers were hidden by the moisture-heavy air. And a sense of calm and serenity prevailed.

"Oh, Daddy, I can't see anything!" Sharon said. "I'm scared."

"It's beautiful," Catherine said.

Sharon pulled a blanket over her head.

They continued downward, but Will slowed the horses to a crawl. "If we're not careful," he said, "we'll walk right into the river."

When the terrain leveled, the teams closed and edged along together.

"Better get out and lead," Will called back through the fog. "We can't chance a broken runner, or worse, an injured animal."

Catherine clutched Emily when her father halted the horses. "We'd never find her if she jumped off the sled."

The men groped through the dense fog as they walked the horses down the slight slope and onto the roadway. When he looked up Will saw a pale, orange globe far away in the western sky.

"Fall in behind me, boys," Will shouted back to the others as he surged ahead. "I'll stop a ways up the road, then pull up close and we'll link together with a lead rope. I don't want anyone to get left behind."

They moved ever so slowly. Will watched the globe descend lower in the sky, their misty world darkening. He plodded through a soft, wet mush.

"Oh, Daddy, will we be okay?" he heard Catherine call from behind. "Don't worry, dear. We're almost there."

But he was worried. He hoped they would get there before the sun fell off the horizon. He didn't want to run blind, not along the river. It was a contest now. Could they make it through this netherworld before the sun went down? Minutes seemed like hours.

A slight breeze cooled Will's face and drove whiffs of white fluff past him. The breeze increased, the fog thinned, and then it was clear. Will saw ahead for the first time since they entered the river valley.

And it was a beautiful sight.

There was a big house which was almost as big as their Ashley Springs house, but it was so different. There were no multiple roof lines, no elaborate trim, intricate shapes, or side-by-side entry doors under a big fan window. It was a box. A big, white, two-story box, its frankness broken by a smaller box that protruded from the back, three roof gables, and a covered wrap-around porch. Tall double-hung windows complimented this tall two story house. It was as plain as the one-seat privy on Grandpa Duffy's farm. But it looked as sturdy as the big red barn and twin silos that stood alongside on this river valley flatland, all having withstood years of wind gusts that tumbled off the surrounding bluffs. It was a house like Will remembered from his youth.

When they stopped by the front porch, Will jumped to the ground. A dog stood looking down on him, and as Will approached, he sat back on his haunches and raised a paw.

Will turned back to his family, still in the sleigh. "This must be Teddy. Mr. Barnes said he'd be here. He didn't have the heart to take him away. It's the only home he's ever known."

Catherine was first on the ground. "Oh, Daddy!" She stood at the bottom of the stairs and looked up at Teddy. "I wonder how long he's been here."

Will could see that she was troubled.

"We shouldn't have kept him waiting."

Ruby and Sharon jumped down and raced toward Teddy, who whimpered and licked their hands as they gathered around to love him.

Mary's face softened and she smiled at her children as they fawned over their new friend. Will scanned the house, the buildings, and his fields. He looked back at his family and warmed to the sight.

He was home.

THE END